DRAGON'S PROTECTION

RED PLANET DRAGONS OF TAJSS BOOK 16

MIRANDA MARTIN

CONTENTS

VICTORIA

*T*he inescapable, oily and repugnant stench from the cooking pot isn't causing the moisture tracking down my cheek. I thought I'd run out of tears a long time ago.

The kitchen is cramped and tiny, with no real ventilation apart from a struggling fan that moves the smoke and air around. It seems fitting for the gray, depressing room I spend a most of my time in. Though "room" might be too generous of a word for the narrow hallway with a stove and oven on one side, a sink on the other, and some shelving and cabinetry. It's all beat up, scratched, and dented metal that has clearly been through a lot. Even the floor is a metal grate that I can see right through to one of the corridors below.

I draw the scrap of blanket I took off the bed closer around my shoulders, the nearest thing I have to outerwear to combat the constant chill in the air. I never thought that I'd ever find myself wishing for the scorching heat of the Tajss desert, but I find myself dreaming about the hot suns and the resulting high temperature more and more.

How the tides have turned.

I eye the soupy liquid in the pot and decide it looks done —or done enough. I don't know what the meat is they brought me to work with, but I try not to think too hard about that anymore. Whether it has six legs or twenty-five, it's what we have to eat. Being ferried around the universe in this ship as maid and cook means I've seen a large variety of prey animals, or at least animals that were killable.

I don't know if that's really the same thing.

I've tasted things at this point that I'm sure wouldn't be eaten by the natives of the planets. There was a particularly bony, slimy aquatic animal that left me with a variety of scratches and tiny puncture wounds when I worked to prepare it. And we only got a few bites each of the oddly spicy flesh at the end of all that work.

Then there was the harshly bitter taste of the bright blue worm-like creature from a planet where everything seemed to be that odd blue color. Even the Zzlo, who seemed capable of eating just about anything, had had to work to get that stuff down. You'd think they'd be a better judge of what was edible in these places after traveling so much, but there you go.

Setting the long-handled spoon down, I grab a smaller spoon and dip it into the broth. Blowing on it to cool it down, I steel myself as I carefully take a sip, not knowing what to expect. This particular creature had come to me with too many eyes to count. I'd had to look away as I cleaned it up and skinned it, feeling like it was watching me the whole time.

Huh, not bad.

I take another careful sip. At least it tastes like meat and not a noxious substance that we shouldn't be digesting. Damn, my bar has really been lowered.

Shrugging and judging it good enough, I reach up and pull out the large bowl I use to serve stew of any kind. There really isn't a lot I can do to make it taste better since I don't have a lot to work with when it comes to meal prep.

The Zzlo don't have much appreciation for seasoning beyond a gray, powdery substance that's vaguely salty. Maybe it's for the best. I was never a cook before so at least there isn't much I can do to mess things up given the limited range of options.

"Ugh-rk." An impatient grunt startles me and I jerk, spilling stew on the counter.

My stomach clenches and for an instant I'm blinded by fear. Glancing over my shoulder I see it's the Zzlo in charge, based on his size and the slight variations in his space leathers. Even after all this time I can't tell all of them apart by their faces, but that might be because I try not to look them in the eyes if I can avoid it. They scare the hell out of me, still.

Their orange-tinted skin has a leathery, worn look to it, matching their outfits in an odd way, but that isn't the worst part. Their mouths are filled with sharp teeth, no molars that I can see. Clearly, any kind of vegetation is not in their diet plan. I'm tired of eating only meat, but even if I could communicate with them, I wouldn't make demands.

My strategy since my capture has been to keep my head down and make myself useful. It took some time, but it's worked. They don't usually pay me much attention anymore except when they need me to cook and clean.

Which is fine. The less attention I get the better. It's one hell of a lot better than when they first took me and I was kept chained to a wall.

Apart from those crazy teeth, they have two spiky protrusions coming out on either side of their mouths. I stare at those to have something to look at that isn't their eyes. I'd stare at the tops of their heads, but there's nothing to anchor my gaze on, only a bald head. Their dreadlocks—or tentacles,

I'm still not sure which they are—ring the backs and sides of their heads with metallic bands decorating the lengths of each lock. I avoid those too because sometimes they seem to move as if they're alive. It's creepy and makes my skin crawl.

The Chief, as I think of him, says something else completely unintelligible and takes a menacing step forward, his hand going to the ever-present club holstered at his hip.

Flinching, my adrenaline spikes and my heart pounds in my ears. I wipe at the mess rapidly and then pour the stew, but my hands are shaking so hard I spill more.

"I'm coming," I say, my voice barely a whisper past my dry throat as I try to move quicker.

Setting the pot down, I grab the serving spoon, set it in the bowl, pick up the heavy bowl, and turn toward the door. He's still standing there, menacing. I'm frozen in place, trying to will myself to move, but my body isn't responding.

Swallowing, I keep my eyes down, staring at the Chief's beat-up boots as I force myself to walk, acutely aware that he's blocking the only way out. He doesn't move until I'm almost upon him, my eyes glued to his hand hovering over his club. One tentative step at a time. I can't stop—it'll be worse if I do—but each step is terrifying. I'm trembling and trying not to spill the stew. When I reach him he finally moves enough to let me pass.

Mind games.

I've learned to spot them, but that hasn't made them any less effective. I can never forget that they can do whatever they want to me and there's nothing I can do about it. No one is going to step in, that's been made quite clear.

I've been dealt a glancing blow a few times since they let me out of my chains. None that were meant to cause real harm, but more as a warning and a reminder.

Stay in line. Obey.

I'm sure the only reason the Chief doesn't give me a shove

right now is because I'm holding the food. The tingle of his attention on the back of my head as I pass makes the hair on my neck stand on end. Fear spikes with each reverberation of his heavy footsteps behind as he follows me down the narrow hall that is lined with exposed pipes and electrical panels.

I focus on the familiar corridor and try to ignore my body telling me an imminent threat is behind me. Primal instinct, fight or flight, but there's nowhere to fly to and I can't fight.

I know that, so I stare at the dull, old metal of the hall. I wonder if the ship started off shiny and new or if the design, such as it is, is more a result of scavenged parts than anything intentional. This ship clearly wasn't built for comfort or aesthetics. It's as hard and ugly as its inhabitants.

I turn left at the correct doorway, running on automatic, accustomed to the walk from the kitchen to the small mess hall. A ripple of reaction goes through the assembled group of ten waiting Zzlo and they growl words that I don't need to understand in order to get the gist of the mood.

It's always the same. No matter how quickly I cook, it isn't fast enough for them.

I set the large bowl down on the long, metal table—more than ninety percent of this place is some kind of old, worn metal—shaking my arms out after I let go of the heavy weight.

If nothing else, cooking for them is a great workout. My arms are stronger than I ever remember them being. As soon as I set the bowl down, one of them grabs the ladle and the others jostle and push, trying to be first. Stew spills all over the table but they don't care. That's my problem, not theirs.

The Chief steps forward and knocks aside a couple of his enthusiastic underlings. One of them growls and raises a closed fist. The Chief slams him across the head with the ladle so fast I don't see him move. The underling stumbles back into two others who push him to one side, letting him drop to the floor. The others laugh at their compatriot's misfortune.

I use the distraction to get the heck out, moving on silent, quick feet. Now I'll have some time to myself while they focus on their bellies.

Back in the kitchen, I pull out the small bowl and spoon I have set aside for myself and pour the rest of the stew from the pot into it. The first few times, I made the mistake of assuming I'd be able to get some from the communal bowl. There hadn't been any left by the time I'd had a chance to get to it, so now I keep some back.

I lean against the counter and eat quickly, listening to the sounds of slurping and conversation from the mess hall. I'm going to have to clean up as soon as they're done or someone will find me and herd me along to do so. That herding comes along with more than a few cuffs I'd as soon avoid, so I listen for them to be done.

As soon as I don't hear the loud chewing anymore—none of them seem to have ever learned that eating with their mouths open is impolite—I straighten from against the counter and hurry down the hall to the other room.

They lounge about, talking to each other in that odd foreign tongue that I'm no closer to understanding than when I first got here. The sounds are just too different, the intonation harsh on the ears, but I can understand body language and tone just fine.

I try to be as unobtrusive as possible while I grab the large bowl to take back to the kitchen, scurrying away with my head ducked. Grabbing a crude tray from the kitchen to lessen the trips I have to make, I hurry back to grab the used bowls and spoons. Stacking them, I do a quick survey of the table and the floor.

I stifle a sigh.

As usual, there's food everywhere. How hard can it be to get it into their mouths rather than dropping it damn near everywhere? At least the floor in here doesn't have holes like the kitchen does but where the stove and sink are. Probably for this reason.

I head out with the bowls, setting them down directly in the sink and getting the water going to wash them. Washing dishes isn't fun, but I don't really mind it much. I can let my mind wander while I do it. A small reprieve from life.

Though my thoughts aren't restful. When I don't have other things to focus on, my mind inevitably makes its way back to Tajss. Back to the desert planet that our ship crashed on. Back to the sequence of events that led to my capture. Led to *our* capture, but Noelle and Albert were sold off what seems like ages ago.

I frown, scrubbing a bowl. How long has it been since I was taken? There isn't a lot here to mark time with, especially while we're in space. Time seems to blend into one long day after another—a gray blur kind of reminiscent of this place or of my life now.

I set the bowl on the rack and attack the next one. Did I make the right choices? Was I stupid to follow Gershom? I bite my lip at the familiar train of thought. I've gone over things so many times that I don't even know anymore.

The natives on Tajss, the Zmaj males, were big, powerful men. Bigger and stronger than anyone I'd ever encountered before, even my father.

My muscles lock for an instant as I take a ragged breath and push aside thoughts of him. He's gone; he doesn't matter anymore. He can't hurt me, not anymore.

The Zmaj were much more powerful than he ever was, and he was able to do so much damage. How much could a Zmaj male do if he wanted to? If he turned on us?

That thought alone terrified me. What if? None of us

could have stood up to even one of them. If one of them got mad? If he decided he was tired of the humans...

So I threw my lot in with Gershom and the rest of his people. It wasn't because of the xenophobic rhetoric they spewed, or their reactionary desire to stay "pure" and human. No, I never bought into that line. I did it because I thought it would be safer not to allow the Zmaj into our lives.

They could do whatever they wanted, and we wouldn't be able to stop them. Or so it seemed at the time. Ironically, I probably wouldn't be here if I had chosen differently. My decision led to being exiled from the City, pushed out by Rosalind and her faction along with the rest of us who were following Gershom at the time.

They offered to let any of us stay, but no, I let my fear rule me. Even then I had an inkling of trepidation, but the fear kept me with Gershom. The dragon men never showed violence toward us, but they were just so big. So... intimidating.

How could I ever live among them without fear? It didn't seem possible.

I yelp and jump when another bowl clatters into the sink, clutching my grubby shirt with wet hands. The Zzlo barks something, gesturing at the bowl pointedly, before turning on his heel and walking away.

I swallow, taking a deep breath and attempt to slow my heart rate. My hands shake as I pick up the bowl. The irony of where I've ended up isn't lost on me. I don't know what would have happened if we'd accepted the Zmaj, but I do know what happened while our group was taking shelter in the wreckage of the Generation ship after we were exiled.

Noelle, Albert, and I were making a routine run to gather supplies, vigilant about the area around us, but familiar with it as well. Realistically, we could have been more careful and it wouldn't have helped anyway. We were no match for the Zzlo, just as we were no match for the Zmaj.

When we saw them we ran, but we were too far out to reach help. I remember screaming when one of them caught me and dragged me by my hair, tying me up and gagging me, but it was no use. I watched them do the same with Albert and Noelle too. We struggled but to no avail.

They quickly tired of our struggling and I saw Albert go limp after being clubbed almost gently over the head. So I stopped struggling and went along meekly. Perhaps that's why they decided to keep me when they later sold the other two to some even creepier-looking aliens.

For the better?

I don't know. I'm a slave same as they are wherever they ended up. As the days blend into each other, hope is fading. I may not have much left soon. At which point...

I shake my head, pushing aside the dark thoughts that sometimes consume me. After finishing cleaning the last bowl, I head to the mess hall with damp rags to clean it up too.

I have to hold on to that dim glimmer of hope if I want to survive. Even if it doesn't make sense. I will get out of here somehow. There is no other option. I *will* get out of here.

I keep saying that to myself while I clean the table, the benches, the floor. God, why are they so damn messy! It's a pig sty. Finishing the mess hall, I go and clean up the trash that accumulates around their stations in the control room. Then I hold my breath while cleaning the disgusting bath room facilities that never stay clean for more than a few hours before those animals come back in to use them.

I will escape. I will get out of here.

I hold on to my mantra all the way through my own shower, which I take with my clothes on, more to wash them than for protection. They don't bother me much for the most part anymore. I'm no sport for them. They just want me to work.

Squeezing the water out of my clothes, I trudge to the tiny closet that serves as my quarters. There's enough room for a cot and a small stool. Not that I need storage space because I don't have anything to store.

Stripping my clothes off, I pull on my only other set of clothes, a shirt and pants I had in my pack with me when I was taken. I sit down on the hard bed and pull my fingers through my hair in lieu of a comb.

The ship shakes so hard I bounce up and down and I grab the cot. It isn't much, but it's at least bolted to the floor. While I'm not. I frown as the shaking intensifies before easing off. I know what that shaking means.

We've pushed through some planet's atmosphere. I wonder what animal they're going to hunt this time. I get up to go out into the hall because there aren't any viewing windows around my quarters. A small spark of hope flickers as I walk, but I immediately quash it.

I've been through the sharp rise and drop of that roller coaster too many times, and we haven't been to the same planet twice yet. I reach the small window in a dim corner of the ship, away from the usual activity. Though it isn't so dim now, with warm light flooding in through the glass rather than the coldness of space. At least it looks sunny.

I squint at the brightness after too much dim light for so long. I blink, wiping at my watering eyes, and try to make out shapes as the land below slowly comes into focus.

Red and white striated sand. A lot of it.

I frown, pressing closer to the glass and my heart skips a beat. A small pool of water with familiarly odd-shaped trees around it.

It can't be.

Can it?

No, no it can't be... then I spot a familiar metallic glint in the distance.

A city. A city with a familiar skyline. Almost too afraid to look, I angle myself and search the sky. I might not have the right viewpoint to know for sure, but... two suns.

Two.

My grip on the small ledge of the window tightens until my knuckles turn white. It's a struggle to stay upright; my knees are weak and I'm lightheaded.

Tajss.

We're landing on Tajss.

LOTHOR

I move slowly, carefully ensuring my movements are smooth and close to the sand. I've been following the guster pack since early morning, waiting for the right time to strike. One guster I can kill; a pack of gusters at once and I'll be the prey.

One of the large creatures swings its head in my direction, opening its mouth to display the razor-sharp teeth that fill it and I freeze in place. If it alerts the rest of the pack now I'm in trouble.

It turns its head away from me and from the rest of the pack. It takes a few large steps forward, its wide webbed feet helping it almost glide across the sand rather than sinking in as a beast of its size would otherwise.

Interesting.

Perhaps it needs a nudge, a reason to stray farther from the safety of its pack. Keeping my eyes on it, I slide back down the dune until I lose sight of it, but this shouldn't take long. I saw a grouping of rocks not far away that should be sufficient.

Reaching the grouping, I find a rock large enough to

hopefully draw the guster's attention, but small enough not to draw the entire pack's. Then I climb back up the dune, still staying low. The curious guster is exactly where I left it.

A little separated from the pack, but not yet far enough to risk a direct attack. Gauging the best place to throw, I aim at a narrow passage between two dunes, out of sight of the others. Pulling my arm back, I throw the rock. I don't use much force, not wanting to draw too much attention.

The rock hits in that narrow passage and the guster's head jerks toward the small sound, its eyes narrowing. Come. Come investigate the sound.

It lumbers forward, the hulking mounts across its back swaying, the hard spines sprouting at various points along its thick hide shifting with each movement. Those hard spikes help ward off predators and certainly wouldn't be a pleasant mouthful. Though gusters don't need that protection—there are no predators on Tajss that would hunt them in any case, except the zemlja. Nothing the guster can do will protect its life from one of them.

I check on the rest of the pack and see that they continue to mill about, not bothering with the one moving away. Good.

I move along with the guster as it gets farther away from the pack, its head swinging back and forth as it attempts to find the source of the small sound. I draw closer, but I have to move silently. I have to kill it quietly. If it lets out the odd hissing howl of its kind, it will alert the others and they may come investigate.

So I follow, biding my time, hoping it continues to increase the distance between itself and the rest. It slows before I would like it to. I inch closer, continuing to travel parallel next to its path. It stops, hesitating.

Did it hear me? Is it planning to turn back?

Its large body shifts to the side, clearly planning to turn

around. It will see me as soon as it does. Throwing stealth to the side, I spread my wings and leap from the top of the dune, above and to the left of the creature.

Swinging my lochaber, I point the blade down. I should have enough force to crack through its skull if I hit it in the right—

The guster looks up at exactly the wrong time, letting out a huff of breath as it pulls back abruptly. I adjust course in the air, but I miss the kill. There is no time to worry over it.

Before my feet touch the sand, the guster lunges forward, hissing, its mouth open wide, ready to take a bite out of me. Swinging the lochaber around, I land a blow on its face with the shaft, startling it and giving me enough time to leap back in the air.

I spread my wings wide, flapping to hold onto the slight drafts of wind. Gliding up and over I jump onto its back. It bucks, attempting to get me off, and then it lets out that howling hiss that I know carries over the land.

Are we far enough away for it not to matter? I don't know, but there is no help for it now.

Dropping down to straddle its neck, I squeeze with my thighs, trying to hold on while I reach for my knife. I'm too close for the lochaber to be an effective weapon.

Making a calculated decision, I toss the lochaber aside and grip the hilt of my knife in both hands. I need to end this sound now. Gritting my teeth, I barely hold on as it bucks once more.

When it hits the ground again, I strike, letting out a harsh grunt, sinking all my strength into that one blow directed at the base of its skull. I feel and hear the distinctive crunch of bone.

The guster's cries turn to squeals of pain, but I didn't penetrate deep enough. I hold onto the handle as it maneuvers, turning in a frenzy underneath me. I barely stay on.

Tightening my legs even more, I hold onto the neck with a viselike grip with one hand and the knife hilt with the other.

Clenching my jaw, I try to get a better grip on the hilt of the knife, the hot blood spilling around it making it hard. It bucks again and I slip, my legs sliding along its leathery skin. Digging my heels in I catch on its ribs and barely keep from losing my seat. There's the briefest point where my backside is in full contact with the beast's spine.

There.

Snarling, I shove down with all my strength, my arms and shoulder straining. The skull gives way reluctantly under the pressure, the knife sinking in another finger-width. The beast bucks again, wildly, with the primal knowledge of death looming.

I stay upon it, sinking every bit of strength I have in the next shove down. The hole I've made widens enough that the blade sinks in to the hilt, buried in the soft matter just beyond and the beast goes still underneath me.

Letting go of the knife, I leap to the side as it topples to the ground, the spark of life fading from its eyes. It huffs once then lets out a long exhale that sounds like a wheeze. I pick up my lochaber, attempting to catch my breath as I race up to the top of one of the rocky dunes.

That was not the quiet hunt I had intended. Burying myself halfway in the sand for cover, I go still and wait. If the guster's death cries were enough to summon the rest of the pack, I'll know soon enough.

I watch the path, waiting.

My breath is easing when the sand trembles around me. The tremble is from footsteps. Heavy ones. Then I hear the distinctive howl-hiss of gusters. It's no surprise when they fill the path below.

I watch as they find their fallen pack mate, circle the body, and sniff the area. Their sharp eyes are searching, but they don't find an easy target. They mill around the body for a period, but eventually they turn around and go back, tracing the same path. Deciding to leave their dead and move on.

When they leave, I follow for long enough to ensure they do not intend to turn back. Satisfied, I return to the fruit of my hunt.

Pulling my knife out from where it is still lodged in the skull, I make quick work of carving the meat off the carcass. Guster meat is good to eat and the beast yields enough for me to cook now and dry for later. I won't waste it.

I fill my pack and another bag I brought along for the purpose, shouldering both, then clean my knife with the desert sand and return it to its sheath. Gripping the lochaber, I turn toward home.

I followed the pack of gusters for some time, but they didn't travel all that far, thankfully. Their path was more a wandering one, with no real destination in mind. The result is I find myself reaching the rocky cliffs riddled with various caves before the suns fully set.

Climbing up the path not easily discernible at a glance, I stop in front of the cave I have made into my home. It's toward the top of this grouping of rocks, situated in such a way that it gives me a good vantage point to scan the area and defend it from attack.

The tough hardened leather I stretched over the wooden frame to make the door blends well with the red-toned, striated rock around it, a deliberate choice that provides extra security. I avoid drawing unnecessary attention at every point I can.

Prevention is a better strategy than any other preparation for a battle. There's a soft mewling before I even open the door. Smiling, I swing it open and step inside, crouching down to slide my hand over soft fur.

"My apologies for being gone so long," I murmur to Sree.

She mewls again, rubbing herself against me, her bright blue eyes only slightly admonishing. If she decides she wants to leave, she can fit her small, compact body through the space under the door. I am under no illusion that I can or should contain her. Sometimes I feel as though I'm her pet rather than the reverse.

She can fend for herself as well or better than I can. Her body is small but strong, her yellow fur tinged with red and sporting dark stripes to help her blend into the desert. Her wings allow her to glide across the sand just as mine do, her fluffy, long tail aiding in balance. Again, like mine.

Greeting finished, she steps away, yawning widely to reveal a small pink tongue and tiny sharp teeth suited to the small prey she prefers. She moves curiously over to my pack, her body moving sinuously as she smells the meat.

"Yes. We shall feast tonight," I agree, standing to unload my packs.

I take out a sizable chunk of meat and set it down in her dish. She prances over eagerly, digging into the meal with a delicate greed.

Sree seen to, I start a fire in the pit lined with rocks just outside the door. Separating the meat, I place some on a spit over the fire to cook, but I place others farther away to dry and preserve. That immediate chore seen to, I clean up and return to the cave, waiting for the meat to cook.

The sunlight reflects the shelf to my right, catching my eye. Though I'm always aware of the shelf and its contents to some degree, I don't let my thoughts dwell on it. I step over to it and pick up a small mirror. The handle of the mirror is cool in my hands. It's well made and there is a delicate design etched into the handle.

The glass is cracked, but I don't have the urge to discard it or the other artifacts I keep on this particular shelf. A hair clip that lost its shine some time ago. A smooth, white ribbon. A dim memory stirs, a flash of laughing eyes, softness... and then the emotions lash at me.

I am unworthy. Lost. Alone.

My hand tightens on the mirror. I don't remember why these objects stir my thoughts, but I know I cannot bear to part with these things. So I keep them, touching them even though they hurt me. Apart from Sree, these dim memories and the confusing feelings are the only companions I have left.

Alone. Yes. I am that.

Sometimes I feel as though I'm drowning in the solitude, the weight of it a burden that is becoming more and more difficult to carry as of late. An odd whistling sound penetrates my thoughts. I frown, setting the mirror down carefully, glancing toward the door.

The sound grows from a whistling to almost a roar, but not one that is coming from the throat of a creature. Sree hisses, running to hide under the table, her fur standing on end. There's a loud boom that causes me to flinch and cover my ears. The ground trembles beneath my feet, the mirror and other objects rattling on the shelf. It grows louder and louder then—

Silence.

Pulse beating hard in my ears, I lower my hands. There is no mistaking that sound followed by the ground itself shaking, absorbing impact. I pick up my lochaber and step out of the cave.

3

VICTORIA

*M*y heart is pounding when I hear the vacuum seal break around the door. The hissing sound is too loud in my heightened state. Bright sunlight streams in as the door swings open and I close my eyes, raising a forearm to shield me from the bright light.

The Zzlo in front step out as soon as the door opens, shoving at each other to get in front. When I don't step forward right away, one of them shoves me hard, grunting and gesturing outside. Swallowing, I take a tentative step, then another.

The ramp shakes a little under my feet and I'm disoriented as my eyes struggle to adjust to the light. It's warm. God, I forgot how warm it was here.

I sigh, tilting my face up to absorb the warmth. I know I'll probably feel too hot soon enough, but the heat is a welcome reprieve from the coldness of the ship. The sunlight feels so good on my skin.

I yelp as I'm pushed forward, causing me to stumble out onto the sand. It's soft and giving under my feet, making it difficult to find purchase after growing so accustomed to the metal on the ship. I fall down, but the sand absorbs the impact. I'm not hurt and the warm sand feels nice.

I glance at the Zzlo, but it doesn't seem like they're paying a whole lot of attention to me. Apparently they've decided all this new space is excellent for beating each other up. I shake my head, getting to my feet while I watch them shove each other hard and cuff one another with closed fists.

One of them tackles another and they roll across the ground, grunting and fighting for the upper hand while the others cheer them on. One of the ones cheering trips and accidentally takes the one next to him down in the fall, and then they're right at it with the others.

I roll my eyes, turning away. They look busy, but I'm not fooled. I know they're keeping an eye on me. They're certain I'm too docile to run and too weak to survive in any case. I feel like a pet allowed to go for a sanctioned walk. Which I guess is basically what I am. It burns, but not enough for me to sulk and not take advantage of this reprieve.

I take a deep breath of the fresh air and walk, my feet sinking into the soft sand with every step. There isn't a whole heck of a lot to see. Miles of red sand punctuated with some rocks and a reddish sky with two suns, but it's more than I've seen for a while. And it's Tajss.

Tajss.

Where I know there are more humans. Not that that's likely to help me. Even if someone noticed the ship entering the atmosphere, why would they come out here seeking trouble? Sighing, I push that depressing thought away and continue to trudge through the sand. I make sure not to wander too far and keep scanning the area, well aware of all the crazy animals here. This place is harsh and the wildlife here reflects it. It's teeming with ferocious predators.

I scan the empty horizon. Okay, maybe teeming isn't the

right word, but it definitely has its fair share of things with sharp claws and teeth that would see me as a tasty, soft snack.

It might be sad and pathetic that I feel safer with the Zzlo than I do alone out here, but I know my limits. I stop moving forward as I crest a rise and turn back to look at the rough-housing aliens. They're still clearly enjoying themselves, fully occupied with their mock fighting.

Biting my lip, I look around. Maybe this is far enough away...

Turning, I circle the ship, not moving farther away and making sure I stay within sight of my captors. I wish there were an oasis nearby. A wash in warm water sounds amaz—

Something bursts out of the sand to my right and I scream, jumping back, flailing my arms as I stumble. There's a flash of focused gray eyes set in a chiseled, tanned face framed with dark, wavy hair. Leathery wings. A tail, with yellow scales edged in orange glinting in the light.

A Zmaj!

Cold ice forms in my stomach, the hair on my arms stands on end, and I'm frozen in place. I try to step back, to get away from the seven-foot-tall, muscled warrior, but my body betrays me, refusing to respond.

He grabs me around the waist and throws me over his shoulder like a rucksack.

"No! Let me go!" I scream, scratching at his arm, beating his back and shoulders with my fists.

He tightens his hold, flares his wings, and leaps away, ignoring my pitiful attempts to escape. The Zzlo shout behind us over my screams, but the Zmaj bounds away, using his leathery wings to glide across the desert, his feet barely touching the sand.

I beat on him and scream, but I don't think he even notices. Once again, I'm too weak to defend myself and someone has decided to take advantage of that fact.

4

LOTHOR

I adjust my grip on the squirming female, attempting to contain her without hurting her. I can't do anything about her high-pitched screaming, so I ignore it for now. There is no doubt the Zzlo have heard her anyway. The best I can do is travel as quickly as possible and gain as much distance from the site of their ship's landing as I can.

The Zzlo aren't native to Tajss, so they have a difficult time giving chase, their heavy bodies sinking into the sand with each step. I skim over it, my wings lightening my weight so I can glide across the desert.

Slowly but surely the sound of their grunts grows distant as the gap between us and our pursuers widens. The female keeps hitting me with her tiny fists and she struggles in my arms, but I ignore the blows, focusing on speed.

I adjust her again, changing my grip to better control her struggling form. Her light, soft weight stirs something inside me. I don't know why I took the female. It doesn't make any sense to risk myself because of it, and it *is* a risk.

I didn't calculate anything while watching her slowly

approach as she wandered the sand, her gaze returning periodically to her captors. She was so small, her shoulders hunched, her long, shining brown hair covering part of her face.

Hiding.

She was hiding behind it while she walked around, hesitant and fearful. I knew where the Zzlo were, their loud grunts and the sound of their wrestling matches easy to pinpoint without looking. That was on the periphery, almost incidental while I watched this soft creature approach. Her bright blue eyes looked worried as she moved, carefully staying within sight of the ship and her captors.

She's alien, strange, no scales. No tail or wings. An unknown species to me, but something about her fear-tinged face and her cautious steps awakened a sharp and primal need to protect her.

Save her.

She clearly didn't want to leave the slavers' sight, but I needed to save her anyway. I wasn't thinking rationally. When she ventured close to my position, instinct took over. I couldn't stop myself from reacting.

Her screams were jarring but not unexpected, her weight even more negligible than I expected. And the softness of her body struggling against me, her scent, the way she moved against me. I registered all of it while turning to run with her clutched to me.

But now that I have her, I'm at a loss.

What do I do with her? The Zzlo will come looking for her. I've made myself a target too, so they'll come looking for me also, most likely to sell me. I know Zmaj warriors can be sold for a good profit. They'll want that profit if they can manage it.

Continuing to move, I ensure I step down only as much as necessary, leaving as minimal a trail as I can for the Zzlo to follow. With a little time, even that trace will be taken away by the shifting sands of the desert.

I keep running until the suns have traveled a few hours, then change directions to head toward home. When I'm certain we are as safe as we can be, I stop within sight of the rock cliff that houses my cave.

The female is clearly frightened. She breathes in ragged gasps, but she isn't attempting to land blows. I would have halted sooner to help soothe her fears, but we needed more space between us and our pursuers. Bending over, I gingerly set her down on the sand.

As soon as her feet hit the ground, she scrambles back, falling to the sand in her haste to pull away from me. Her eyes are wide, the whites showing, strands of hair falling over her pinched face. Her chest rises and falls rapidly, her mouth slightly open as she sucks in air.

My gaze falls involuntarily to the soft mounds covered by the thin fabric of her shirt. Are they? Could they be, so exposed, with no protective covering? Strange alien female, so different than my dim memories of a Zmaj female.

When she says something in a shaky voice, her soft voice as feminine as her appearance, my eyes quickly jerk back up to her face. Fear is written across her features. I hold up my hands in a placating gesture and take a large step back, trying ease her fear. She searches my face, repeating the same foreign words. I shake my head.

"I cannot understand you," I respond slowly, alert for any sign she understands me more than I understand her, but nothing registers on her face or her body language.

She shakes her head warily, climbing to her feet while keeping her eyes fixed on me. As though I am a guster that may strike at any moment.

"I am not going to hurt you," I murmur.

I know she can't understand me, but I still feel compelled

to say the words. She frowns and shakes her head. She says something in that lovely voice. My scales itch as I tighten my jaw and shake my head. I've never wanted to understand anyone more.

She wrinkles her brow and looks away for a brief moment before turning back to me. She speaks once more, but this time incorporates gestures. Crouching down, she buries her hands in the sand and then bursts up, snatching something invisible from the air.

She stares, extending her hands out in a clear question. There's no mistaking she is asking why I took her.

"Why did I take you?" I sigh.

If only I had an answer to give. I say the only one I can think of. Taking a few more steps back to give myself room, I move forward using the distinctive gait of the Zzlo, grunting and wrestling with an unseen opponent.

She looks away, clearly understanding. When she looks back, I turn in the direction that we came from. I point to her, and then back in that direction, adopting a questioning look on my face.

Does she want me to take her back to her captors? I do not know who would want to return anywhere as a slave, but perhaps she finds them more familiar and thus less dangerous than myself. There's a moment where she doesn't answer, her meek eyes meeting mine.

I hold my breath. If she wants me to return her... I don't think I can. I couldn't return anyone to known slavery, let alone a female I feel such an inexplicable urge to protect. After a heavy pause, she slowly shakes her head, saying something to accompany the gesture.

She doesn't sound certain of her choice, but I breathe a sigh of relief nonetheless. I will not have to stop her from returning. We stand there in silence after the exchange. Now what?

I look in the direction of my cave. If she is staying with me, my home is the safest place for her. We will need every advantage we can find. The Zzlo will not be abandoning pursuit of their slave and another potential slave any time soon, but I can't simply grab her once more.

Not only do I not want to frighten her, but her screams could draw predators other than the aliens, beasts even more dangerous than our pursuers. A large part of what keeps the cave secure is that I am careful not to lead anything there.

"I want to take you to my cave," I say, gesturing to her and then to the rocks.

Her frown deepens as she looks between my finger and the rocks. I can almost hear what she is thinking. Why would she want to go over there? I must try to explain differently.

Crouching down, I use the sand as she did. She leans forward, her eyes intent on my hands. I shape a mound and then draw my knife. The instant I do she tenses. Moving slowly, I wiggle the hilt of the knife through, fixing the sand around it so the end is flush with the edge. The dark base of the hilt is the best I can do to approximate a cave's mouth using the sand.

"There is a cave. My home," I say, pointing to the hilt of the knife and then to the rocks.

Her face clears when she seems to understand what I'm trying to say. She glances around, almost as if just realizing how vulnerable we are here in the open. Apart from the rocks, there is only desert as far as the eye can see from this vantage point, but the dunes can obscure much behind them.

There are threats waiting for us. Waiting for everyone. Looking back to me, she nods. Though she doesn't look any less frightened. I don't know what else I can do to reduce it. She will have to learn herself that I mean her no harm.

Pulling the knife out of the sand, I return it to its sheath. It would be faster to pick the female up, but she is still too skittish. I know it will only scare her more, even if she doesn't scream. So I step forward and turn to look at her over my shoulder, waving her to follow. She takes a step, her feet sinking into the sand.

Good. She's following.

I turn back to our destination, my senses hyperalert while I listen to the female struggling behind me. If I sense any imminent threat, I'll have to pick her up and move quicker, noise or no noise. I force myself to slow, to shorten my stride so she can maintain the pace. The journey feels interminably long. My shoulders tense the entire time.

Eventually, we arrive at the base of the obscured trail. I slow even more, looking back often to see if the female is able to follow. She is. In fact, now that we are on rock more than sand, she is able to walk faster.

Good.

She's nervous, trying to look everywhere at once while still keeping an eye on me, but I see a confused expression the farther up the trail we go. The cave isn't readily apparent. Perhaps she wonders if I lied about where I'm taking her.

I wish I could reassure her, but the best way to calm her fears is to reach the cave. I increase the pace slightly, seeing she can keep up now. When we reach the cave, I watch her as I open the door. She cranes her neck to look inside with curious eyes, but she doesn't step forward or go inside.

Hmm. I consider various ways to show her it's safe when a small blur runs past me.

Sree!

I turn to lunge for the small creature, worried she'll cause the female to run, only to find the female crouching down, crooning something sweet to the kedi in that beautiful voice, and petting the soft fur with her delicate hands.

Sree rubs against the female's legs, soaking up the attention, preening, her eyes half closed in pleasure. I stare, taken by surprise by both the female's and Sree's reactions.

The kedi didn't even look at me before she ran to the female. And the female accepted the strange creature without even a hint of the fear she has shown toward me, even though I saved her from the Zzlo.

Confusing to say the least. I sigh silently to myself. I'm glad something is able to calm her.

I step into the cave, aware that the female is watching. Perhaps the best way to lure her in is simply to not try. So that is what I do.

I set down my lochaber inside before I check on the meat and clean up the remnants of the scraps. I'll need to set up another pallet for the female, so I look through the stores and find enough bedding that she will have a comfortable place to sleep.

I lay it out toward the back of the cave, a safe distance from my own pallet, which is situated between the door and where she will be. If anything happens while we sleep, I need to be between her and danger. She is too soft to survive a true threat without protection.

While stacking the layers that will protect her from the hard rock underneath, from the corner of my eye I see the female finally step into the cave, Sree held comfortably in her arms. I don't look over, not wanting to draw attention to her action.

I can only hope her fear will dissipate with enough exposure. Perhaps Sree will be able to help.

Finishing with the pallet, I very deliberately do not look at her as I continue on with my chores, allowing her some space in which to let down her guard.

Or, at least, that's my hope.

5

VICTORIA

I keep my eyes on the big Zmaj. Not that I don't know exactly where he is at all times. He's difficult to miss and not just because of his size.

He has a... presence that is undeniable. An electrifying energy around him, like he could explode into action at any time if necessary. Like a wolf or a tiger. Not that I have any real experience with either, but I remember how arresting the big predators were in the nature documentaries preserved on the ship.

Predator.

He prowls out of the cave, the muscles of his back flexing as he props open the door, his thigh muscles clearly delineated as well though he isn't doing anything more than walking.

Yes.

My body and mind both tell me that I'm in the presence of a predator. Seven feet tall and all hard muscle, he could do a lot of damage. Even to the Zzlo. Have I jumped from the frying pan into the fire?

Yes, the Zzlo were bad. They didn't care about me at all. They saw me as a commodity, something useful. They gave me food and a place to sleep with the expectation that I would be a domestic slave for them. It was bad, but I wasn't naive. It could have been a lot worse.

I could have been sold to some aliens, like Noelle and Albert were. Someone or something that wouldn't have even bothered to feed me or would have actively abused me. I tense when he walks back into the cave, but he goes to a pack, rustles through it, takes something out and leaves the cave again, ignoring me.

What does he want?

I can't believe that he risked himself because he wanted to save me from the Zzlo, not without some ulterior motive of his own. Maybe it's harsh, but I just can't see someone I don't know—someone from a completely different species—rescuing me out of the goodness of his heart.

He hasn't done anything yet, but that doesn't mean he isn't going to. I know the Zmaj have all the working parts that are compatible with human women. At least with the Zzlo, I never worried about that. I still have no idea what's under their suits. I don't know if they ever take them off.

A mental image of the Zmaj flash across my mind's eye. The brief covering over his hips doesn't leave a whole lot to the imagination. He's all tanned, gleaming skin over hard, combat-formed muscle. A flash of heat stirs deep inside but is quickly followed by fear.

Sure, he's pretty, but all that muscle means he doesn't need me to say yes to anything. As he's already clearly proven. I shift on the softness underneath me, considering this particular offering.

I haven't been on anything this soft in... I can't remember. He didn't have to make this pallet for me. But does that really mean anything?

Ugh!

I'm double- and triple-guessing everything until I feel like I don't know up from down! An inquisitive mewl draws my attention down to the cat. Or the cat-like creature. I guess that would be more accurate. Not that it matters. For all intents and purposes, the cutie seems like a cat. And she's really sweet. A silver lining to this otherwise murky situation.

"Come here, sweetie," I murmur, picking her up and setting her in my lap. She hasn't strayed far from me for long since I got here, which I appreciate. Stroking her soft fur calms me down more than anything else has.

"I don't have to worry about your motives, do I?" I croon to her, watching her bright eyes close with pleasure. "I know you like food and scratches. Simple and straightforward."

I wish more things were as simple. I sit for a bit longer, but I can only sit idle for so long. Even before the Zzlo took me and expected me to work around the clock, I liked to keep busy. And what am I going to do? Stay huddled in the corner forever?

All right. Time to get up. Taking a deep breath, I set the cat onto the pallet. She doesn't appreciate the interruption of her petting, giving me a rebuking look, but she appears to be mollified by the softness of the pallet underneath her.

"Sorry, sweetie. I can't sit all day."

I look around the cave. It isn't a pigsty, like the Zzlo's quarters—and their entire ship really—but it could do with some tidying up. So I get to work.

First, I smooth out our pallets, noticing how much larger the Zmaj's is than my own. It drives home how big he actually is, not that I need the reminder.

I find a broom-like object and sweep the floor next, wondering if it's possible to ever not have sand inside on Tajss. It's likely a losing battle, but it's worth a try. The cat watches me work, eventually getting to her feet and following along behind me, watching curiously.

When she bats at the broom experimentally, I wave the broom around, laughing as she tries to pounce on unsuspecting prey.

"We'll play more later," I promise, putting the broom away after a few minutes. "Let's get through the rest of this place, okay?"

Moving on to the rough dishes, I organize them in a way that makes more sense, stacking them neatly on the shelf next to the door. There are a few small bags on that same shelf, and when I open them, the scent from each of them smells distinctively herbal. Spice maybe?

I reach into the first bag to get a better look at the small green leaves. Huh. It would be nice to have some food with actual flavor for once. A bubble of excitement rises as I look at the fresh meat in the corner not yet processed. Maybe I can make a rub of some kind and cook it directly over the fire. Hmm.

Grabbing one of the shallow dishes, I mix together a couple of the herbs, going light on the one that smells spicier. Taking a few pieces of the meat, I coat it in the mixture. I take it outside to where I saw the fire earlier and set the experimental meat closer to the fire than the strips I think the Zmaj is trying to preserve.

I look around but don't see his large figure anywhere nearby.

His cave is set up high in this rocky terrain and gives a good view of the area around it. I can see why he set up his home here—there's advantage both to the view he has and the higher ground, but I don't see him after my quick glance. I wonder where he went?

Shrugging mentally, I head back into the cave, looking for

something else to keep me busy. My eye lands on a shelf deeper into the cave, oddly separated from the others. When I step closer, the assortment of objects set atop it are odder still.

An ornate hand mirror with a delicate design carved into the metal, what looks like a hair clip, and a ribbon made of some smooth, satin-like material. There's more space on the shelf, but there are only those three items there and they aren't in pristine condition.

The mirror has a large crack running down the center, the metal tarnished and in need of a good polish. The hair clip looks as though it was shiny at one point, but the stones set in it are dull and lack luster now. The ribbon has a ragged edge, the length of it grubby and dirty where it must have once been a smooth, creamy white.

Maybe I can at least clean the objects up. I can use one of the rags I found to polish the hand mirror. I reach for it—

I gasp as a hard hand clamps on my wrist in a punishing grip. I try to jerk back, but I'm not strong enough for it to even register with the Zmaj. His gray eyes search the shelf frantically, as if to ensure I haven't damaged the trio of items there. Then they turn to me, narrowed in warning.

Cold grips my guts like an icy hand. My eyes are wide, my mouth dry, and I'm trembling.

He says something, his tone low and harsh.

I wish I'd learned some of their language despite Gershom's ban on it, his fear of the alien race leading him to outlaw any and all possible human association with the Zmaj, including their culture and language.

I wish I had done a lot of things. Still, I don't know what he's saying—but the meaning couldn't be more clear. He doesn't want me touching the collection of objects on that shelf.

"Sorry! I'm sorry, I didn't know!" I gasp, fighting against tears welling up and pulling against his hold once more.

Something flickers in his eyes before he abruptly lets go. I almost lose my footing when he lets go, stepping back quickly as I try to regain my balance. He takes a step toward me.

Turning, I run away, my instinct to create distance between me and an obvious threat. I hear him say something as I slam through the door and out into the open, but I don't register it. All I can think of is getting away. I can't let him hurt me. He's too big, too strong, and I can't—

The cat mewls next to me, cutting through the wild fear. Looking down it's easily keeping pace. I slow my run, glancing over my shoulder to see if he has followed. I don't get very far out of the cave before fear of everything else here on Tajss hits.

Where am I running to? There isn't anywhere safer. I slow and then stop, only a few paces from the door to the cave. Turning, I survey the space around me.

Rocks, sand.

Nowhere to go.

Gulping air, the fight drains out of me.

Helpless.

Once again.

I drop onto a flattish rock, utterly defeated. The cat creature jumps onto my lap, a low purr coming from it as it rubs against me. Offering me comfort. I hug the warm, soft body to me, trying to calm down. Trying to catch my breath while my instinct keeps telling me to run, to get away from here.

I jerk my head back up when I hear the heavy approaching footsteps, and scoot farther down the rock. The Zmaj stops abruptly, watching me with steady, calm eyes, but I don't trust it.

Whatever he sees on my face has him taking a step back. I stay tense, even when he turns away, going back to the cave. Leaving me alone with only my thoughts and the cat for company. I bury my face in the soft fur. What am I going to do?

6

LOTHOR

I am careful to maintain some distance between the female and myself. I frightened her when I first met her, which was unavoidable. She needed to be saved from the Zzlo. I do not regret that, but then I needlessly frightened her again with my harsh reaction when she almost touched the most precious objects I own.

I regret my unthinking, instinctive response. Now she is even more wary around me. I watch from the doorway, staying at the edge of it so she does not notice. I want to look at her—a desire that has only grown the more time I have spent in her presence.

She is simply beautiful.

Small and soft, with curves that my hands itch to touch and explore. Her skin is fine and silky, branded into my palm after the rough manner in which I held her wrist. The sensation of it is alien and strange, lacking any scales or protection.

She smiles at Sree and her eyes sparkle, her soft pink lips curving in delight as the kedi jumps at the piece of thread she holds out for the animal to play with. I wish she would look at me with such joy. My attention turns briefly to the kedi. She has mostly abandoned me in favor of the female. I do not blame her.

The kedi is much softer and sweeter than I am. I begrudge her no comfort when she clearly feels so alone, so vulnerable, frightened of anything and everything around her. She smooths a shining lock of her rich brown hair away from her face. I want to run my fingers through the mass of it. I close my eyes and take a deep breath, but it does not help.

The air is tinged with her sweet scent and it's as lovely as she. A flash of heat, of possessiveness. I suppress a growl. My inner dragon is stirring to life, rising to the surface after... I don't know long.

In truth, it has been asleep for so long that I did not think it would ever rise again. Didn't think that it could. I open my eyes, finding her once more. I know why I was seized with the need to take her when I saw her. Why I could not leave her. She glances over to the door and her eyes clash with my own, but only for a moment.

She looks away as quickly as she looked over, allowing her hair to shield her now-guarded expression from me. My chest tightens as pain stabs into my heart like a blade. Am I seriously jealous of Sree?

I step into the cave, keeping my steps slow and measured, trying not to startle her. I want her to accept me. I need her to. Somehow I must break through this prickly shell, this state of fear she lives in.

Sree hardly looks at me when I walk in, following the female to the other end of the cave, looking up at her with adoring, liquid eyes. It is clear she moved to avoid being too close to me, her hands moving to clean a corner of the cave that does not need it.

She is an industrious little creature, her hands usually

busy, finding things to do. I understand a desire to be moving and doing. Perhaps that is a good way to begin to break this barrier between us? I walk over to the basket I use to gather various herbs. They need to be cleaned and the leaves picked off the tough stems so they can be added to the food. I saw her testing the already separated herbs on pieces of meat earlier.

Picking up the light weight, I walk over to the female. She stills but doesn't shift away when I stop two armlengths away from her. I wait patiently until she cautiously glances up. When I see her eyes my hearts stop and my breath catches in my throat.

I hold up the basket, drawing attention to it, then set it down on the sturdy table I eat at. Opening the top, I reach in and pull out risa, one of the tougher plants to clean, especially for my larger hands. Hers will be much more suited for the task, her fingers more able to pick out the leaves from the claw-like bases. I hold it up between us, twisting it between my fingers.

"Risa," I explain.

I take off a few of the easier leaves to pick off, dropping them onto a small bowl I keep in the basket for that reason. She watches my motions carefully. It looks like some of the tension leaves her shoulders while she watches me work. I hold the small branch out to her, offering it silently. She jerks back at the motion, but then stops, her gaze going from my face to the plant.

"Can you finish?" I ask slowly.

A pause. I hold my breath. I can see her gauging the distance between us, looking down at the plant and wondering if it is a trap. I stay in the same position, waiting for her to take it. Or not.

Finally, her gaze locks on the plant and she reaches out. Her hand has the slightest tremble as she does. I remain frozen, not wanting to scare her away from a movement that seems to be taking her a good amount of mental effort. Her small fingers close around the stem. I immediately let go, pulling my arm back.

"Risa," she repeats in a low voice, looking up at me.

She is obviously wary, but I grin at the word.

"Yes, risa," I agree, then I press my hand to my own chest. "Lothor."

"Lo-thor," she repeats, her brow knitting in concentration as she sounds out my name.

"Yes, Lothor," I encourage her.

I give her a questioning look. I want her name, want to refer to her properly, not as just the female. She presses her own hand to her chest, inadvertently drawing attention to her curves. I force myself to look back up to her face, ignoring the stirring in myself at the sight.

"Victoria," she says, going as slowly as I did for my name.

Exotic and pretty, just as she is.

"Vit-ira," I try.

She smiles slightly, humor lighting her eyes. My chest swells at the sight. I would make a fool of myself hundred times if it means she will light up in such a manner.

"Vic-tor-ia," she repeats, breaking the name apart.

"Vic-tor-ia," I repeat, forming the sound more carefully.

Her smile widens.

"Victoria," she agrees, nodding emphatically.

I step back, not wanting to push her too hard with our interactions.

"Risa?" I ask, pointing to the herb.

She murmurs something I don't understand. It must be assent because she sits down, her nimble fingers getting to work. She is fast, much better at the task than I anticipate. By the time I gather some vegetables from the small garden I have coaxed to grow at the base of the path, she is almost finished with the entire basket. I give what I hope is an approving look and reach to take some of the herb.

"Thank you," I say quietly, knowing she cannot understand me, but wanting to voice my gratitude nonetheless.

She says something back. Something I wish I could understand. She shakes her head, pointing at the basket I brought back.

"Food?" she asks.

"Foo...?"

She mimes putting something in her mouth.

"Food?"

Ah. I nod.

"Food," I agree, storing the word away in my memory.

A useful one. I take what I have gathered and some of the meat I cooked earlier with me to the fire to prepare a meal. I find myself taking more care than usual, knowing I have another mouth to feed. Knowing I have Victoria to take care of.

Cleaning and trimming the vegetables, I re-season the meat with the risa and more salt, adding the same to the vegetables I roast with rendered fat. Victoria wanders out of the cave to check on me when the scent of the cooking food wafts over and I smile, more to myself than her. It does smell appetizing.

I fill two plates with food—and Sree's dish with meat alone—carrying them all inside at the same time.

Sree mewls in demand when I walk in, but I set Victoria's plate and my own down on the table before I squat to serve the kedi. Sree attacks the food with the same vigor that a starving Zmaj warrior would after battle.

"I know you are more than well fed, Sree," I admonish her, shaking my head.

Not only does she eat the food I provide for her, she also disappears sometimes to hunt on her own. When I rise back up to sit at the table, Victoria is hovering, looking at the plate. I gesture for her to sit.

"Food," I say.

She hesitates. I sit down at one end of the table, nudging her plate toward her. I hope, at some time, she would sit next to me, but I do not want her to force her. I don't want to create even more trepidation than she already does being even this close.

I take a bite of the food, encouraging her to eat with a glance. She bites her plump lower lip, looking at the food. She is clearly hungry, but I cannot force her to sit and eat. That will undo all of the progress I have managed to make. I think the scent and sight of the food is what finally convinces her to take a seat, much as I might wish she is warming to me.

Drawing the stool back, she sits down lightly, ready to stand back up at a moment's notice. I drop my eyes briefly, not wanting her to see my troubled expression. Was she always such a frightened, small presence? Or did her time with the Zzlo make her so?

The thought tightens my jaw, anger rising, sharp and hot. The thought of her trapped with those animals...

My hands close into tight fists, the urge to go back and destroy her captors very real. And also very stupid. I force my fists to unclench. If I go back to exact revenge, there will be nobody here to protect Victoria and care for her. And what if I were taken or killed in the attack? She cannot survive here alone.

No.

I do not have the luxury of allowing emotions to dictate my actions. A hum of enjoyment draws my attention back to Victoria. Her eyes are closed while she chews, a look of such decadent pleasure on her face that I am enraptured with watching her. A heat of a different kind rises. I want her to look like that. Underneath me.

She opens her eyes and smiles. It's a little unsure along the edges, but it is still a smile and it is freely given.

"Food...good," says slowly, smacking her lips in obvious enjoyment.

I tilt my head to the side. I know the first word.

"Goo...d?" I repeat.

Her smile widens.

"Good," she repeats, taking another bite and humming at the taste.

I grin as warmth fills my chest. She is enjoying the food I provided.

"Good," I repeat, and take a bite myself.

She nods, swallowing.

"Good food," she proclaims.

I nod as well.

"Good food," I repeat dutifully, basking in her enjoyment.

I watch her while I eat. I have a rising desire to take care of her, feed her, shower her with every luxury I can. I want to see her glow like this again and again. Heat gathers in my belly as darker thoughts enter. I know what else I want her to glow after.

7

VICTORIA

I look up at Lothor's footsteps. He smiles when I make eye contact, his eyes crinkling adorably at the edges. The expression pushes his already handsome face over the edge to downright devastating. My heart skips a beat and my breath catches in my throat. For a moment, brief though it is, the constant fear is gone.

Lothor without a smile is already a lot to take in. Seven feet of tanned muscle, a handsome face, that wavy, sun-streaked dark hair that frames it...

It takes me a second to realize he's holding out a freshly filled waterskin, offering it to me.

"Oh!" I reach out and my fingers brush his. My heart pounds at that small touch. "Thank you," I murmur, face warming.

His face lights up.

"You are...welcome," he forms carefully.

I can't help my smile widening when he steps back, clearly pleased with himself for the pronunciation of the words. He's a quick learner, especially considering it's difficult to fully explain the meaning of some words.

Water delivered, he lingers for a moment, scanning my face, but then turns and goes back to doing whatever he does when he isn't in the cave. I take a sip of the cool, clear water, sighing at the taste of it.

I hadn't even realized I'd gotten so used to the metallic edge of the water on the Zzlo ship until I drank the water Lothor brought to me. I lower the waterskin, staring at it. Maybe he isn't so bad. He hasn't done anything but take care of me so far. Hasn't made any kind of demand. A now-familiar furry head nudges my hand for pets.

"Feeling a little ignored?" I murmur, scratching behind her ears. I laugh when her eyes close in pleasure, her left ear twitching. "Why don't we go clean up a bit, huh? And check on the garden?"

She perks up at the word garden, knowing it means we're going outside.

At this point, Sree is more my kedi than Lothor's. I still sometimes think of her as a cat, though Lothor taught me the proper word. She's so close to a cat that she may as well be.

I take a second to fix my pallet and Lothor's—not that he leaves it a mess, I just like smoothing it out—and then I sweep the floor and wash the dishes. By that point, Sree is running back and forth between the door and me, clearly ready to head outside. I laugh at her impatience, setting down the drying cloth and rolling my sleeves back down.

"All right, all right," I say, trying to calm her down as I walk to the door. "Let's go outside."

As if she understands my words, Sree bolts out the door. Shaking my head, I follow behind her. Maybe I'm more hers than she is mine. I walk to the garden, more for the walk than any need. Lothor does a good job tending it and I don't know what to touch and what not to touch yet, but I like looking at the small patch of growing things.

Raising my face to the sky, the warmth of the two suns

44

soaks in. It's different now; I hated it when we crashed here. Hated it worse when I left the protective dome of the City with Gershom, but after being on the cold Zzlo ship for so long, now I welcome the warmth.

Yes, things could be much worse.

Reaching the garden, I turn and look back at the path I just walked. Lothor has done an excellent job of disguising it. It appears like a random assemblage of rocks with no rhyme or reason, the route deliberately curved and jagged in places to further that impression. Even the small garden appears as though it may have simply sprung up here on its own.

Smart.

He knows his best protection is to not be noticed by threats in the first place. Turning back to the desert, I look to the horizon, searching for any sign of the Zzlo. Butterflies dance in my stomach thinking about them, about being forced back to the way things were. Did they give up?

Maybe I'm not valuable enough for them to expend resources to recapture me. I frown considering that. Even if it's true, Lothor would be a valuable catch, and if they run across either of us...

Yeah, better to stay vigilant. A hand settles on my shoulder and I shriek, whirling around and stumbling back. I surprise myself by not tripping over any rocks.

Maybe if I hadn't just been considering my captors— wondering about a possible return to my enslavement—I wouldn't have reacted so harshly, but there you go.

A small blur rushes past and Sree spreads her leathery wings, fur standing on end as she hisses, a sound I've never heard her make before now. Her mouth is open wide baring her razor-sharp, tiny teeth, and she paws the air in front of her with claws fully extended.

It takes me a second to register that the tall figure is Lothor.

He stays still, his hands up, glancing between me and my security, his expression contrite. I press my hand against my chest, shaking my head. My heart pounds under my hand and I'm shaking as adrenaline drops out.

"I... Don't sneak up on me like that, Lothor," I mutter, rubbing my face.

He makes a soothing sound and steps back carefully. I look up. Maybe to tell him it's okay, maybe to stop him, I'm not sure, but he's walking away.

My frightened response is scaring him off. I shake my head, crouching down, and Sree decides it's safe again and trots over.

"You know that's your actual master." I point at Lothor's retreating form, petting her back with a slightly trembling hand. "I'm the newcomer. What did you think you were going to be able to do anyway?" I point out. "Lothor could defeat you with a pinkie."

She leans into the pets, her eyes closing to slits.

"Silly goose," I admonish, picking her up.

But there is a warm glow in my chest at her valiant effort to protect me from the threat, even when it was Lothor.

Lothor.

Who backed off immediately when he saw I was scared. It clearly wasn't because of my fierce little guard. He reacted to my fear by giving me space. He didn't have to do that.

I linger for a bit, getting myself under control before I start back up the path that leads to the cave. A flicker of movement above draws my eye and I see the familiar, tall Zmaj figure at the top of the path, but his eyes aren't on me.

They're on the path behind me, on the desert beyond. Watching. Standing sentry.

He does that whenever I go for a walk anywhere. He never stops me from leaving the cave, just watches over me, making sure I'm safe. He's more a protector than a captor.

Maybe I'm being naive? But he hasn't done anything to counter that thought. When I reach the cave, I realize he must have come down to call me up to eat. The table is set with vegetables from the garden, delicious-smelling meat, and berries.

Xara berries, I think he called them. My stomach rumbles loud and my mouth waters at the scents and sight of the food.

Lothor glances over at the sound, setting down another clean fork-like utensil next to one of our plates. He smiles, gesturing to the seat, then moves to the other end. I feel a pang of guilt at the way I reacted at the bottom of the path, even though it wasn't personal.

I like to cook too, but I can't deny having food served to me is great. And Lothor's a good cook. His food is simple, but also flavorful and filling.

"Thank you," I offer, taking the seat. "Smells delicious."

I know he can't understand what I'm saying, but I want to say it anyway. He nods.

"You are welcome," he says, sounding the words out carefully.

It's amazing how quickly he picks things up. I take a bite of the meat, humming as the tender morsel almost melts in my mouth. I think I've put on a good five to ten pounds since I've gotten here, all due to Lothor's fixation on feeding me.

He watches me eat and the satisfaction on his face clear. It's almost like he enjoys watching me put food away. I sigh.

I wish I could ask him some things rather than just guessing. I watch him back, discreetly. It's a little overwhelming being the object of such focused attention. Even when he's not looking directly at me, I have the feeling he's completely aware of my position and what I'm doing. That's not only one-sided.

My eyes track the breadth of his wide shoulders, noticing

how his biceps flex even when he's doing something so simple as bringing food to his mouth. My eyes lock on his lips as he chews on the food. *Get a grip on yourself, woman.*

I shift my attention away from his mouth. It isn't all that helpful, not when his chest and abs are on full display. Why do the Zmaj only wear pants? Ugh. My hands itch with the desire to touch that scaled skin. It looks warm, but I wonder if it feels soft or stiff? Are his muscles hard as they appear?

I shift in my seat, squeezing my thighs together which puts pressure on my clit. A small shudder races up my spine as pleasure signals race through my body.

Clearly, I'm going insane. I force my attention back to the food. I need a distraction.

Quick.

"I'm sorry I screamed when you touched my shoulder, Lothor," I say, trying to divert my attention. "But...I'm not strong. Not like you." I look up at him, noting the frown between his brows, his eyes watching me intently. He can't understand, but something about his full attention, his willingness to listen anyway, opens up the floodgates. I haven't had anyone around who wants to listen in so long. "Not even when we were all on the ship, heading for a planet to colonize." I shake my head. "I'm no idiot. I know a large part of why I'm so weak, so scared, is my father. He wasn't a nice man."

That's an understatement. My father was violent, prone to taking out his frustration on me when things didn't go his way. And he was frustrated at a lot of things. Work, his lack of love life. Basically his whole lot in life. I don't know why he thought he deserved more, where he got such a sense of entitlement, but he did, and I paid the price for it.

I spent a lot of my childhood tiptoeing through our quarters, hoping not to catch his attention, but anything could set him off. A burnt piece of toast, my shoes where they shouldn't have been. Sometimes even just the sight of me.

I learned to wear long-sleeved shirts and pants. People may have suspected, but he was careful never to hurt me where it would show and never to hurt me so much that I needed medical attention. Now that I'm older, I know the real damage wasn't even the physical violence. It's what it did to my brain, to my emotional state.

"I think that's why I have so much anxiety and fear," I continue after a pause. "And why I was so triggered by your people." I look over at him, skimming his large frame. "He was large, liked to box. Not nearly as big as you, of course." I'm sure that didn't help and wasn't it ironic that Lothor's frame and muscles trigger a fear response in me while at the same time attracting my attention? It's like a cruel joke. "Anyway. That's why I fell in with Gershom's crowd, though it clearly wasn't the smart or logical thing to do. Humans aren't built to survive here, while you guys clearly are. It would make sense to team up and work together. It doesn't make sense to alienate you, to turn insular and racist."

Looking back, it's downright embarrassing thinking of the hateful rhetoric Gershom spouted. And how scared I was of the Zmaj, so scared I could overlook it so I wouldn't have to interact with them.

"And look at me now. Living with a Zmaj. And surviving." I smile and he smiles back, though there isn't any comprehension in his eyes. I'm grateful for that. I'm not sure I could say all of this out loud if he understood. "Life can be strange."

I prop my elbows on the table, meeting open gray eyes. He's so easy to talk to.

"Falling in with Gershom wasn't a great move. There's safety in numbers. Being exiled from the City wasn't good." I smile grimly. "As evidenced by the fact that I was taken prisoner while we took shelter in the wreckage of the ship.

Gershom talked a big game, but he wasn't a leader. The only thing he was really good at was capitalizing on fear, stoking it. Maybe if he hadn't been around, those who followed him would have adjusted."

I shrug. "Maybe. They weren't all bad people, just frightened ones trying to hold on to what was familiar. I know Noelle and Albert didn't have bad intentions. They were acquaintances on the ship, but we got close after the crash. And they helped me out more times than I can count, when I needed a shoulder to cry on or some water when we didn't have any to spare."

There's an empty pang of loss at the thought of them. "I have no idea where they are now, what they're being subjected to. If they're even still alive. All of it happened because we were too afraid to face the unknown." Tears well in my eyes but I rub at them, forcing the tears away. Not productive, and I don't want to cry in front of Lothor, don't want to feel that vulnerable right now.

I drop my hands when I'm back under control. "I do miss some things about the ship," I continue, trying to get back onto a lighter path. "The temperature control, for sure. I sometimes dream about it being cold enough to snuggle with a blanket and have a hot bowl of soup, maybe watch one of the old movies from Earth we had saved in the vid database. And I miss my friends who didn't make it…"

I talk for a while and Lothor listens, at least appearing interested and watching my expressions. I relax as the words flow. And some of the emotional burden I didn't even realize I was carrying starts to lift.

8

LOTHOR

*B*efore I leave the cave in the morning, I check to make sure Victoria is still asleep. Her breathing is light and even, her pale cheeks flushed with sleep, her soft palm upturned next to her face, the fingers slightly curled.

I scan down her length. She kicked off her light blanket during the night, and her shirt pulled up to expose the soft skin of her belly. Soft, pale, a beautiful curve. I want to kiss that swath of skin, that section that does not usually see the suns' light.

My eyes stop at the waistband of her pants, pushed low from her tossing and turning. Her delicate hipbones press up against her smooth skin, the fabric of her clothing starting just where more may begin...

I look away, feeling guilty at the track my eyes and my mind take more often than not when I am near Victoria. Reaching down, I pull the blanket up and over her limp body. She will be safe here while I am gone. I should have sufficient time to hunt down what I want before she wakes. Sree raises her head to look at me, keeping guard next to Victoria's head.

"Keep her safe while I am gone, little one," I whisper.

She settles her head back down on her paws, watching me with her reflective eyes. With one last look at Victoria's relaxed countenance, I leave the cave, shutting the door quietly behind me. The dawn's light is just now breaking through the darkness of the night.

I want to be back before the suns are too high in the sky, preferably before Victoria wakes. I head down the path from the cave, considering the best places to track down my prey for the day. I want to find something to give to Victoria, something that she will enjoy. Something more than the necessity of food or shelter. Something pretty and feminine. Like her.

Not wanting to travel too far away from Victoria, I start with the cave system that is a part of the very rock face where I made my home. Our home now. My chest swells with that thought.

Our home.

It is as though Tajss heard me, listened to how lonely I was, and sent Victoria to assuage that emptiness inside. But I cannot force too much too fast. I must win over this lovely creature that I found.

Resolved to come back with something pretty, I look through the caves that I know have openings above to allow sunlight in first. The deeper caves have fresh water, one of the sources I use to replenish my supply. Water and sunlight could mean pretty plants in some areas where enough soil has accumulated.

I have not seen any recently in the paths I usually travel, so I expand my search, alert for any dangers that may arise. There are many creatures that prefer the coolness of the caves, using the protection from the searing Tajss suns.

I don't sense anything dangerous as I prowl on silent feet. But I make the novice mistake of looking away from the path in front of me, distracted by a gentle breeze I try to track down the source of.

My foot hits a rock and pain lances up my leg. I hiss, but that is the only thing that keeps me from stepping forward and falling into the narrow but deep crevasse directly in front of that rock.

I stumble back from the edge, my pulse racing, hearing the echo of the rock hitting the sides of the opening as it drops down the crack. It drops for a long time. Too long for me to have survived.

I take another step back from the black abyss of the hole, resolving to pay more attention to where I put my feet. If I injure myself or worse, who will take care of Victoria? I must be more alert.

Deciding that is enough exploring of the cave system, I turn around to retrace my steps, but the ground trembles

What...?

Then I hear it.

The distinctive susurration of wings. A lot of wings. Almost afraid to do it, I look back just in time to see a dark cloud burst up through that crack in the ground. Oh no. Turning back toward the exit, I no longer walk forward with care.

I run.

As fast and hard as I can.

There is not a sufficient place to take cover in the narrow tunnel, not enough to protect me from a swarm of this size. A few sismis I could handle, could cut down, but one of this size with this limited a space to maneuver in?

I'm better off attempting to reach the end of the cave system. The leading edge of the dark cloud nips at my heels, one of the large winged creatures attacking my head with its talons, fangs gleaming in the indirect light of the sun streaming through a crack above.

Making a tight fist, I punch it away, not slowing my forward momentum. It screeches, hitting the side of the tunnel with a cracking thud.

I don't stop to see if it is dead as I may very well find myself in that state. The sismis are mostly blind, hunting by sound. I know they hear my footsteps, but if I can just get out of the tunnel...

Their screeches sound behind me, the beating leathery wings drawing closer. I swat away another one, but this one manages to dig in a talon before I shake it off, drawing blood, the wound stinging.

Almost there.

I burst out into the sunlight and dive to the side, taking cover behind a boulder. I cover my head with my arms and freeze.

No movement, no sound, and they might miss me completely. The vampiric creatures aren't known for allowing their food to live when there are this many to feed.

I hear them above, feel the breeze from so many wings flapping at the same time. I don't move.

Hopefully, my patience will reward me.

Time drags past as I lie there for what feels like half the day, but it is likely no more than a moment or two before the sounds of the swarm abate, changing from a rush of sound to a trickle.

I open my eyes cautiously and see only clear sky above. No wings. No dark cloud.

Letting out a breath, I sit up, looking around to see if there is any sign of the swarm I inadvertently disturbed. A few stragglers are flying back into the cave, returning from where they had been roosting before I so clumsily threw a rock down into their home.

I stand up, dusting myself off. Perhaps it would be better to search some nearby oasis for what I seek. Taking a deep breath, I adjust my lochaber in my hand and continue forward, feeling foolish.

Victoria does not have to know of my mistake. Perhaps the barrier of our words is for the best in this case. Sighing, I head out into the desert, traveling in a direction I do not usually go.

I have been to the nearest oasis recently and know it does not have what I seek. Perhaps one of the those in the opposite direction does, however.

Spreading out my wings, I snap my tail to help balance as I skim across the desert sands, my eyes constantly scanning the area, listening intently to any shifts in the normal sounds around me. I cannot allow another threat to take me unawares.

I travel farther than I intend to, having to change direction when I do not quite remember the location of the oasis I search for, but I eventually find the tall baoba trees that mark the area. There are enough of them that I know there is a fair amount of water still at this oasis.

The trees are tall, many times my own height, with wide trunks that narrow dramatically toward the top. Large, flat leaves grow at the very tops, offering some shade to the spring below. I move through the vegetation carefully, my sight on the water.

It looks clear and cool. A drink would be very welcome. I don't see the rustle of any larger creatures, which is a good sign. Water means more than plant life, after all.

I skirt around a large baoba but freeze as bright color catches my eye. Long leaves with an orange and red center. Pretty. Attractive. Deadly.

I step carefully back from the cvet, noticing the tendrils spread across the sand, shifting across it with a soft sound, ready for prey.

I take another step back. And feel movement directly

underfoot. I freeze, but it is too late. Multiple tendrils burst up from the ground to grab me.

I whirl my lochaber around, cutting through three of the four before they can grip me. But the fourth wraps around my arm and jerks me forward. I grunt as it pulls me, slowly but inexorably toward the trembling, carnivorous center.

If I reach it, that is the end.

The paralytic poison will ensure I won't be able to fight as the plant digests me. Snarling, I drop the lochaber, the length of the weapon a hindrance in this case. I pull out my knife, digging my feet into the sand as I try to slow down my progress toward that deadly center.

I hack at the tendril, no delicacy or finesse in the attack. My goal is simply to cut through it, not look pretty while I do so. I'm pulled forward another arm's length.

Two.

My feet drag through the sand as I hack desperately. The plant shudders, going still. With a grunt of effort, I pull my arm out of its grip, fluid bursting out of the now-severed tendril.

Flaring my wings, I leap back, gaining as much distance as I can with the movement. Just in time, as it seems.

Other tendrils burst out of the ground where I was standing, but close on air rather than my body. I take a moment to search the area around me, now hypervigilant.

But I am on the edge of the spring now, the sandy part fairly safe. Not that I let down my guard while I walk. I scan the area around me, impatient. I'm running out of time. I have been gone too long from Victoria as it is. I'll have to leave without anything to show for my efforts if I do not find something—

My eyes stop on a burst of color.

Fihibs.

Each one as big across as my hand, five large petals with

frilled edges in an overlapping spiral, the edges a mixture a bright yellow and orange, the colors fading into a pretty green and then a vibrant blue, ending in a blood-red center with a deeper orange funnel at the very middle.

One of the few flowers on Tajss that isn't poisonous. Not only are they beautiful, they are known for the thick, golden nectar in their centers. It is a deliciously sweet delicacy.

Crouching down, I cut away three of the prettiest, excitement rising in me. I know Victoria will love these. I cannot wait to see her surprise and pleasure.

Taking out a small cloth from my pack, I dampen it in the spring and wrap it around the flowers, tucking them carefully away for the journey back. A few sips of water for myself, and I leave the oasis. This hunt was much more eventful than I expected it to be.

I almost float back to the cave, my feet eating up the distance. The look upon Victoria's face will be well worth the effort. I know it.

I can't stop grinning as I hurry up the path to the cave, anticipation bubbling. I wonder if she is awake...

When I see the door is open, I hurry faster. She must have opened it for some air. I walk inside, my eyes going first to the empty pallet, and then to the empty table. I falter to a halt, excitement quickly shifting to worry.

Where is she? Did she go for a walk?

Telling myself she must be safe somewhere nearby, I clamp down on my fear, leaving the cave to search for her. She cannot have gone far—

A piercing, female scream rends the air around me. My hearts freeze. A wave of dread rises.

Victoria.

9

VICTORIA

*W*hen I wake up, Lothor is nowhere to be found. I'm not surprised; he sometimes leaves for brief stints, so I don't worry about it. He's never gone for very long.

I run my fingers through my hair, working out the tangles, and then rinse my mouth out with some water. Taking the waterskin, I pour a touch into the small bowl for Sree then place a piece of meat down for her. She sniffs the meat and looks at me reproachfully. I figured out a while ago that she isn't a fan of the smoked meat. She prefers her food raw.

"Sorry," I say, scratching behind her ears. "It's that or nothing."

She sniffs it again, looks up and makes a sound close enough to a meow to reinforce that she could be a cat with wings. She drinks the water, lapping it up with her soft pink tongue and ignores the meat. I have no doubt she'll disappear later to find her own food, but I leave the piece there for her in case she changes her mind.

My stomach grumbles so I grab a piece of the flavorful

dried meat and step outside the cave, chewing on it and sipping some water. Usually he'd be back by now, so I scan the area searching for him. I frown, the edge of concern growing to worry.

He's already been gone longer than he ever has been. I'm probably overreacting though. Yes, Tajss is dangerous, but Lothor has survived for this long on his own. He clearly knows what he's doing.

Sree rubs up against my legs, mewling, her wide azure eyes meeting my own. Maybe she can feel my unease.

"Come on, Sree. May as well be productive while we wait for him to get back, huh?"

I go back inside and Sree follows on my heels. I neaten the pallets, sweep the floor and clean a couple of dishes. There's herbs in the gathering basket that need to be separated, so I start on those next. It keeps my hands busy and diverts my attention for a little bit, but as the minutes stretch into at least an hour, I can't curtail my rising anxiety.

Where is he? Did something happen to him?

What could I do if something did? I don't have any idea about where I would start looking for him! I finally abandon the herbs and get to my feet pacing the cave. It feels too small in a way it never has before this.

It's possible he got hung up on something. Maybe he found something to hunt and is stalking his prey, making sure we have food to eat. Or he traveled farther than usual for some other reason. Fear for his safety eats at me.

Yes, we can't really speak to each other. And I don't really know a whole lot about his past, but he's been kind to me, helped me when he didn't have to. He freed me from slavery.

I care about him.

Maybe I should be more worried about what I would do, how I would survive without him to hunt for us, without him to protect us from the dangers of Tajss. But I can't even think about that right now.

My worry is all for Lothor.

Sighing, I turn on my heel and continue pacing. Sree's compact body sprints past me and right out the door.

"Sree!"

I rush after her in time to see her sprint down the path. She's never done that before! Where is she going?

Heart in my throat, I run after her. Maybe she heard something? Maybe she knows where Lothor is?

Whatever has happened, it's clear she has a specific goal in mind, her direction sure and unwavering. God, she's fast!

I try to run faster but I'm woefully out of shape when it comes to cardio. It isn't like I was spending my time jogging on the ship. Life's been all about survival ever since we crash-landed on this ridiculous planet.

Sree runs up a dune, her wings helping her skim across the sand. When she reaches the top, her wings snap wide, she leaps, and disappears.

"Damn it!"

I slog up the dune, wishing I had wings too. Or wide, webbed feet to help distribute my weight. Anything to help me not sink in so deeply into the sand with every step. I reach the top, gasping for breath, looking ahead to find Sree rather than looking where I'm going.

Mistake.

Big mistake.

I gasp as I trip over a rock I didn't see and fall down, slipping and sliding down the dune. That's when I see the fissure directly in front of me. My heart stops. My throat closes and I can't even scream. I can't see the bottom from this angle. For all I know, it could be a mile deep.

I try to slow myself down, digging my hands into the sand, but it's loose and my descent barely slows. There's nothing but sand to grasp. I'm going to fall into the crack. There's no help for it.

With nothing else in my control, I shut my eyes, not wanting to see how deep it is. The sand turns hard under my back, scraping against me, but that pain doesn't last long before it's replaced by...nothing.

Only air.

My stomach becomes weightless as I fall. If this is how I die, after everything I've been through and survived so far—

"Oof!"

Thoughts are knocked right out of my head when I hit the ground. Along with every ounce of air in my lungs in a whoosh of exhale. My mouth moves as I try to gasp, eyes blurry with tears, desperate for air. All is pain, the sharp initial edge of it slowly giving way to a dull throb.

My vision blurs more and everything becomes gray, then a trickle of air works its way into my lungs. They suddenly expand, and I gasp.

Well, I'm still alive, I guess. Woo-hoo.

Everything hurts but the gray recedes with each fresh intake of hot, dusty, sand-filled air. Each breath is the sweetest thing. I slide my hands across the hard ground underneath me, trying to orient myself.

Rock. Rock with a fine layer of sand. You'd be hard-pressed to find anywhere on Tajss that didn't have the distinctive red sand. All right. I have to open my eyes. It's an effort of will but I crack them open a slit, afraid to look.

I blink away the tears, then shield them with one hand. The sky is bright above me, but I only see it through a crack. A cave. I'm in a subterranean cavern of some kind, the sandy red rock above and around me rough and uneven.

Hmm.

I wiggle my toes experimentally. They obey the command. Good toes. I move up to my calves. Then my thighs and hips. My arms. Everything seems to be in functioning order despite the dull aching pains. I'm hurt, but not too badly.

All right. No need to panic. I just need to—

A scuffing sound penetrates my haphazard attempt to get myself together. My stomach clenches and I freeze in place when I hear it again, followed by an odd, low cry, kind of like the horrifying child of a dog's howl and a cat's hiss.

A hard shot of adrenaline pierces through me. I sit up, even though what I really want to do is keep lying there with my eyes closed praying whatever it is will go away, but that won't help.

So, I breathe past the increase in pain the movement causes and force myself to look toward the sounds. I don't see anything; the cavern is larger than I expected. It's a lot darker deeper in, the light not penetrating across the entire space.

Then I see the glimmer of a pair of eyes. And then another. Are my eyes adjusting to the darkness or are the eyes getting closer to the light? I make out the edges of their silhouettes.

Big. They're *big*. My knees shake, almost refusing to hold me up as I back away.

Hulking mounds sway as they close the distance between us, the outlines of sporadic spikes coming into focus. I scramble to my feet, eyes glued to the approaching creatures.

They step into the light, the one on the right opening its mouth and hissing, displaying razor-sharp teeth.

I swallow hard, staring at the fast-approaching giant lizards. I don't think they just want to say hi. I back up, unable to tear my eyes away from my impending death. That's what I see in those hungry eyes. My death. I hit the rock behind me.

Looking to either side, there's nowhere else to go. This is

it. Nowhere to run. Looking back at the monsters, I do the only thing I can, though I know it's pointless.

I scream.

Scream as loud and hard as I can, sinking my fear, my frustration, my despair at this hard ending to a hard life. This is what all of this was leading to all along? Dying alone in a cavern, filling the bellies of these monsters?

I close my eyes, not wanting to see the end coming. I'll feel it soon enough.

There is a vibration through the ground and a *whoomph* sound as something heavy hits the ground in front of me.

What?

I open my eyes in time to see Lothor swinging his lochaber, the light glinting off the sharp blade as he whirls it in front of himself, blocking the reptilian monsters' approach.

His face is grim, his eyes sparking with rage, the muscles of his arms and torso twisting and contracting with the force he puts behind the swing, his feet braced shoulder-width apart. The blade cuts halfway through one of their skulls in one blow.

The light in the monster's eyes goes out just like that. I gape at Lothor, unable to process that he's here. The other beast howls and hisses at Lothor, its jaws gaping open as it darts its head toward him.

Lothor isn't there anymore. Leaping up and drawing his long knife, he lets go of his lochaber, clearly embedded too deeply in bone to pull out quickly. How is he going to kill the second one with just the knife? He's going to have to get too close!

He baits the second one as the first drops to its knees and then to its side. The second turns away from me chasing after Lothor. He's drawing it away.

My hands clench tight, nails digging into flesh as I wish

there were something more I could do than just stand on the sidelines. Lothor proves quickly enough that he doesn't need any help.

Sliding under the monster's head as it lunges, he stabs up with his knife and penetrates deep into the thick hide. He yanks the knife through, opening a deep, almost perfectly straight cut from neck to chest.

He ducks out from under the creature as blood gushes out of the fatal wound. The creature isn't done yet, snapping its tail at Lothor as it bleeds out. Lothor almost dodges but the tail glances off him.

I wince and he stumbles to the side, but recovers almost immediately, running deliberately in front of the dying beast. He keeps its attention and forces it to move with him. Forcing its heart to pump faster, to spill its life's blood more rapidly. The thing obliges, running and lunging.

Its movements slow, each step heavier and slower, until it lunges one last time then drops down to the ground, hard and without any control. The ground shivers under us, dust rising at the heavy impact.

Dead.

I barely spare a glance for it. I can't look away from Lothor. The muscles of his chest and abs contract with his heavy breathing, his eyes narrowed on the creatures. His hair is a wild, windblown mane around his face and shoulders, his hand clenched into fists at his sides while he searches the dark around him.

Ready for anything.

I watch him assess the situation quickly and realize there are no more threats. Those hot eyes turn to me, the battle intensity in them still at the forefront. I shiver involuntarily when he covers the distance between us in one leap, his body a stunning work of art.

Hard and strong. Beautiful.

"Victoria," he says hoarsely, his eyes desperate as they scan me.

Searching for injuries? He reaches for me but then stops himself, his jaw clenching. He isn't touching me like he clearly wants to, needs to, because he thinks I wouldn't like it, but I'm feeling a little... crazy.

Maybe it's the adrenaline. Maybe it was watching him single-handedly defeat two of those things to save me. Maybe it's just how sweet he's been to me.

I don't know.

All I know is I want to touch him. I want his hands on me. I take a step closer until I'm only a hairbreadth away from him. His eyes meet mine, a question in them. They widen when I brace my hands against his chest, rising to my tiptoes. His hearts beat a rapid tattoo against my palms. Holding his eyes until they blur from how close we are...I set my mouth against his.

Oh...yes.

10

LOTHOR

*M*y pulse pounds in my ears, my senses still on high alert after the battle. I feel every minute detail of the moment. Victoria's scent swirls around me, heady and sweet. The touch of her soft palms against my chest burn like a brand. And her lips...so soft, so lush.

Tentative.

Her taste slowly permeates, her mouth moving gingerly against mine, her hot breath sending tingles through my body. I feel those few points of contact...everywhere.

From the top of my head down to the tips of my toes. My fingers curl into my palms. All I want to do is wrap my arms around her, pull her in against me, rub my hardness against her. She has set me on fire with the delicate touch of her lips against mine.

Her lips open against mine, shy and careful, her tongue making a delicate foray. I groan, deepening the kiss, twining my own against hers. Taking in her taste. I want more, so much more than this.

I want her naked, want to touch and taste every inch of her. I dig my nails into my palms, holding on to a thin edge of control. She's finally touched me of her own accord, after maintaining an invisible but very real barrier between us. The last thing I want to do is push her too hard, too fast. Scare her back into the shell she erected around herself.

I force myself to take only what she gives and no more. No matter how difficult it is. How much I burn to do more, the desire a scalding wave pulsing through me. Pushing me to take what I so badly need. In that moment, something inside me awakens. A part of me that I thought was forever buried, too badly damaged, asleep to survive.

Mine.

That statement courses through me. Through my mind. Through my body.

Mine.

A fire scorches through my body, my nerve endings singing with it. I'm alive, present. Fully and completely *here* in a way I did not even know I was not before. My dragon is awake and he has chosen Victoria.

It is a knowing that is undeniable. Victoria is mine.

She pulls her lips from mine, a breathy sigh escaping and caressing my kiss-wet lips. I beat down the urge to slide my hand around the back of her neck and bring her back to me. To kiss her like I want to. To claim her.

Mine.

Her cheeks are flushed a deep pink, her lips slightly parted and reddened from contact with my own. Her eyes flutter open, the heat in them making my dragon buck in response.

Mine!

Her hands fall from my chest and she looks down, but she does not step away. Still, she is clearly not ready for more. And what she needs is what is important. What I will abide by.

"Come," I say, voice hoarse with desire denied. "Let us return home. I need to see to your wounds."

I know she only understands that I want to leave, but that is the most important part of what I said in any case. She nods, watching me expectantly. I look up through the opening above that led down to this cavern.

It's too high, the handholds too precarious for Victoria to climb up on her own. I'll need to leap out using my wings. Which means I'll need to hold her. I take a deep breath, steeling myself for another test of my control.

I meet Victoria's eyes, holding my arms out to her. She looks up, clearly gauging the distance herself. Biting her lip, she looks at me, nodding. I let out a silent sigh when she steps trustingly into my arms. She is learning that I am safe.

That knowledge helps me maintain the strong leash I must keep on myself. Swinging her precious weight into my arms, I pause when she winces.

"Am I hurting you?" I ask frowning, hoping she can glean what I mean by my expression.

She says something I do not understand, but gestures to her back before patting my chest carefully. Telling me her back is hurt and that it is fine. I hold her as gently as I can, but I need to maintain a firm grip on her for safety. I move quickly.

Crouching, I propel myself into the air, spreading my wings to help with the lift. Victoria squeaks, her hands tightening on me as we rise up. I land as softly as I can, using my knees to absorb the shock of the impact.

Rather than putting her down, however, I turn toward the cave and travel the distance with her still in my arms. We are not far and it will take at least three times as long to reach our destination if Victoria walks.

She's hurt. She doesn't need to put more strain upon her body if she does not need to. I hurry, using my wings to help leap across long distances, reaching the cave in only moments. It's lucky we didn't travel very far.

When we reach the welcome coolness of the cave, I set her on a stool. I grit my teeth as her soft body rubs against me.

"Stay," I order when she tries to get up.

She sits back down, familiar with that word. It's an important one for safety, so I made sure she knows it. I pick up a freshwater flask, some clean cloths, and the jar I keep filled with healing paste made with sismis claws. It's potent, aiding in rapid wound healing.

Turning back to Victoria, I set everything down on the table next to her. She watches curiously as I begin with her hands. They are raw, with a few minor cuts and bruises, most likely in an attempt to stop her fall.

Taking them one by one, I wet a cloth and clean them off. I know it must hurt to do so, so I preform the necessary cleaning as quickly as I can. Victoria stiffens and holds her breath but stays still and allows me to do what is necessary.

"Done," I murmur when they are clean. Setting down the cloth, I pick up the jar, removing the lid. Victoria leans forward, her eyes on the paste. "Healing paste," I explain. "For wounds."

I scoop out a healthy portion and point at her cuts and bruises. Comprehension dawns on her face and she nods, holding out her small, battered hands.

I clench my jaw, holding back the growl that wants to come out. I don't like seeing her hurt like this. Even with wounds that are relatively minor. I rub the ointment between my palms and take her left hand first, gently rubbing it all over her palm, the back of her hand, making sure to get it between her fingers and at the very tips where some of her nails have torn.

Victoria sighs. A sound of relief. I look at her face and see her eyes are closed. The paste is quite soothing. Setting that hand down lightly on her thigh, I move to the other, trying to ignore my reaction to her response and to touching even such an innocuous part of her body.

How can hands excite me? I don't know, but my cock presses up against the cloth straining to cover it. I force myself to stop when her other hand is covered in the paste. Clearing my throat, I stand up, stepping behind Victoria.

I am hoping she does not see the clear evidence of my desire. I don't want to frighten her with my need. Then I am confronted with another test. Her shirt has a few small tears and drops of blood are seeping through here and there. I must clean her back.

Taking the material between my fingertips, I tug on it. Victoria stills, but she doesn't stop me when I lift the shirt over her head. Raising her arms, she allows me to pull the material completely off.

Baring her delicate shoulders and narrow back, it's interrupted only by a thin band of cloth across the center. Some kind of breast band.

I force my breathing to slow, and reach out to gently gather her thick, silky hair and move it over her shoulder. I'm distracted from the softness of it under my hands when I can finally see almost the entirety of her back.

I hiss out a breath, taking in the already-forming bruises and the red marks that will almost certainly become bruises if not tended to. On top of that, her skin is raw from rubbing over sand, and she has a few small cuts.

A drop of blood slides down from one of them as I watch, probably from pulling the shirt off of it. I reach for a clean cloth to dampen it, focused mostly on my task once more.

Mostly.

I don't think anything will allow me to forget that her torso is almost completely bare. Moving the other stool over so I can sit behind her, I take a deep breath. It doesn't help. I breathe in the distinctive scent that is Victoria.

Reaching out, I carefully wipe the cloth across her back, ginger with the bruises and cuts, especially the one still bleeding. Victoria stays still, allowing me to minister to her. I hit the breast band, accidentally wetting it.

"Sorry," I murmur.

Even as I say it, she reaches back and unhooks that small piece of cloth and shrugs out of it, holding it only to her front. Exposing her entire back. I don't know why it makes a difference, but it does.

My cock is trying to drill a hole through the cloth. My hand isn't completely steady when I continue on with the rest of her back. Where it is not wounded, her skin is smooth and pretty. Utterly pettable.

I want to wrap my hands around that slender waist, trace the delicate furrow of her spine. Kiss my way down it. Her breaths come faster, her small ribcage rising and falling under my hand.

And then it is clean. I set down the cloth. Now the hard part. Not that maintaining any kind of sense so far has been an easy task. I reach for the jar, scooping out a larger amount this time. Enough to cover her entire back.

Rubbing it between my hands long enough to warm it, I stare at her back for a moment. At the utterly feminine shape of her. At her shining hair, her beautiful neck. I should not do this. I do not know if I have the control.

Reaching forward, I press my palms against her. She shivers slightly under my hands, but she does not move away from my touch. I shift the stool closer, watching my hands smooth down her back, the slick paste helping them slide. It does not take long to cover her entire back. One of my hands is large enough to span her waist, but I don't stop rubbing the paste in, unable to break the skin-on-skin contact.

"Lothor..." Victoria sighs, her head falling back against my shoulder, her eyes closed.

Just a little more...

I slide my hands around her waist to the softness of her belly. I'm on the edge, playing with fire, too entranced to stop myself from going farther. Breath harsh even to my own ears, I raise my hands. She trembles underneath the touch, but again, does not move away.

Reaching the breast band, I pinch the fabric in the middle and tug. Her hands fall and I pull that scrap of fabric away. My eyes immediately go to the now-exposed curves of her breasts.

Pale and soft, with pink tips, the sight of them has my cock surging once more. I'm so hard I almost reach climax at the sight of them alone, but I do not care if I have.

Kissing the translucent skin of her temple, I slide my slick hands up to her breasts and cup the heavy softness of them.

Victoria gasps, arching slightly into the touch even as she trembles. I squeeze them, but not too hard.

Gentle, gentle.

Her skin is so soft, her body so vulnerable. The pink tips are hard under my fingertips.

Victoria jerks against me when I rub at them, her hands reaching down to grip and squeeze my thighs. I shudder against her, shutting my eyes at the sight of her.

Of my hands on her.

Of hers on mine.

She hasn't stopped trembling.

She isn't ready, not yet comfortable enough with me even though she doesn't reject my touch. I must stop. I don't want to extend this beyond her limits. Letting go of her breasts and sliding my hands down to her waist is difficult. Carefully pushing her upright even more so.

"Sorry," I murmur when she opens her eyes, using the word I learned from her. "I must..."

I stand and her eyes drop to my erection tenting my pants. There's no hiding it. Her eyes widen at the sight.

Fear?

I don't know, but I am large everywhere in comparison to her. I take a step back, my eyes raking over her naked torso, her mussed hair, her flushed face. She is tempting. Too tempting for me right now.

I turn away and stalk out of the cave, closing the door behind me. I don't walk off, unwilling to leave her unprotected, especially after what just happened, but I need to be away from the sight of her, the smell of her.

How am I going to contain myself? She sleeps near me, we eat every meal together, spend most of every day together...

Groaning, I slide down the door and sit on the ground. This is going to be a slow kind of torture.

11

VICTORIA

*L*othor brings in some more vegetables and the light glints off his hair, emphasizing his high cheekbones. It plays off the small horns that emerge from his hairline and curl backward, making them sparkle as they reflect the light.

He flashes a quick smile, his face wonderfully familiar and comfortable. My pulse increases and my breath quickens. Now it's for a completely different reason than the fear it used to be.

"Good food," he says, setting down the basket.

I nod, stepping forward and looking at the overflowing basket.

"Good food," I agree.

I sort through it, separating out the ones that need to ripen fully and those that should be stored in a cool, dry place until we eat them. Lothor goes to the food store and takes out a piece of dried meat, offering it to me.

"Hunger?" he asks, in that accent I can't help but think is cute.

We've exchanged a few words, both in his tongue and my

own. The ones that are the most practical for us definitely had priority, so we can communicate a little better now. Maybe we can eventually have a full conversation without miming things out.

I can't help smiling as I remember some of the odd-looking gestures Lothor came up with to tell me he had to relieve himself. That was different.

"No, thank you," I return, using the Zmaj language.

He nods, taking a bite of the meat. I turn my attention back to the produce. He always does that. Asks me if I want or need something before he takes it himself. Always prioritizing my needs over his own. He's been so gentle with me, so careful. He hasn't tried to make any moves or tried to capitalize on the fact that we've exchanged those intimate moments.

I glance over and warmth suffuses my chest. My heart is definitely softening. How could it not? He's been nothing but sweet, which is not a word I thought I'd ever use to describe a Zmaj, but there it is.

Surreptitiously I watch as he finishes his food and then looks through the food stores. I know what he'll find; there's not a lot of meat left. He turns back to me and I immediately look away, trying to appear like I wasn't watching.

"Victoria."

"Hmm?"

Is he buying the nonchalant act?

"You, stay," he orders, pushing his hands down toward the ground. "I hunt." He pats himself on the chest and points toward the door.

My stomach tightens and cold chills run down my arms. How long will he be gone? What if something happens to him this time? I'm under no illusion that he's invincible. He's powerful, but he could still be killed by one of the many dangers out there.

He frowns and takes a step toward me. He raises his hands partway and I take an involuntary step back. He drops them without finishing the gesture. Why did he raise them though? To offer comfort? I'm sure that's what he meant, but damn it that simple gesture triggers me so hard. I clearly didn't hide my fear. He stares, his frown deepening, then he nods as if deciding something.

"You...come hunt."

"Come...hunt?" I repeat, not sure I heard him right.

He nods.

"Come hunt." Going to the door, he opens it, and looks back at me unexpectedly.

Oh boy. I hesitate. Do I want to go hunt? Maybe the more relevant question is do I want to stay here alone? I step toward Lothor, still undecided. Looking around the small space we call home it hits me how empty it is when he's not here.

Nope. Not staying here alone again, not after the last incident. I walk out of the cave and wait for Lothor to lead the way. I have no idea how to hunt or where we're going for that matter, or even how long we'll be gone.

Unprepared is the mildest word I could use for how I'm feeling. Lothor moves past me, carefully avoiding getting too close despite the small pathway leading down. I watch his broad back as he walks in front of me, down the path and out into the desert.

Doubts assail me, thoughts spinning around in a storm. Fears. Fear of being alone, fear of his size, fear of this planet, fear of dying, fear of everything. Through it all though one thing becomes certain: I trust Lothor. Enough to follow blindly into the expanse of sand.

When we're out among the dunes, he turns with purpose, so at least he knows what general direction he wants to go in. I struggle to keep up, my feet sinking in with each step. He moves so easily across the loose sand and I know he's going much slower than he would if he were alone, but it's still a good clip for me.

He looks over his shoulder, his gaze assessing. He stops in place, waiting for me to stop as well.

"Walk...with me," he says, holding his arm out to his side, but he doesn't close the distance between us, his eyes watching me patiently.

Waiting to see what I'll do. Biting my lip, I consider my options. I'm going really slow in comparison to how fast I know he can move, and the slower I go, the longer we'll be out here. Which means we're potentially in danger longer...

Closing my eyes I take a deep breath, hold it, and push down the sick feeling in my stomach. Stepping into the space he's made for me at his side, I ball my hands into fists waiting for the panic to hit. He wraps a brawny arm securely around my waist.

Any second it's going to hit, but I feel that innocent touch more keenly than I should. Feel the relative coolness of his body against mine like a brand. I never thought I'd be so drawn to that coolness that's just so...other. It's one of the things that shouts that Lothor isn't human. That he's alien.

It's funny, but I've kind of stopped seeing the horns, the tail, the scales, and the wings. The sight of him is as familiar to me as the cave that is now home, but the coolness of his body is still more new. It stirs something deep inside me, something so long dormant I can't put a finger on what it is exactly, except that the panic doesn't come.

I don't have time to ponder over that, however. Held securely to his side now, Lothor *moves*. There's a whispering rush as his wings flare and the shadow of them shades my back when we travel, our feet skimming over the sand. We're going fast enough that a warm breeze blows on me. It's almost nice.

My heart rate spikes but then settles only a bit above normal as we traverse the desert together. What must it be like to feel so powerful out here? To know you could fight if you needed to, could possibly run and leave danger behind if necessary?

I'm envying his strength. Maybe I wouldn't be as easily frightened as I am if I were stronger. Faster.

"Bivo," Lothor grunts, interrupting my thoughts.

"Hmm?"

He's scanning the sand to the right, his strong profile stunning in the bright double sun light. Following his gaze I see what has caught his eye. Footprints. A lot of them, leading away in a river of disturbed sand.

Bivo, assuming Lothor is right, as he'd know more than I. I couldn't tell what kind of animal it is from the prints. The dry, blowing sand doesn't allow clear-cut prints, and what do I know of hunting on Tajss or anywhere for that matter?

Bivo. I can't come up with a visual off the top of my head. Have I heard of them before? Shrugging, I follow Lothor as he adjusts our path so that we're following the very obvious trail of what I have to assume is a large pack.

The tracks grow deeper in the red, drifting sand and I guess I won't have to wonder what they look like for long. Lothor tempers his speed, moving more carefully as we stalk the pack. We travel for a bit longer, following the trail, and I know we must be close when Lothor slows even more.

He stops at the base of a swelling dune, his head tilting to the side, his eyes sharp. He lets go of me and I feel vulnerable once more. Wrapping my arms around myself to push down an instant of panic, I look around nervously. Lothor leans down close to my ear.

"Victoria, stay," he whispers. It's a breath of sound.

The animals must be close. I nod, not wanting to be

stupid and argue about going with him. I'm not an idiot and he knows what he's doing out here, which I definitely do not.

I watch him go up that dune in a low crouch, his hands digging into the soft sand as he moves. When he reaches the top, he lies down and inches up that last bit in almost an army crawl, his tail whipping out behind him, jerking left to right.

He stays there for a minute or two, his head swiveling slowly as he takes in whatever view he has. I stay exactly where he put me, looking around carefully before turning my attention back to him, only to find him skimming back down the dune. Stopping in front of me, he holds out an open hand, his expression encouraging. Swallowing, I set my own, much smaller one in it.

The contrast of his darker skin and massive hand against my own is oddly sharp in that second before he tugs me up after him. Maybe because of the adrenaline everything feels a little sharper, a little clearer as I follow Lothor up, mimicking him and staying low.

Before we hit the top, he stops and makes a down gesture with his hand as he drops to his belly. I drop along with him, lying down so that we're hopefully even less visible. We inch up that last little bit, just high enough so we can see and no higher.

"Bivo," Lothor repeats.

I nod dumbly, my eyes glued to the sight below. It's definitely a pack. Or maybe herd is a better word for them. They look like giant, hairy buffalo, animals I only know from some of the nature documentaries about Earth I saw while we were still on the ship. They are...big.

Huge doesn't even do them justice. Their heads are enormous, with protruding tusks, crimson eyes, and massive necks. Probably to hold up those impressive heads.

Currently, they appear to be milling about, rooting around in the sand with those tusks.

One of them stands to one side, apart from the herd. This one appears larger than the others, eyes a bit meaner, with scars in its fur along one side. From fighting? Maybe it's the leader or something? I can't be sure about that, but one thing seems clear even to my untrained eye—they don't seem intent on moving anytime soon. Perfect for us.

"Stay," Lothor whispers, his breath brushing my ear, warming my skin and making my cheeks heat more than the double suns above can account for.

He's gone before I can agree, sliding down the dune the way we came. Where is he going?

I lose sight of him a couple of times while he circles around the herd, only to find him once more to my left. I hold my breath as he slithers over the top of the dune, half buried in sand, his eyes focused below. I follow his line of sight to one of the bivo.

It's a medium-sized one that's rooting around at the base of the dune, a little bit away from the rest. My eyes shift back to Lothor. I'm too afraid to even blink as I watch him creep down to his prey, but he doesn't come down directly on it or even super close. Instead he slides down behind it and then slowly scoops up some sand?

What the heck is he doing? He throws the sand and it spatters against the bivo's backside. Hard, judging by how quickly it jerks its head up and gallops forward, away from Lothor, who has buried himself in the sand once more. Forward and away from the rest of the herd moving out of sight.

As I watch the herd mates around the bivo shift restlessly, snorting as they move their massive heads around, their nostrils flaring in an attempt to pick up a stray scent. The biggest one raises its head in response, watching the others with hard eyes.

Lothor must have ice water in his veins because he stays so still. I can barely find him again. After maybe a minute of high alert, the tension in the heard ratchets down once more. Maybe they think their fellow comrade just caught a wild hare and wanted a run. I don't know, but I'll take it.

Once things have calmed, Lothor slithers back up the dune, his body moving half under the sand to stay hidden. Once he's passed the dune's crest and out of sight of the herd, I breathe a sigh of relief. Only then do I think about where the heck that other bivo may have gone.

Even as I think it, there is a snort from behind me. My breath hitches and I freeze. Did it come up behind me? Am I about to be trampled by one of those giant hairy things?

Swallowing, I turn my head slowly, trying to mimic how I saw Lothor move. I don't see anything right away. Not until I look down. And find the stray bivo.

It's farther away than the sound suggested, trotting slowly along the bottom of the dune, its attention on the path in front of it. Not on me at all. I breathe a sigh of relief. That I immediately suck back in when I see Lothor leaping along behind the bivo, swift and silent.

By the time the bivo realizes that it's being hunted and whirls around, baring its teeth, Lothor is on top of it. His lochaber slices right through one of those red eyes and straight into the beast's brain. It doesn't even have a chance to howl a death cry. I let out the breath I sucked in once more. Okay.

The fur ripples as it falls over into the sand, landing almost softly in that cushion. Bracing a foot against that massive head—he looks almost small next to it, something I didn't think was possible—Lothor pulls the resisting blade out of the creature's head.

I can't hear anything from this distance, but I wince anyway, imagining the odd slurp it probably made coming out. Lothor turns to me, his chest rising and falling with deep breaths from the expertly executed hunt. Raising a hand, he waves me over.

I nod, sliding down the sand carefully. I don't want to alert the rest of the herd that we're here. It takes me a bit to trudge through the sand, Lothor's eyes scanning the area around us constantly. He's still clearly in battle mode when I reach him, his jaw hard, nostrils flared, eyes narrowed.

Warmth plunges through my belly to my sex, forming an empty ache. Why do I find that so sexy? My cheeks warm as it happens and I can't meet his eyes, looking anywhere but him. Not that there's anything to look at, just sand and more sand rolling on and on.

When I reach him, he sets down the lochaber and pulls out two long knives. Flipping one of them over, he hands it to me hilt first. I take it, unsure about what exactly he wants me to do with it.

"Meat," he murmurs, turning to the animal.

He sinks the blade through the side, cutting through the thick hide. I wrinkle my nose at the sight, but also at the fur and manure smell coming off the animal. All my carnal thoughts are washed away with the sight and smells. I can't even imagine how the herd must smell if we were down in the thick of it. I watch as he skins the side of the giant beast, blood coating his hands.

Swallowing, I steel myself. This is no time to turn squeamish. Stepping up next to him, I follow Lothor's lead. I'm sure my hacking at the creature isn't very impressive, but Lothor looks at me with approval in his eyes, smiling in encouragement. It almost makes the blood worth it.

To my surprise, I get over the gore of the situation pretty fast. The practical side of my mind takes over. This is food.

We're not going to waste Lothor's hard work or this animal's sacrifice, and that means dressing it and harvesting the meat.

Even more surprising than the sudden practicality, I realize I'm actually enjoying working alongside Lothor. Sure, this isn't the most enjoyable task, objectively speaking, but I can't deny I like that we're working together. Like a real team.

I look over at Lothor's intent profile while he works alongside me, quick and efficient. The butterflies dance in my stomach for an entirely different reason as I study him, letting my hands do their work. It's good, nice, maybe even something more.

I refocus on the task in front of me, purpose infusing me in a way it hasn't in a good, long while. And it feels damn good.

LOTHOR

*V*ictoria seasons the fresh cuts of meat, her brow furrowed in concentration as she rifles through various herbs.

"Salt, of course...this...or..."

I listen to her talk, half to herself. I love listening to her speak, even though I can only understand a fraction of what she says. Her voice is so soothing, the chatter making this place I call home actually feel like it. That is what it is, is it not? Victoria has made the cave into a home. I cannot imagine not having her in it anymore.

"...this?" she asks, holding up an herb that can be particularly bitter.

"A small amount," I say, holding up my fingers in a small pinching motion to help convey the meaning of my words. "Can be bitter." I make a face to show that is not good.

A smile breaks across her face that sets my pulse racing. She is so lovely. Both inside and out.

"You know... cooking."

She says more words in between that I do not fully understand, but the intent of her words is clear enough.

"I... remember cooking before the Devastation," I say as an empty ache blooms in my chest.

My attention is drawn to the artifacts on the shelf, something about Victoria's comment pulling it to them. What is it about them? The fog of the bijass swells, rising and falling, refusing to give up the memories attached to them. I force myself to look away from the shelf that stirs so many disjointed emotions.

"Are you okay?" Victoria asks.

Focusing on her, I force myself to smile, pushing away the empty sense of loss of whatever it is I can't remember.

"Yes, sorry. I remember cooking and the mistakes I made."

She bites her lower lip, her eyes narrowing. Her hands motion, as if going to reach for me, but then she drops them to her sides. She nods at last and finishes spicing the meat without more questions.

"Done," she announces, stepping back with a nod of satisfaction. "I think it's good."

"I am certain it will be good," I return.

I know she understands *good*, but I make sure to convey my approval with my tone and expression as well while I pick up the meat. I am certain it will be good.

Once Victoria learned all the spices and herbs and what flavors they imparted on the food, she became remarkably good at finding combinations that I have never thought of. The mix she used today smells particularly appetizing, wafting up to my nose when I pick up the platter and take it to the fire burning just outside the cave.

Once I place it on the spit and on the rocks for cooking, the scent strengthens, drawing a growl from my stomach. Victoria laughs at the grumble, a joyful and carefree sound that sets my thoughts soaring and my loins to burning.

I stare at her glowing face, wishing I could take her in my

arms and taste the laughter on her tongue. Touch that wonderfully curvy body.

With an effort of will I go back to the meat, turning it to ensure even cooking. I must exert complete control over myself. She is not ready.

I do not know why she hesitates, but I do not need to know. I will not push the issue, not when she has only just begun to trust me. So I content myself with listening to her talk about anything and everything. The food, the cave, or Sree, the kedi who is never far from her new mistress.

When the food is done it brings some relief, giving me something to do with my hands and mouth. It's a poor second place to what I want to be doing with them, but not because the food is not delicious.

"Good," I remark, taking another bite with gusto.

The flavor explodes on the tongue, but also manages not to be overpowering.

"Thank you," she responds, clearly enjoying the food herself. "But...nothing...without the hunt."

I nod, accepting her thanks, my chest swelling and my hearts pounding. It feels good to provide for her, stirring memories, but more than that giving my life meaning. A purpose besides surviving day to day for no other reason than I didn't know what else to do.

Good food, good company. Yes, my night could be much worse.

We relish the food, talking to each other in a mixture of her tongue and mine, neither of us fully understanding every word. We don't need to in order to enjoy ourselves.

When we are done eating, my body feels heavy and my chest constricts. Soon, we shall sleep. A necessity, of course, but all I want to do is spend more time with Victoria. There is no way to satiate this need I have for her. Every moment with her is magical and I never want them to end.

Victoria does not stand right away either, though she does not reach for more food. Perhaps... she is enjoying my company as well? I linger, waiting, unsure what to say or do but unwilling to break the moment. There is nothing but the sound of our breathing, the delicate whisper of hot wind traversing the desert sands, and the two of us. She's outlined in silvery moonlight, making her even more beautiful. My scales itch and my tail shifts in the sand making a dragging sound then Victoria stands.

"Clean up," she sighs glancing at me with an indiscernible look.

I nod, standing with my plate, not able to justify dawdling any longer. I reach for her plate as well, stopping when my hand lightly touches hers as she reaches for it at the same time. A flash of heat races through my body from the brief brush of her fingertips against the back of my hand, and my prime cock stiffens.

I still at the unexpected touch, savoring it. Waiting for her to pull back.

One moment turns into two.

And then three, but she does not pull away.

No, she does the exact opposite. I take a shaky breath as her small, slender fingers trail up my arm, her eyes cast down, not meeting mine. Her other hand joins in, trailing up my left arm.

I watch as they slide up, across my biceps to my shoulders, hesitating a moment before sliding onto my chest. I tremble under the delicate touch.

Facing a bivo is simple, easy, the stakes low in comparison to... this.

I raise my eyes from where she is touching me and they clash with hers. Her cheeks are flushed, but she meets my gaze without flinching. Heat simmers in that look. Desire.

It calls me, pulling at the same rising tension in myself.

My cock throbs, my breath catches, my heart pounds loud in my ears.

"Victoria..." I sigh, reaching to wrap my arms around her slender waist.

Moving slowly, carefully. Not wanting to frighten her away with the enormity of my want. She does not pull away when I shift her closer to my body. Does not turn her head when I lift her up and lean down, closing the distance between our heights.

Then my mouth is on her soft one, the taste of her seeping into me. I groan, clenching my hands on her. I want to touch more of her. Holding her close, I kiss her carefully, delicately, while I carry her over to my pallet. I want my hands free.

Dropping down to the soft cushion of the pallet with her underneath me, I deepen the kiss. I shudder when her tongue makes a foray into my mouth, rubbing against my own.

Careful not to put too much of my weight on her, knowing I could easily crush her under my much larger body, I position myself over her. She shifts under me, sighing.

My cock jerks at the soft sound. The kiss turns a little wild, a little less controlled, my hand sliding up her side to cup the soft curve of her breast, but I am frustrated at the feel of her shirt rather than her skin.

Growling in the back of my throat, I slide my hand under her shirt and back up, forcing the small covering she wears under her shirt up.

I cup her now-naked breast in my hand, kneading it, rubbing the hardened tip. It's exotic, strange and alien, her breasts protrude out unprotected, so different than a Zmaj female. I want to taste it.

Breaking the kiss, I have a brief glimpse of Victoria's face, her eyes glittering with heat, lips slightly parted, but then I must focus on what I reveal when I raise her shirt. Round and perfect, the pink tips tight with excitement.

"Beautiful," I murmur, knowing she cannot understand me.

I hope she can understand how much I want her. Not able to hold back for another moment, I take her exposed breast into my mouth.

Sucking, licking.

"Lothor!" she cries out, her hands sliding up my shoulders, my neck, and into my hair, gripping a touch too tight.

But I enjoy the tug, enjoy her obvious desire for me. Her hips thrust up against me, the jerky movement seeming almost involuntary. There is another part of her she wants touched.

My cock is so hard, it aches, throbbing with need. All I want to do is glut myself on her. I slide my hand down her soft, trembling stomach and under her clothing.

Straight to the hot, wet core of her.

I pull off her chest to look down, watching my hand move under her clothes. I want to remove them, but I also do not want to pull my hand away yet. Or ever.

I slide my fingers down the drenched softness of her folds, listening to her gasp. She arches into the touch. I could listen to her, pet her like this, forever.

Suddenly she stiffens underneath me. I still, pausing. Did I hurt her?

"Victoria?"

I look up to her face, but she does not look back at me, shaking her head, her small hands pushing me away.

I grit my teeth and pull my hands off of her. It hurts to do so, but I will not force anything. Especially not this.

"I'm sorry," she mutters, shoving her shirt down to cover herself and climbing to her feet. She still does not look at me. "I-I can't do this."

She hurries out of the cave, followed by her furry shadow. I listen, hearing her stop just outside. She will be safe this close. I drop onto my back, taking a deep breath.

My cock stands straight up under its now too-meager covering. It does not understand, aching with unfulfilled desires. Closing my eyes I ignore it, focusing on what matters.

What did I do wrong?

Did she not want any of it? But then why did she touch me?

I scrub my hands over my face, unsure what I can glean from this encounter. All I know is that I feel even more alone now without her softness and heat next to me.

13

VICTORIA

I run out of the cave without any thought about where to go. I mean, there isn't really anywhere *to* go, is there? I stumble to a stop right outside. Looking around, lost, I go over to the low bench by the firepit and sit.

Sree jumps up, curling in my lap. I bury my face in her soft fur, beyond frustrated with myself. What is wrong with me? How could I do that to Lothor—again? Heck, how could I do that to myself again?

I want more with him. Want to go that last step with him. Want to share my body with him. He's so sweet, so caring. And God, he's hotter than fire!

But even though I feel that downright raging desire for him, constantly thinking about what it would be like to be with him like that, I'm still afraid.

"Victoria."

I jerk at his deep, gentle voice. I raise my head, but I can't look. My cheeks warm as I cover my face with my hands as a tingle sweeps up my neck and across my face.

"Go inside," he says carefully, gently. "I am outside."

I miss a couple of the words, but nod in understanding. I

peek through my hands, catching a brief glimpse of his face. I can't read much off of it. He's not looking at me directly, staring off to his left. He's moved as far away from the path to the cave as he can, leaving it open for me.

"Okay," I say, picking Sree up.

Ducking my head, I hurry back into the cave. Even now, he came out and sent me back in to keep me safe. It's unbelievable, he's so kind, so perfect. I'm in awe of him yet unable to open myself. I go straight to my pallet and pull the covers over my head.

Sree paws at me lightly, mewling in complaint. Sighing, I pull them off my face, blowing my hair out of my eyes.

Okay, logic. Assess it out. Here's what I know.

I want to have sex with Lothor. I'm also scared of having sex with Lothor. Why am I scared?

He's never done anything to deliberately scare me. If nothing else, the last two times I've stopped things have shown me he'd never do anything I wasn't comfortable with.

I turn over onto my side, staring at the rock. Deep down I know what this is. It's the same reason I joined Gershom's group even though I didn't share his racist views.

Father. And all the scars he left me with.

I know, intellectually, that Lothor isn't him. He would never use his physical strength against me, a fact that he's proven repeatedly.

I guess I've been so conditioned to view male strength as a threat that my heart just can't let it go. Can't fully accept that Lothor is safe. That he won't hurt me. It's so damn frustrating!

Especially when it keeps running up against my desire to be closer. I cover my eyes with my forearm, my mind working over the problem. That I've gotten as far as I have in terms of physical closeness is a testament to how much I want Lothor.

There's something about surrendering myself, about making myself as vulnerable as a woman can be with another person that triggers that fear. How do I get past that last hump, no pun intended?

I drop my arm only to find Sree's eyes focused on me, wide and unblinking. I shut my eyes. I can't think about this with her staring at me like that. I take a deep breath and let it out.

All right.

Maybe I'm overthinking this. Maybe I just need to desensitize myself to the thought of him a little, in the context of intimacy in particular. I look at the cave door, listening intently. I know he's gone outside somewhere. I also know he hasn't gone far, even though I can't see him. Regardless, he isn't here right now.

With how much time we spend together, maybe I should take advantage of that, use this time to help with this issue. Besides that I also need a release. Still listening intently, I slide my hand down my stomach.

Imagining it's Lothor's big, gentle hand. He has the best hands.

I slide my much smaller one down my pants straight to where I'm still wet and hot from everything he did. I sigh, sliding my fingers through my slick folds, thinking of Lothor.

Of his scent.

His taste.

The rapt look on his face when he kisses me, touches me.

I push my other hand under my shirt, gripping my breast like he does. Wishing it were him doing it. I bite my lip, feeling the tension build. The heat rise.

Sensations race through my body, pushing aside fears until I forget that he likely isn't that far. Forget that I'm not really behind closed doors. It feels too good...

14

LOTHOR

I pace outside the cave, but not far. I will not leave Victoria vulnerable, but I need to keep moving., I'm too agitated to remain still. My mind circles around Victoria, around what might have gone wrong.

I failed. Failed to help her feel comfortable. Pushed her too fast, too far? Perhaps.

Perhaps she simply wanted a kiss and I began to paw at her, my voracious hunger for her taking over as soon as she made the slightest gesture like the starving man that I am.

Raking my hands through my hair, I growl. I failed. Failed Victoria when she placed her trust in me. Took too much from her.

I frown. Is that right? It is part of it, but there is something more, something I can't put my finger on. The bijass throbs, its cloudy covering struggling to contain the past trying to break through. The sense of failure triggers something more. Victoria is not quite...all of it?

A hollow pit forms in my guts, a feeling that is not quite failure, but something deeper.

Older. Heart-wrenching.

I turn, continuing to pace as I try to name this emotion, swirling so very completely with that sense of failure. I am failing Victoria... too?

Confusion lies over everything. I shake my head, trying to clear it, but nothing resolves. Nothing makes sense. This has ignited something else inside me, emotions without a tether to any event or moment. Or, at the very least, a tether I cannot quite recall.

This sense of failure and loss, what happened? What is my mind protecting me from?

I try to go deeper, attempting to scratch that surface layer, look underneath as to the cause, the origin of it, but it is as though I hit a wall. A hard surface in my mind that simply bounces my forays back.

I try to find a crack, a grip, something, but to no avail. Snarling, I walk faster, balling my hands into fists and digging my nails into the soft flesh of my palms.

Looking around, I'm on top of the dunes. I cannot go any farther; it's too risky to be too far from her. I turn back toward the cave, abandoning the frustrating, fruitless search of my mind. Of myself.

With enough time, perhaps there will be a way to push past that wall, crack through it to what eludes me on the other side. Find the source of this vague pain that never quite leaves me. If I could...

My steps slow as I hear something. What was that?

I hear it again.

Low and quiet, but unmistakable. A moan. A very feminine one.

My cock jerks in response, knowing immediately what that sound is. My feet move forward silently, drawn closer by the soft sounds coming from the cave.

Stopping outside the door I hear a gentle rustling sound and then a gasp. Breath coming quicker, I lean forward, slowly and carefully. Only for a moment, but it is long enough to sear the image into my brain.

Victoria, lying down on her pallet with the covers kicked off of her, her shirt rucked up to expose one breast, her hand inside her clothes. Between her thighs. Working rhythmically.

Her back arches as I watch, her teeth biting her lip, cheeks flushed, eyes thankfully closed as she concentrates on her pleasure. I bite back my own moan as I quickly pull back from the door, leaning against the rock next to it.

My hand finds my cock of its own accord, squeezing the throbbing organ hard. Closing my eyes, I grit my teeth, trying to resist the pulsing need. Her soft moan slips through the door, caressing my hearing like the soft touch of her fingers on my scales.

I cannot hold back any longer. Shoving the cloth aside, I grip my thick length in my fist, imagining it is Victoria's soft, small hand rather than my own larger, callused one. Her hand sliding up and down. Her hand rubbing the wet tip, twisting slightly at the top...just...so...

I groan as I stroke, my balls pulling up tight, ready to explode. Long denied need pounds in my cock, pulsing with every beat of my hearts. Then she gasps louder, reaching her own climax, and I can hold back no longer. I spill onto my hand, climaxing so quickly it leaves me shaken.

My legs tremble from the release, so necessary. I take a deep breath, hearing the quiet inside. Knowing Victoria has reached her own end herself. Wishing I was the one who made her feel that pleasure.

15

VICTORIA

"*A*re we almost there?" I ask.

Lothor nods as he adjusts his grip on me, then he takes another long leap across the desert.

We never really addressed what happened between us, but I'm totally fine with that. At least the language barrier means awkward conversations like that are harder to have. Silver linings, right?

Right.

Mentally I sigh, trying my best to not notice how good Lothor's hard side feels against my own. I'm failing miserably, of course.

"Look," he murmurs, pointing.

I follow the direction he's pointing and blink, trying to decide if I'm seeing a mirage. A verdant green meets my eyes, which is more than a little disconcerting after all the red that makes up Tajss.

"Oh," I breathe.

The oasis probably isn't huge by any standard, but it isn't tiny either. It's at least a few hundred feet long that I can see, with multiple trees and brush. There's a glimmer of water just peeking through. Water. A pool of it. Oh, that sounds amazing.

Lothor slows as we near, coming to a stop a few yards away from the edge of the green patch.

"Follow me," he orders, stepping forward. He stops and scans the area with sharp eyes, then looks over his shoulder at me. "There is...danger," he explains haltingly.

I nod, looking at the oasis with a more critical eye. Danger. Right, of course there is. This is Tajss.

"Here," he says, holding out one of the empty bags he brought along with us.

Right. We're here to gather food. I need to keep my eye on the prize, but that doesn't mean I can't enjoy being here either.

I follow Lothor as he steps through the brush, careful to step only where he does. If there's one thing I know about Tajss, it's that it has come up with a whole lot of creative ways to kill us. It's always better to take as much care as I can.

The shade from the tall trees is lovely on my skin even after that relatively short trip through the desert. My eye snags on something yellow with darker yellow stripes. It looks sort of like a lemon? Interesting. I reach for it—

"No!"

Lothor grabs my wrist in a strong but gentle grip, startling me.

"What's wrong?" I ask, not fighting his hold, putting my trust in him.

He must have a reason to stop me from touching that fruit. He says a word I don't understand so I shake my head.

"What?"

"Not...good," he says, clearly struggling to communicate something.

Giving up on words, he mimes eating the yellow fruit and then bends over, fake retching.

"Oh." I shake my head, looking over at the fruit again. "Poison."

"Poi-son," Lothor repeats. "Bad to eat?"

I nod, lowering my hand.

"Yes. Bad to eat," I agree.

All right. Note to self—don't touch anything Lothor doesn't touch any more than I step anywhere he doesn't. Lothor doesn't let go of his grip on my wrist when he turns and continues deeper into the foliage. I don't pull away, letting him guide me through the lush landscape.

When we stop again, it's because Lothor points at some small, purple, berry-like fruits.

"Good to eat," he says, reaching out to pluck one and placing it in the bag.

I nod, doing the same. I feel a little nervous after my last failed attempt to touch something, but the berries don't bite back as I place them in the bag. Okay then. After we've plucked enough to fill our bags halfway, Lothor moves on.

We're getting closer to the center of the oasis, closer to the water, but we're going in kind of a spiral pattern so Lothor can harvest whatever he thinks will be useful. We stop again near a reddish green herb that looks familiar. The scent when we pluck it reminds me of dried strands I found in Lothor's pantry. It adds a nice savory taste to dishes.

Next we find some green pods that look almost like peas. Lothor seems really excited by them, urging me to gather all that we can, but when curiosity has me raising one to my mouth for a taste, Lothor stops me with a gentle touch to the wrist.

"Must cook," he explains.

"Ah." I put it in the bag with the rest. "Okay."

We continue moving forward. I see another flash of red in

one of the openings between the trees and stop. Maybe there are more berries or something through there?

"Lothor?" I call out stepping toward that opening carefully to get a better look.

When I do, I realize the color is part of a plant with a huge orange and red core. I don't get any closer, frowning as it starts to tremble. Clearly not a fruit—

"Victoria!"

I'm jerked backward, stumbling as a hard hand grips my arm tightly. At the same moment long, green leaves shoot up from the ground, encompassing the area I just was.

I hadn't noticed the plant extended that far. I press a hand to my chest, my heart pounding hard and struggling to catch my breath.

"Cvet. Dangerous," Lothor admonishes, pulling me away from the still-moving plant.

Its prey gone; the plant slowly unfurls once more. Waiting for something else to come along. I shudder, turning away. Damn, I was trying so hard to be careful. Okay then.

I dog Lothor's steps so closely after that that I have to apologize for stepping on his heels a couple of times, but I've definitely learned my lesson. I don't know enough to stray from the path he sets for us. Not even close. I'm learning fast, so there's that.

Maybe soon I'll be able to walk through an oasis like this and know what can kill me. Fingers crossed. I shake my head as we near the thinner area of foliage right before the sandy edge of the actual water.

Oh, it looks gorgeous. Sparkling and clear. A different kind of excitement runs through me at the sight. Suddenly, I'm acutely aware of every speck of dirt and sweat on me. All I want to do is rush forward and jump right into that welcoming pool, but I stop myself. I'm not an idiot.

I'm not doing anything without Lothor clearing it first. If

he isn't rushing over to the water, I'm not rushing over to the water. As if on cue, Lothor stops, holding an arm in front of me to halt me as well.

I freeze, my eyes scanning the area around the water. It takes me a second to find what has him stopping this close. The movement is what alerts me. Oh jeez.

The creature raises its head from where it was drinking, its face oddly reminiscent of a human's. A primate of some kind? It looks kind of like a gorilla, hunched over with its meaty fists resting on the ground, and it looks strong. Really strong.

Its arms are thick with muscle, its shoulders and chest matching that size. Thick, shaggy fur coats its shoulders and the upper parts of its arms. Oddly, its bottom half is without any kind of fur, its skin a deep blue color.

Even hunched over as it is, it looks about as tall as me. Large and strong. And, judging by Lothor's reaction, not necessarily peaceful. We remain still, watching as it scans the area with sharp brown eyes. Its gaze pauses, lingering on the thin foliage that offers us cover. My heart clenches and my breath hitches.

Does it see us? Are we going to have to fight it? We, as in Lothor? Is it alone? What if a whole group of them are here, just waiting for unsuspecting prey?

All of that goes through my mind as we stand stock still, not moving. I don't know about Lothor, but I don't even dare to breathe. Luckily, after a few beats, its eyes continue on. It raises a large hand to scratch at its cheek, then turns around and lumbers away from the water, its fists swinging forward on the ground to help it move.

It disappears into the foliage on the other side. However, Lothor stays in place, his eyes on where it disappeared. Copy that. No moving yet. I stay still, waiting. And waiting some more. Finally, the tension drains from Lothor's body, at least a little.

I don't think he's ever actually relaxed. Maybe in the cave, but even then I can see him periodically checking on things. He turns to me.

"Majmun," he murmurs.

Majmun. I file that information away.

"Safe?" I ask, looking at the water.

It would be a shame if we left without being able to use it. Lothor nods.

"Yes."

Taking my hand, he leads us through the last bit of greenery and out to the narrow strip of sand around the water. I immediately feel more vulnerable without even that thin cover. Watching Lothor's watchful eyes continue to take in the surrounding area is comforting. Nothing is going to sneak up on us, not while he's on watch anyway.

"Water," Lothor murmurs, keeping his voice low.

He takes out his waterskin and fills it at the pool. I follow his lead, crouching next to it, noting the apparent current as I fill my own waterskin. Looks like the water is constantly circulating and being filtered by the sand, which must be why it's so clear. Beautiful, clever, what a design. I bet that is how it keeps from drying out in the massive heat of Tajss.

I drink some of the water from my waterskin, sighing at the cool, refreshing wetness in my parched mouth and throat. Refilling what I drank, I set the skin and the now-full pack I used to gather food aside and turn to Lothor.

I'm not making the mistake of jumping in if it isn't safe, but damn I hope it will be.

"In?" I ask, pointing at the water.

He nods without hesitation and I grin.

Yes! A tingle races down my limbs as my pulse races and my grin grows to a wide smile. The water is so inviting and

I'm so filthy. Reaching for my shirt and starting to undo its fastenings, I stop.

There's no way I'm going to get any kind of privacy here. I don't want to undress in front of Lothor, not when I'm not ready for anything more. After all I've done to him, pulling back and denying his needs, I can't do that to him, not again. I'm not some evil bitch playing with him.

Okay, think this through. My clothes are dirty too and could definitely stand a wash. Shrugging, I make the decision. Tugging off my shoes, I step into the water.

Oh, that feels good. The water isn't really cool, just cooler than the hot desert air. Glancing at Lothor, I can't wait anymore. I wade into the pool, reaching the deeper middle of it where my feet can't touch the ground. Closing my eyes, I submerge myself.

Oh, yeah. It feels so good, even with my clothes on.

I scrub at my hair, trying to get all of the oils and gunk out without soap. Scrubbing my scalp with water feels beyond good. I shake my head under the water then move closer to shore where it is shallower so I can stand.

Then I start on the rest of my body, using the cover of the water to scrub underneath my clothes. I don't know if anything could feel better than the fresh water on my skin.

Lothor watches from the shore, his head swiveling as he scans the area. When his eyes land on me, I smile, which he returns before he's back to scanning. Apparently satisfied at last he strides into the water too.

He doesn't take his clothes off either. I know it's for me. He doesn't want to make me uncomfortable. My heart melts for the thousandth time. He's just so...

Wonderful.

Surreptitiously I watch as he ducks underneath the water as well, coming up with his hair slicked down onto his head. It draws attention to his beautiful face, all masculine angles and soft lips. The way his horns, so alien yet perfect for his face, curve back from his forehead, not large but an accent. To his shoulders, broad and hard with muscle.

I swallow as familiar desire rises in me once more. He's sexy in a beautiful, primal way, but this is so much more than his body. My body responds to his, sure, but I know in that moment that it'll never be far from the surface. Not when it comes to Lothor, because it's so much more than physical.

He moves to shallow water, still watching around us. Turning his head side to side as he scrubs his body. It's so that he can defend us more easily if needed, I know, but it has the added benefit of revealing him down to mid-thigh.

My eyes take that journey with relish. Down his beautiful face. To his muscled chest. Hard stomach, the almost delicate dent of his navel. And straight to the massive cock tenting his pants.

I swallow hard, wondering at it, but then I see where his glittering eyes have landed.

Not at my face.

Or at our surroundings, where maybe they should be.

I look down.

I've inadvertently moved closer to him, slowly but surely. The water is only waist deep on me now and my white shirt isn't doing a very good job of covering much at all.

I bite my lip at the sight of my nipples pressing hard against the transparent cloth of my shirt and bra, the curves of my breasts so clear I may as well be naked. I look back at Lothor. His attention is still focused there.

His desire for me is as clear as it can be, but he doesn't make a move on me. Maintains a respectful distance. What if I no longer want that kind of respect? I take another—this time deliberate—step toward him.

16

LOTHOR

I am not being subtle, or even respectful, but I cannot stop staring at Victoria. At the way her shirt clings to her breasts, shaping them faithfully, the fabric sheer from the water. She may as well be wearing nothing at all. I'm entranced, desire pounding through my veins with every beat of my hearts. My cock throbs, jumping up and down under the thin cloth of my pants.

"Lothor."

I look up at my name, not realizing she has been slowly drifting toward me this entire time, so taken was I by the sight of her. I open my mouth to apologize, wondering if I have made her uncomfortable or if I should turn away, but when I meet her eyes she does not look uncomfortable.

The apology dies in my throat. There is no denying the flush to her cheeks, the slightly parted lips, the way she is looking at me. If all of that was not enough, she closes the distance between us and sets her hands on my chest.

"Victoria?" I whisper hoarsely, not moving to reciprocate, knowing if I move a muscle, I'll lose all semblance of control.

Rather than answering with words, she grips the back of

my neck, tugging me down. I follow without hesitation. A sigh escapes when she sets those soft lips upon my own.

Somewhat hesitant, her lips rub against mine before deepening the contact. The combination of bold and shy makes my cock ache, but anything she could do would have the same result, would it not?

Still, I keep myself under tight control. I do not know what made her pull back last time, but I do not want it again. I stand still, not touching her back, resisting every screaming fiber of my body demanding more. I allow her to kiss me sweetly and touch me softly. I kiss her back, but that is it.

It is all I can allow myself without losing all control. Even this strains my limits; I don't know how much more of it I can stand.

A small hand slides over the length of my erection and I shudder, clenching my jaw, balling my hands into fists, stilling further under her soft mouth. Small fingers grip me through the wet cloth.

My control is simply... gone.

Growling, I cup my hands under Victoria's backside, picking her up and walking her out of the water, my mouth plundering hers.

I take over the kiss, my tongue sliding against hers as I explore her mouth, pressing my lips firmly against hers. Her hands clench on my shoulders, her breath coming out in a shuddering sigh as I sit her down on the soft sand, reaching for the bottom of her shirt.

I break the kiss only long enough to pull her shirt and scrap of fabric under it over her head. Then I reach for her pants, hooking my fingers into them and the small piece of cloth she wears under it as well, stripping it both down her legs. Leaving her completely, deliciously, naked.

I take a moment simply to stare. This is a picture I will never forget, not just because she is beautiful, which she is, but because this is Victoria. Her form is familiar yet alien. Zmaj females breasts are not left exposed like hers. They rise on her chest coming to hard, pink tips that make my mouth water.

She watches me through half-closed eyes, her pulse fluttering in the side of her neck, her arms lying at her sides. Not attempting to cover herself from my gaze. I trail my eyes down. Down to the delicate collarbones. To the round curves of her breasts, so perfect, so soft.

Down to the soft curve of her stomach, the small indentation of her navel. Her small waist flares out beautifully to meet the curve of her hip and then her rounded thighs and slender calves. Even her feet are pretty, with their high arches and small toes, but there is one part of her I want to see the most.

I set my hands on her calves, sliding them up to her knees. When I start to push them apart, Victoria sets her hands on mine. I look up to meet her eyes.

"No?" I ask, ready to stop if she wants me to, no matter how hard it will be.

I do not care how far we go. I will always stop if she needs me to. She meets my eyes, biting her plump lower lip. I can see her wavering, unsure which way she would like to go.

"Safe, Victoria," I murmur, pushing her knees gently apart. This time, she allows me to do so, her eyes locked with my own. As if reassuring herself it is me. I do not break the eye contact, hoping my eyes can anchor her to the now. Can help her leave behind whatever past plagues her, at least for this moment between the two of us. "Safe with me."

She sighs, closing her eyes and letting her legs fall open to my eyes.

Perhaps it is good she cannot see me. Because I know I am now looking at her like I am starving and she is the only sustenance that will do.

Soft and delicate, like the rest of her, she is pink and flushed between her thighs, her desire a slick dewiness that I can see even before I reach out to touch.

Victoria's thighs quiver when I slide my fingers up that wetness. Find that hard little nub at the top of her melting cleft, the part of her that gives her the most pleasure. She makes a small mewling sound, one hand coming up to cover her mouth.

I stare down at my hand, watch myself touch her, but I want to do more than this. I want to taste her, want to feel her pleasure against my tongue. I push her legs farther apart, making room for my shoulders between her thighs. As I lie down between her I whine and adjust my cock underneath me.

"Lothor?"

I look up to see Victoria propped up on her elbows, her eyes wide. I do not answer her. Not in words. Leaning down, I lick up the seam of her. She jerks under the touch, her thighs attempting to close. I hold them apart with my hands, licking her more firmly, concentrating on that small part just at the top.

"Lothor..." she sighs, dropping back down onto the sand.

It is not a complaint. Humming at the taste of her, I attack, sucking and licking, closing my eyes to savor her body. I glut myself on her and know I will only want more.

Her hands slide into my hair, clutching as she moves restlessly. Her hips rock against me in time with my touch. I look up at her face, taking in that delicate frown, that hot flush.

Her taste changes under my mouth and I know she must be close. I lick harder. Suck longer. Slide a finger slowly, carefully into her, her desire easing the way.

She cries out, her body stiffening as the climax overtakes her. I hold down her bucking body, keeping my mouth on her, keeping her pleasure going as long as I can. My cock weeps in response.

With one last, low moan, she drops back down, her breath coming in gasps. I kiss softly up her fur and onto her soft belly before rising to rid myself of the last of my clothing.

I admire her nakedness, splayed, welcoming as I drop my wet pants. Completely naked, I settle onto my knees between her legs, ready to take her, but I pause.

My body is more than ready, more than willing, but that whisper of loss...

It flows through me followed by a tinge of guilt. Sadness. My vision blurs as something tries to come into focus, some distant memory attempting to break free of the bijass and overlay this special moment.

"Lothor? Are you okay?"

Her soft voice jerks me out of the vague memory. Victoria is sitting up, her hand on my forearm, watching me with concern.

"Yes," I say firmly. "Yes."

The past, if I remember it or not, is gone. Whatever happened then, I will not let it interfere with my future. With our future.

I push my hips forward carefully until my cock is nudging her entrance. Victoria's eyes widen at the touch.

I lean forward while wrapping one arm around her and taking her back down to the sand with me. Her eyes on mine, she cups my face, pulling me closer so my forehead rests against hers. Holding me there, with her eyes so close they blur, she thrusts her hips up toward me.

I hiss in response and she gasps her pleasure. I am in just past the head, her hot grip so tight I wonder that I do not ignite right then and there. Gritting my teeth, I press in further. I want to be fully inside her when I reach my climax.

Victoria moans, her legs wrapping around my hips as I gently make room for myself in her tightness. I go slowly. I am large and she is so very small, but she is drenched in her pleasure, easing my way considerably.

I watch her every reaction, noting any hint of pain and adjusting course accordingly. It takes time. And patience, but I will take all the time Victoria needs.

Finally, I seat myself fully inside her, my hips meeting hers. I suppress a shudder at the feeling of my cock being so completely encompassed by her body, holding and savoring the sensations. Slowly I begin to move in earnest.

Victoria makes a small sound in the back of her throat, her neck arching, her body gripping me tightly. Gritting my teeth, I keep my thrusts slow and smooth, angling my hips so the ridges at the top of my erection strafe against her where it will do the most good. The reaction is instant.

"Lothor!" Victoria cries out, her nails digging into my shoulders as she thrusts toward me, her movements involuntary.

Holding her down, I increase my thrusts, watching her face. Noting her internal response.

Close. She is close.

I tremble, holding back my own release. Only a little more. I watch the way her breasts sway with each thrust, the tips tight. Look down to see how thick the root of my cock looks as it disappears inside her...

Victoria cries out, her legs pulling me deeply into her, grinding up against me as she reaches another climax. I cannot withstand it. I groan, my eyes shutting as she squeezes me, my pleasure drenching her inside.

I climax so hard my feet are tingling from it. Victoria drops down once more, her hands sliding off my shoulders, and I take a deep breath. The scent of her, of us, swirls around us.

I need more, my appetite is only whetted, my need for her too much to sate so easily. I pull my softening member out, my second cock rising to replace it from under my tail. I thrust back in.

Victoria's eyes snap back open, her mouth opening in shock at the new intrusion.

"Lothor...you..." There's surprise in her voice.

"Two," I grunt, peppering her face with kisses while adjusting her hips. If I do this correctly, I know she can join me again. She is already sensitive...

"Oh!"

She squirms underneath me, tossing her head from side to side, squeezing her eyes shut tightly. I reach between us and pinch that small nub. She screams, a short, sharp scream that I should worry about because we're not in the safety of the cave. I can't, not when my own pleasure is tackling me, taking me down on top of Victoria's slick body.

I thrust hard and fast, the pleasure riding me hard. Victoria is there with me, pushing back against me, her small cries in my ear spurring me on.

I thrust all the way in, the last of my orgasm pouring out of me. Taking a deep breath, reality finally intrudes.

The desert breeze, the dappled sun. The rustle of small creatures in the brush. I should rise, should...

Victoria wraps her arms around me, kissing my temple, and everything else fades to the background. She is all that matters. She is mine, my treasure, no matter what happens next, I know this is true. My dragon has claimed its mate. She is the one and I will do anything for her.

If I only knew that'd I'd lose her in a year.

17

VICTORIA

*E*verything changed after we made love, yet nothing changed at all. Sometimes life is weird like that. Lothor hasn't changed, except if anything to become even more attentive than before. He's less distant than he was, or maybe it's more that he doesn't hold himself stiffly back now that we've crossed that line.

I guess, really, I'm the one who's changed. It's good, if odd. It's been a week since "it" happened, and there's been no repeat performance. I've thought about it, God have I ever thought about it, but I keep holding back.

These barriers took a long time to be built and I can't really help that they're not going to come down completely in one day, but it's better. So much better. The butterflies in my stomach when Lothor is near feel completely different than they did. It's not fear, well at least not completely, but interest. Almost I feel like a schoolgirl with my first crush.

The week has flown as we fill each day with living. Living on Tajss is so much more work than it ever was on the ship. On the ship I had a job, we all did, you go to your job, you put in your eight hours, and then you go do what you want. I never once thought about food, especially where it was going to come from or how to get it.

There were restaurants and grocery stores to buy what you wanted in, I'd go home and cook most nights, alone or with one of my handful of girlfriends. Friends isn't something I had a lot of back then. They would want to go out and see and be seen but I didn't. I was scared, even then, of 'out there'.

On Tajss there are no such conveniences. You want to eat? You have to gather it or kill it. That's something I'm trying to come to terms with. When I was a prisoner on the Zzlo ship they did all the hunting and killing. I cleaned it up and tried to make whatever "thing" they brought me into something edible, but I was never witness to the killing part. Lothor doesn't like to leave me alone so he brings me along when he hunts.

Sree rubs against my legs demanding attention, so I stop trying to sweep the incessant sand out the door and kneel to scratch behind her ears. She purrs or something close enough to call it such.

"You like that don't you?" I coo.

"She does," Lothor says.

"Ah!" I exclaim, leaping forward and away from his voice.

I try to whirl around and I'm sure in my thoughts somewhere it was meant to be cool and effective, but I'm not that coordinated. Still in a crouch I swing around, trip over my own feet, and fall backward onto the pallet. My heart pounds and I'm breathing in ragged gasps as the adrenaline spike settles out.

"I am sorry," Lothor says, holding his hands up, palms toward me.

He hasn't moved any closer, carefully standing as far from me as he can and still be inside the cave.

"How do you do that?" I grouse as much as ask. "You're so big you shouldn't be so quiet."

Climbing back to my feet he starts forward to help I'm sure, but I flinch involuntarily and he stops, backing up slowly. Tears well in my eyes. Damn it, I should be better than this by now. We've slept together. How much more intimate can it get and yet I'm still scared?

"Are you okay?" he asks.

"Yes," I say, tears falling, then I shake my head. "No. I don't know!"

I throw my hands up in the air and then cover my face with my hands. He's silent, lost I'm sure, and I can't blame him. I'm lost too. What is this? Why is this? Why can't I get over it?

Because I can't, that's really the answer, isn't it? A lot of damage. A lot of broken goods. That's me, broken.

God above, get a grip!

Wiping furiously at the tears I take two deep breaths and shake my head, then push myself to my feet.

"I'm sorry," I say. "That was uncalled for."

Slowly I force myself to face him, to look at him, full on. It's an effort. Fear tells me to look down, don't meet his eyes, don't see what is there. The inner struggle takes a long moment but I win out at last and meet his soft eyes. I see the kindness in them. The compassion and the fervent desire to help.

"You have nothing to be sorry for," he says.

He doesn't move, holding still and waiting for my permission. My heart aches; his patience is more than I deserve. More than anyone could ever ask for. He's amazing. If only I could be as amazing to him back.

"Yeah," I say, trying to keep the defeat out of my voice.

I know I don't succeed but it's all I can do for now. Standing up, I wipe at my face to get rid of the last of the uncalled-for tears and then look around the room. My eyes land on one of the waterskins and a small clay bowl. I go over, pour out a small bit of water, then wash my face. The cool water helps and at last I feel halfway together again.

Stupid that such a small thing causes this much drama. I feel bad about it, but what can I do? I feel his eyes staring at my back, boring into me with a weight that needs to be answered whether he's demanding it or not. Except I don't have any answers to give. So I do the only thing I can: I change the subject.

"We're going to need more water," I say, hefting the waterskin.

"Let's do that," he says, rolling with me. "There is time today for a trip."

Smiling, I shake my head. He really is perfect.

A trip to the oasis is always an adventure in and of itself, and I welcome the distraction. I gather up the waterskins and the leather carry bags that I have no doubt Lothor created himself. He takes most of the bags and the full waterskins, leaving only the empty ones for me to worry about. He doesn't ever say a word about it. It's automatic that he shoulders the heavy items.

It only makes sense that he does. He's huge and those muscles that ripple under his scales as he adjusts the straps...

Focus. Good Lord, I'm a mess. One moment I'm scared to death and jumping away from him, and the very next moment I'm fantasizing about him. He must be extra lonely to put up with me. Which I've no doubt he was, but still.

Sree mewls as we gather at the door, obviously aware that we're leaving and not really having it. She darts over and blocks the door, mewling louder, her mouth opening wide to show her sharp little teeth.

"Sree," I say, shaking my head.

"I've never seen a kedi act the way she does with you," Lothor says. "She really likes you."

"She's spoiled and rotten," I say, kneeling down to scratch her ears again. Sree purrs and moves to rub up against my legs. Lothor grunts in response and steps around us, going outside to wait. "I have to go, you silly beast."

Sree hisses, arching her back as if she understands my words. Still, I'm supposed to be the mistress here, I think. So I stand up and stare at her, and she glares back at me. We stare each other down for quite a while until Lothor clears his throat outside the door.

"Enough," I say finally. "You like to eat and drink? Then let me do my part."

I stride past the kedi and she stays inside the cave mewling. It breaks my heart listening to her cries as we walk away, but I'm right. If she wants to keep eating, we have to do the basics of survival. On Tajss nothing is guaranteed.

VICTORIA

The trip to and from the oasis is much harder than I remember it being the previous time. It was only a week ago. Surely my memory isn't so bad? Am I romanticizing the last trip because of what happened?

I don't know, but as we walk back into the cavern I'm wiped. Lothor carried me the last half of the way home and I couldn't argue with him doing it. I couldn't have made it if he didn't. He sets me down inside the door and my blood rushes from my head.

"Whoa," I say, reaching out for something to stabilize myself.

Lothor gives me his arm and I cling to it as the room spins. Every muscle in my body feels like it's quivering. It doesn't last long but it sucks. Closing my eyes, I take deep breath and look back to see what that was.

"Are you okay?" Lothor asks.

"Yeah, I think so," I say, touching my brow and wiping my forehead.

Only then does it hit me. I'm wiping away nothing. No

sweat, but I should be sweating. It's Tajss; I'm always sweating. How can I not be sweating? Oh…

"What is it?" Lothor asks.

"Sweat," I say, shaking my head.

All the humans back in the city were taking it. Damn it, I never did because Gershom said it was bad. He forbade it to all of his followers, for better or worse. I heard the rumors, if you took it you were stuck here forever. It changes you, somehow, on a basic level. Like on your DNA or something. It's instantly addicting, which is what always scared me the most about it. Instant addiction, I've never been one for drugs and one with an instant addiction? No thank you.

That still scares me. Instant addiction. Maybe it's something else? No, but there has to be some way to handle it besides epis. I don't want to be addicted to anything.

"You're not producing water," Lothor observes. "That's a good thing, right?"

A half smile forms on my face as I shake my head. I'd give him a full smile but it's too much effort and I don't have the energy. Producing water. Despite the fact he looks like a cross between a dragon and a man with the dragon taking on the bigger half I find it so easy to forget he's alien. He doesn't know anything about humans.

"No," I answer. "No, I'm afraid it's not."

"It's not?" he asks. "How is this not good? That's a waste, you putting out the water you need to survive."

The confusion on his face is clear as the suns in the sky. He doesn't get it. It's so foreign to him as to be unreal.

"My body doesn't…" I trail off.

Doesn't what? Science wasn't my strong suit in school and biology was a snooze fest. I don't know the details of it; I only know that sweating is important. I know there was something about it, something from biology.

Lightheaded, it's hard to focus my thoughts, but I know

it's there. Lizards, we studied lizards, didn't we? Yeah, we did, cold-blooded, that's the term.

"It's blood," I start to explain but his eyes go wide and he steps closer.

"Blood?" he asks. "That is bad—"

"No," I cut him off, stumbling the rest of the way to the pallet and plopping down. My head is pounding. "No Lothor, not like that, it's… your blood, I think, is what we called cold. You can take the heat because your body temperature is low without it. Mine is heated internally somehow, and because of that I have to sweat to regulate my temperature. It cools me."

"Oh," he says, but the tone of his voice and the look on his face make it clear he doesn't understand it any better than I really do. Which isn't at all.

"I don't know," I say, lying back. "It's bad, that's all I know. I need to hydrate and rest a bit."

"Hy-du-ate?" he repeats the word back and my head throbs worse.

Damn the language barrier!

"Water," I say. "Can I have some please?"

He doesn't take time to answer, bursting into motion so fast he's a blur. It's nauseating to watch him move so fast and my stomach lurches. I wretch before I can get it under control. In what seems the same instant that I'm throwing myself forward to avoid getting sick on our furs he's there. His strong arm wraps around me, supporting me. He raises the skin to my lips, tilting it back and I drink the cool water, slowly at first then gulping it down.

My stomach roils as it hits the bottom and I'm certain I'm going to lose it all. It takes a moment, but I get it under control and manage to keep it down. Leaning into Lothor I let it all go, closing my eyes and focusing on breathing.

"How do I help?" he murmurs, concern obvious in his voice.

"Sleep," I murmur, turning in his arms to get more comfortable.

My head throbs incessantly and so I give myself over to the blackness waiting behind it.

19

LOTHOR

*S*he drifts to sleep in my arms. I listen as her breathing settles, becoming shallow but regular. Watch her chest rise and fall and feel her temperature against my scales. She's warm, warmer than usual. I know, now, that this isn't good.

Tajss is laying its claim on her. Insidious, creeping in, slowly draining her life. I can't let it happen.

In the depths of my bijass, the swirling fog, something pushes up, trying to break free. It surges at the edges of my thoughts, spinning below the surface. All that comes through is an empty ache, almost a sense of despair.

I can't lose her.

There has to be something to be done for her. Something she needs that I can get for her, something I can kill. Anything. I'll do anything for her.

My tail twitches fitfully as my agitation grows. Sree watches it move, her eyes reflecting the fading light, making them seem to glow. Her head moves side to side in time with my tail, then she pounces on it, claws out.

I stifle a yelp of pain and swat her to one side, unwilling to risk waking Victoria with her silly antics.

Shadows stretch in from the door as the suns above set and full darkness falls. I hold her in my arms through the night, listening, making sure she is breathing, not daring to move a muscle. My arms go numb, my legs tingle, but I don't move a muscle. I cannot disturb her rest; she needs it. It's all I can give her.

Only when the suns' rays are sneaking past the makeshift door to our home does she stir. She shifts, rolling over and snuggling closer. I curl my tail around her protectively and Sree stirs from where she'd curled up next to her breasts.

"Mmm," she groans, her eyes fluttering open. "Is it morning?"

"Yes," I answer.

"Damn, I slept through the night?"

"You needed the rest," I say.

She closes her eyes, touching her head, then sitting up slowly.

"Well, I do feel better," she says. "Mostly. My head isn't hurting as bad as it did."

"That is good," I say, studying her face.

"Yeah," she says, holding her hands in front of her face and staring at them as she turns them front to back.

"What is it?" I ask.

She shakes her head. "I don't know."

Rising to my feet I wrap my tail and arms around her, holding her close. A deep sadness fills me and somehow, it's as if I'm holding empty air no matter that she is here in my arms. Something deep in the fog that shrouds my memories aches, throbbing, a pain that makes my chest tight and my blood pound in my ears.

She is here. In my arms. I don't understand this pain. Fear. It's fear I'm going to lose her.

"How do I help?" I ask, my voice betraying me.

I don't know if she hears it but I do, a hint of the desperation I can't suppress. She shakes her head, leaning her head back against my chest and resting her hands on my arms.

"It's dehydration," she says, soft but matter-of-fact.

"Water then? I'll get you all the water you can drink!" I exclaim, excitement rising. A solution!

"No," she says, and this time her voice is barely a whisper. "It's not enough."

"It's not? What then? What do you need? I will get it for you," I say, that suppressed desperation creeping further into the tone of my voice as I struggle to press it down.

Her fingers trace lines up and down my arms, leaving warm trails along my scales. She doesn't answer for a long time. The tension in her body grows until she is stiff in my arms and I know she's worrying, debating something.

"In the City," she says, "before I was exiled, there was a plant. A lot of the humans took it because it made them able to stand up to the heat. Gershom forbade his followers taking it, said it was all part of the 'alien plan' to subsume us, dehumanize us. That it would fundamentally change who we were, steal our 'humanity' from us. I don't know about all that, but I do know, and believe it to be true, that it's highly addictive. Once you take it, you can't not take it. You're stuck having to have it, forever I guess."

"What plant was this?" I ask.

"The Zmaj in the City called it 'epis,'" she says.

The world stops. Epis. Of course, why didn't I think of it? The plant of life, the soul of Tajss.

"I see," I say, thinking it through.

Epis is difficult to farm. Difficult being an understatement. Dangerous in the extreme would be more accurate. As little as I recall from before I do remember we never farmed it alone. Epis was the lifeblood of Tajss, the industry, our purpose even. Tending, gathering, and shipping epis was what we did.

The caves where it grows are the tunnels left behind by the giant beasts, the zemlja, that burrow their way constantly beneath the surface. The apex predators of Tajss, hundreds of feet in length, dangerous in the extreme. They hunt by vibrations; the slightest movement could attract one if it's close. They are why I made my home here up in this cave, far enough above the earth that the sounds of living wouldn't bring one's attention.

I've never faced one alone. I'm not sure that it's possible. Even if it is, they're not the only threat in the tunnels. Many of the creatures of Tajss use them as their homes in the wake of a zemlja's passage.

If this is what she needs I will find a way. Failure is not an option. I will do whatever it takes to save her.

"Lothor?" she asks, her voice trembling.

"Yes," I ask, biting off the word I want to add. She's not ready for it.

I want to say my love, my treasure, my everything, but I can't risk scaring her. We're still too early in our relationship. She's still scared and not ready. I am not going to push her.

"I'm scared," she whispers.

My hearts throb in agony. The pain in her voice, the fear… I have to fix this.

"It will be okay," I say, and every fiber of my being pours into those four simple words.

It's on me. I will make it okay. No matter what it costs, no matter what it takes, no matter because I can't lose her.

She snuggles against me and I hunch over, enclosing her with my body. Kissing the top of her head, I play out possibilities, rejecting scenario after scenario as I try to find a solution.

"I know," she says. "I trust you."

It's barely a whisper now, so soft I almost doubt she said the words, but she did. She said the words, she trusts me. My chest swells and my hearts race, causing blood to rush to my head. Silently I swear that I will be worthy.

Tajss witnesses my conviction, but I have no idea how sorely that will be tested or how, in the end, I'll lose her anyway.

20

VICTORIA

"Damn it," I curse as I stumble and barely catch myself on the wall of the cave.

Sree hisses, back arching as she looks around for a threat. A moment later she looks at me with her head twisted inquisitively as if asking me if I'm crazy or something. I guess, to a large degree, I am. I'm sick and it's getting worse.

It's subtle, really, the way it's creeping in on me so damn slowly that I didn't notice it until it was really hitting me hard. Headaches. Who doesn't have a headache once in a while? Tremors in my muscles, but only now, looking back, do I see the signs for what they were. My body dehydrating no matter how much water I take in. Something is missing from my regular intake and it's taking its toll.

Before I was taken by the Zzlo, when we were living at the wreckage of the ship, we had supplements that kept us going. It never got to the point where it affected me or any of us. Not like this. This is awful.

I'm lethargic, it's hard to move or want to. My muscles ache and my headache is blinding most of the time. Worst of all is the nausea. I can barely keep down water and the idea of eating is abhorrent, which is making me weaker and feeding the entire cycle of my physical decline.

The door shuffles aside noisily and I turn my head to see Lothor racing through it.

"Are you okay?" he asks, grabbing me by my waist and supporting me.

I hate myself for needing his support so much. I'm grateful for it, for sure, but I hate that I need it. That I'm sick, that I can't support myself. It's all too damn much.

"Fine," I grouse, pushing myself up and forcing myself to stand on my own two feet.

He watches me. Stares is too strong of a word, but it's close enough. Every motion I make he's evaluating, thinking, planning, and clearly he's worrying. Which makes me hate this all that much more. I never wanted to worry him. I don't want to be a hassle. We're only starting to come into something that could be considered a normal relationship and here I go screwing up everything.

The dark truth I don't want to admit is I have a really good idea of where this is going to end. What do I do then? How can I invite him in, let him get close to me, form a budding relationship when I know that it's going to end badly? I'm not that selfish. I can't let him get close to me, I can't let him in, because he'll never forgive himself.

The only thing I can give him now, no matter how hard it is, is to keep him at a distance. I'm struggling to not give in to despair over it. All my life I've lived in fear and I finally, finally meet someone who helps me through that. It's a major breakthrough, a big win, only to have it snatched away before it even has a chance! It's not fair, damn it. Tears fall and I can't stop them. It's too much, too unfair, it's all bullshit.

"Victoria," he says, grabbing me again by my waist and forcefully turning me to face him.

He wipes away my tears with his thumb, his eyes boring into mine.

"What!" I exclaim, furious at myself for crying, furious for caring, furious that I'm losing everything I never even imagined I could possibly have and there's nothing I can do about it.

"I will fix it," he says. "You have my word."

"How?" I shout. "What can you do? What can either of us do? I heard the stories in the City about how dangerous harvesting epis is and they don't do it alone. You can't get it on your own, no matter how you might try, I can't let you. I can't let anything happen to you, damn it…"

I trail off as the tears and despair overwhelm me and I can't force more words past the lump in my throat.

"There will be a way," he says. "Do not give up hope."

"Hope," I choke on the word.

"Yes," he says. "Hope. We were not brought together only to be ripped apart."

His jaw tightens, his eyes narrow, and he purses his lips. Something passes across his face, but I can't read what it means. He looks like he bit off the final words he wanted to say.

"Say it," I tell him. "Please, say it. Whatever it is don't hold back."

There's a pained look on his face, but his eyes warm as his entire body tenses.

"You are my treasure," he says. "I cannot lose you. I will not."

My heart melts at his words. His treasure? I heard Ladon, the Zmaj back in the City, say that once about his love Calista. The word, when said by a Zmaj, carries a weight with it that I've never heard from a human saying it. There's a magnitude that seems to resonate in the air after a Zmaj names a person as such.

With tears staining my cheeks I'm a mess, but I stare into his eyes and the weight eases. It's not gone but it's less, easing off my shoulders knowing that he's shouldering this with me. We're going to face it together.

"Don't do anything stupid," I mutter, unsure what to say and unable to put the massive mix of emotions into words.

He smiles, nodding. I touch his cheek, trailing my fingers along his jaw, passing them over his lips. He leans in closer and kisses me with a soft yet insistent gentleness. His tongue licks my lips, easing its way into my mouth as the kiss becomes filled not with passion but with love. It's not fiery or lustful like our previous kisses; it's a completely different kind of kiss. One filled with need, sure, but more with certainty, with love.

I return his kiss and let down the barriers the best I can. They're not gone—I don't know that they ever will be—but they're less and he's inside of them. So that's progress. He kisses me until the black despair pushes back away from me.

21

LOTHOR

*S*he's getting weaker, sicker. Today she didn't rise from bed until the suns were almost all the way overhead. Her skin is pale and she trembles often as not. Sree will barely leave her side and I trust the instincts of the kedi. She knows something is wrong, very wrong.

No matter how brave a face she puts on it, she's sick and getting worse. It's only been two days, but her decline is happening faster.

I've been planning a fix, but it's not going to be easy. It would be hard if I didn't have to take her along, but there is no way I'm going to leave her behind. Something about that stands out in my mind, sticks at me with razor-sharp claws that tear at my mind. No, there's no way I can do that; it's more dangerous to leave her here then to take her.

Hunting a zemlja alone isn't reasonable either, which leaves me few choices. Years ago, so long now I barely remember it, I saw other Zmaj. I know where they were, but it was outside the territory I'd claimed as mine so I've never bothered with them.

Instinctively I don't want to go to them, especially with

Victoria in tow. She's mine; I'm not going to share her or risk her being taken by another or kidnapped. No, I'll have to hide her somewhere when I find them.

Them. That's what I remember that was the most strange and why I avoided them when I ran across them. It wasn't a lone Zmaj; there were three of them and they weren't fighting. Somehow they'd overcome or resisted their bijass and were working together.

Three on one were stupid odds for me to risk then. They're stupid odds for me to risk now, but now, unlike then, I have a reason to risk it. She has to have epis and soon or I'll lose her forever. No risk is too great at this point.

"What are you thinking so hard about?" she asks with a wan smile.

Closing the small distance between us in a stride, I wrap my arms around her and kiss the top of her head.

"We're going to have to travel," I say into her hair, inhaling the soft scents of her.

"Oh," she says, disappointment in her voice but giving no argument. "Far?"

"A ways," I say.

"Okay," she says. "I'll start packing."

"I'll take care of it all my love," I say.

"Are you sure?" she asks.

"Of course," I say.

I set to work, packing what we'll need and maybe more than we'll need. This will take a few days and I don't want to not have something.

When I get done there's nothing left to do but leave. Sree weaves a crisscrossing circle between Victoria's legs. The beast knows, somehow, that she's about to be left alone. Victoria crouches down and scratches her behind his ears.

"Ah," she says, softly cooing to her. "You're worried, aren't you? You'll be fine. I'm sure we won't be gone long."

I hope not. If we are... Victoria won't make it.

What a dark thought that is, but I know I have to find a solution fast. There's no time to waste, which is why I'm leaving this late, why I'm taking her. It's the only reason this is going to happen at all. Because I know beyond a shadow of a doubt if I don't I'll lose her for sure. This is my one chance at saving her.

"We should be on our way," I say, hefting the pack I've prepared and tying it over my shoulder so that the leather ropes lie between my wings. She rises and stumbles back-ward, falling onto her rear before I can catch her.

"Oh!" she cries out as Sree screeches, rushing toward her.

I race forward at the same time but step on Sree and stumble forward instead. I catch myself on the rear wall of the cave, leaning over her, but beneath me Victoria has raised a protective arm and curled into a ball, her already pale face somehow more whiter, her eyes clenched shut and fear written across all of her.

"I'm sorry," I say, pushing myself back and away from her, giving her space.

She shudders, cracking her eyes open and looking at me.

"Fine," she says, her voice trembling. "Fine, sorry, I'm sorry."

"No," I say. "It was my fault. I tripped."

She uncurls from the ball she'd pulled herself into and pushes herself into a sitting position, one hand on her head and the other resting on the ground next to her.

"Head hurts so bad," she mutters, slowly moving it side to side while rubbing her forehead.

"I will carry you," I say, starting to move forward.

She smiles, glancing up at me. "I'm afraid you may have to. I'm so sorry."

She half laughs, shaking her head, then closes her eyes and I can't miss the glistening moisture forming in them.

"Do not be sorry," I say.

"I'm such a pain," she says. "This is stupid. I'm stupid. I never should have followed Gershom. How could I let fear rule my life for so long? Here I am, still being stupid and afraid. Damn it, I don't... I don't know."

Kneeling beside her, I wait until she looks directly at me. Slowly I reach out and touch her arm. She doesn't flinch or move away so I rest my fingers on her.

"Then I will know for both of us," I say. "The past doesn't matter. You were afraid. It is fine, I forgive you for your fears and do not hold it against you now. I am large, you are small. I am stronger and bigger, why would you not be afraid?"

"Because it's stupid and you've never done anything but be nice to me!" she exclaims. "You're kind and gentle and attentive and everything I could have ever asked for in a guy. Well, I mean, you're a guy if a bit different and certainly not the guy I would have ever seen myself going for," she laughs.

The sound of her laughter echoes off the stone walls and fills my heart with joy.

"You are my treasure," I say, my chest swelling with pride and love for her. "May I pick you up?"

"Yes, please," she says. "Are you sure you can do this? I could stay here, wait for you to come back."

I stop mid-reach for her and think about her words. I've already thought this through many times, and each time I've decided it was too risky to leave her behind in this condition. I can't put my finger on why, but leaving her behind, especially like this, makes me feel... sick. Sick to my stomach, my hearts beat faster, and it becomes hard to breathe as if the very air is too thick to take in. No, I can't leave her behind. I'm not sure why, exactly, but I know it's a bad idea.

"I am sure," I say, scooping her into my arms.

She wraps her arms around my neck and leans her head against my chest. She's light, too light really. She's lost weight and she wasn't big to begin with. Another sign I must hurry. Walking out of the cave, I make my way down the ramp to the ground and move as fast as I can across the desert.

She sleeps in my arms as I run as fast as I can, racing across the rolling dunes in search of the others I saw so long ago. I'm running on hope. It's all I have left. My thoughts spin and the fog of my past surges with them, something trying to break free of its clinging grasp. The bijass does not surrender easily and holds its deep secrets.

Eventually, as the suns are setting, exhaustion settles over me. Victoria stirs in my arms, rousing from the half sleep she's stayed in through the day. She blinks several times, raising her head, then collapses back against my chest.

"Are were there?" she asks.

"No," I say.

"Okay," she says, not really rousing.

Kneeling, I set her down then take up the waterskin, holding it to her lips. I notice now they are chapped, not their normal softness. She drinks some, then sputters and turns her head.

"I can't," she sputters. "Sorry."

"Are you sure?" I ask.

"Yeah," she says, rubbing her face and sitting up straighter. "I'm kind of nauseous."

"Food?" I ask.

"Oh God," she says, her face turning somehow paler still.

I hold her as she retches, waiting for the nausea to pass away, keeping her hair back and feeling helpless. Primal instincts rage under all my thoughts. There should be some-thing that I can take a hold of, something I can hold in my hands and destroy. Something I can *do.* Anything.

At last she leans back against me, spent, pale and exhausted. Still she gives a half smile and shakes her head.

"Sorry," she says, as I brush the hair out of her eyes.

"No," I say. "I am sorry. I will get you epis, soon. I swear it. By the stars above, by the sand below us, by the soul of Tajss itself I swear I will get it for you, no matter what it takes."

She touches my face, her fingers trailing across my cheek. The softness in her eyes, her lips trembling... my throat closes and it's hard to breathe. My hearts pound as if fighting against each other to see which can beat faster. It makes my chest hurt and my lungs burn with the need for air that I can't force past the lump in my throat.

"I know," she says, softly. "I know."

"We have to move," I say.

"Okay," she says, trying to push herself up, but I don't give her the chance before I sweep her into my arms and take off again.

I run through the night. It's dangerous but no more so than not getting her the epis she needs. At one point I circle out from the straight path when I see a flight of sismis, but it's the only problem. Now the suns are rising over the dunes, their first rays of light stretching across the sand, making it sparkle and throw up pretty colors into the air.

She's sleeping still, her breath shallow and hitching when she takes a deep breath. My muscles burn; I've run past the aching, through the pain, and now all that remains is the fire that rages through them. Nothing will stop me. I'm not going to fail.

Closing my protective lenses over my eyes, the rising light filters out and I survey the land, looking for any sign of others. Something that will tell me which direction to go. An empty sensation that is cold at the edges claws its way out of my core, spreading through my guts. Something. *Anything.*

Estejan, the primary sun, breaks over the horizon. As the large fiery orb climbs over the dunes like a god of fire crawling out of the black abyss, an oddity catches my attention. A tower?

It's well hidden, blending into the landscape. If the light hadn't caught it right at this moment I'd have missed it, but luck is with me. I knew they'd have to have someplace to stay, and now that I've spotted the outline of something not made by Tajss itself I see their construction.

Nodding to myself, a joyless half smile forms. I can't take her with me. I don't know these others or what I will run into. If they're deep in the bijass they'll try to take her and I can't fight and protect her at the same time. Especially if there are multiple opponents.

Where do I leave her?

Turning a slow circle, I find nothing. There are no cliffs or natural protection within sight. Smart, really. Why would they build their home in a place where enemies could sneak up? Kneeling down in the sand, I consider hundreds of options, discarding them all as fast as I think of them until there is only one possibility.

"Victoria," I say, softly, not wanting to startle her.

"Hmm?" she murmurs, stirring in my arms. Her eyes flutter open, taking a moment before they focus on me. "Oh, I'm dreaming."

"No," I say, shaking my head, pain stabbing through my chest. "Wake up, Victoria."

Her eyes flutter again and she sighs heavily.

"It's too hard," she mutters, frowning.

"I know," I whisper, unable to speak louder past the lump in my throat. "I know."

At last her eyes open and focus. She forces a smile or attempts to by the twitching of the corners of her lips. It never makes it to a real smile.

"Lot-hor?" she whispers.

Her lips are cracked and peeling, her pale skin is a deepening shade of red, and her normally bright eyes are dull.

"Yes," I answer her.

"Nice," she says, then coughs.

"I'm going to hide you," I say, forcing the words out. "I won't be gone long."

"Hide?" she asks, her eyes widening. "No. Take me with you."

"I can't," I say, shaking my head. "It's too dangerous. I'm going to hide you, so you can sleep. Rest. I will be back shortly."

She inhales and for a moment her eyes flash with the bright light of her. I'm sure she's going to argue, but then the breath exhales out heavily and her eyes drift closed.

"Fine," she says, not opening her eyes.

The ache in my chest is so deep I wonder that my hearts are still beating. Each breath, each pump hurts so much that I can't believe any of it. This isn't fair. It isn't right. I have to make this right and I'm going to. These other Zmaj will help. They will help or I will make them. We will not end like this.

Her breathing evens out, telling me she's asleep again. She's sleeping too much. I lift her up with one arm under her shoulders and rouse her enough to drink some water, which she gulps down gratefully.

Digging through the pack I get out a leather blanket, then cocoon her in its folds. Once she's safely ensconced I dig a trench in the side of the dune we rest on and lay her in it. I carefully shift the sand until all but her head is hidden. Nothing will be able to see her or find her without stepping directly on her.

Rising, I look her over. It's a terrible idea. Every fiber of my being hates this, but what choice do I have? I can't take her with me and I can't leave her out here in the open where any wandering Zmaj or a guster could take her. No, this is the only option I have.

Clenching my jaw and steeling my resolve, I kneel beside

her and kiss her feverish forehead. My only choice is to make this fast, so that is what I will do.

Spreading my wings I leap across the sands, moving with a speed that surprises even myself. I'm exhausted, muscles burning with the effort, but digging deep I pull on some reserve of strength. A well of power I didn't know I had. As I leap into the air gliding as far as I can it occurs to me, I never had this before. No, this is new, this is her. The effect she has on me. She has awakened the dragon in me, and the dragon is limitless in his power to protect his treasure. I will do whatever it takes for her.

The distance to the construct closes quickly now that I'm moving unencumbered. Each leap brings it closer until now there's no mistaking it for a natural formation. I leap into the air once more, but as I do the sand in front of me explodes and two forms explode out, intercepting my path.

Twisting my tail and leaning to the side, I move but I can't avoid both of them. An instant before I collide with one I see it's another Zmaj.

We slam into each other with jarring force and my head cracks against his. Stars explode in my vision and the bijass swells, bringing rage with it. Roaring, I grapple my opponent as we slam back to the sand, rolling over and over.

We come to a stop and he's on top, a fist flying at my face. I slam my tail into the back of his head, taking him by surprise and lessening the force of his blow. Pain explodes in my jaw but nothing broke at least.

I return the favor, slamming my fist into his jaw, knocking him off-balance. Throwing my weight to the side, I roll the two of us and come out on top. Drawing my skinning knife, I hold it to his throat ready to slice him open, but at the same moment cold steel rests against my own throat.

The shock of it cuts through the bijass and I freeze.

"Enough," the other Zmaj says. "Let him go."

"No," I say, pressing my blade harder.

A cool trickle of blood makes its way down my throat from where the lochaber sliced through my protective scales. It doesn't matter. I can't give in now; Victoria depends on me. The only leverage I have is the life of the male below me.

"You're insane," the one holding the lochaber hisses.

"No," I say. "I need help."

"Help? With what?" he asks.

"Epis," I say.

A long tense moment ensues, none of us moving. I stare into the eyes of the man below me and see he's resolved to his own demise, accepting of it even. No fear or worry mars his face. I wait, unsure what's going to happen next, but knowing I can't bend in my own resolve.

"Fine," says the male with the lochaber, and he pulls the weapon away from my throat. "Let him go. We'll talk."

I wait a moment, then two, before I pull my blade away. The instant I do I leap up and backward, ready for an attack. Two on one isn't easy odds but they aren't undoable. I can win. I will for her.

The male on the ground climbs to his feet, then moves to stand by his compatriot. The two of them stare, watching me closely. None of us speak, each waiting for the other apparently. Only after I'm relatively certain they're not planning to attack me the moment I let my guard down do I break the silence.

"I need epis," I say, repeating my earlier statement.

"Why?" the one who has the lochaber asks.

"Does it matter? I'm willing to trade for it," I answer.

"Trade? What do you have that we could possibly want?"

Glaring at him, I tighten my jaw and shake my head. "Furs, foodstuffs, leathers."

The two of them exchange a glance and then the speaker shakes his head.

"That is nothing we cannot get on our own," he says. "We do not need you and we don't deal in epis."

"What do you deal in then?" I growl, anger rising at their dismissiveness.

"Nothing that concerns you," he says. "What do you need epis for? You can't be an addict, not without a source already. Why do you need this?"

"Nothing you need to know," I say, bristling at their comments.

His eyes narrow as he tilts his head to one side. His frown deepens and he shakes his head at last.

"Well enough," he says. "Stay out of our territory or it won't go so well next time."

They turn dismissively, walking away. My stomach sinks seeing them leaving. I can't let them go. Victoria is a dune away and sick. I have to get the epis, and doing it alone is too dangerous.

"Wait!" I call to their retreating forms. "My mate. My mate needs it."

They stop and the one who's been speaking looks over his shoulder.

"Your mate? Are you gejem?"

"What? No!" I exclaim.

"Then you're lying. No females survived, so you're gejem or a liar," he says, turning to face me again. "Which is it?"

Balling my hands into fists, I don't want to lie, but I can't tell them about Victoria either. It's disgraceful, a stain on my honor not to tell the truth. I can't claim to be gejem as I am not, though there is no shame in it of itself, but to claim it when it's a lie is a bigger stain than to lie about Victoria. I'm trapped between boulders with no easy way out, so I say nothing.

"Which is it?" he prods me, taking a step closer.

"Will you help or not?" I ask, desperation in my voice.

They exchange another look.

"No," he says, shaking his head. "We do not have epis. I am sorry for you and for your 'mate.'"

They turn their backs again, walking away. It can't be, I can't let it end like this. Blackness swells with the bijass through my thoughts, consuming everything.

"No!" I shout, the word ripping out before thinking. The two males stop but don't turn around. "No, it doesn't end like this. I need your help. I will trade for it, but right now I don't have time. There is no time and I need help. I must have epis. Now."

They turn around again, staring at me.

"And why are your needs our problem?" the speaker of the pair asks. "We do not know you. We do not owe you anything."

"No," I agree. "You don't. Nothing. But we are all that is left. Our entire race is gone, dying. Pointless. We are the dregs that cling to an empty and pointless life more out of habit than out of any purpose or reason.

"Now I come to you with little to offer, but I ask you for help. If you turn me away now, like this, then our kind truly does not deserve to live. The planet itself will be better off when we are gone, for what good is a male if he does not give unto others? What purpose does any male have if he does not help when he sees someone in need? Is this what we've become? Is this all that remains of the once-mighty Zmaj Empire?"

The words pour out of me, coming straight from my heart. It's the awakening of what we were, though I barely remember it myself. The ideals of who we were, of what we could be. Victoria awakened that, pulling me away from the empty abyss that my life had become. She gives meaning to every day and a reason to live.

"Wise words," the speaker says, and exchanges a look with his partner.

My hearts pound, lungs scream for air, but I don't dare breathe, waiting for them to answer my plea. Waiting for them to agree. They have to, they must, or I'll do it on my own. Help or no help.

The other shrugs and then the speaker nods. He whirls his lochaber through a basic kata, ending with it sliding into its straps on his back.

"You will help?" I ask.

"No," he says, crossing his arms over his chest. "We cannot, I'm sorry. Best of luck. May Tajss be with you."

The air rushes out of my lungs, my knees turn to water, and it's all I can do to remain standing. The two males stare, and I cling to the faintest glimmer of hope that this is a joke. Some cruel prank before they say that's all it was. That they will come along, that they will help.

The jaw tightens on the one who has not spoken, eyes narrowing and tail shifting quickly side to side. He takes a step toward me but the other blocks him with an arm across his chest. His eyes drop from mine as he nods and turns away.

"You can't!" I yell at their retreating backs.

They don't dignify my shout with even a glance.

I'm on my own. Fine.

Resolve forms and devours the bitter disappointment. The bijass throbs with my beating hearts, pounding out its primal calls. On my own is the way it should be, the way it is supposed to be. She's mine and mine alone to protect. Somehow.

22

VICTORIA

I'm floating on a sea. Funny. I've never been on a sea, but I know, somehow, that's where I am. Surrounded by a warm, fluffy cloud as I drift along with the swells of the water. It's nice, so I relax and go with it until warmth stabs at my face, becoming uncomfortable.

"Victoria," someone says.

Who's Victoria? Strange; it sounds familiar, like someone I should know....

"Victoria, wake up," the voice says.

It's a man. A man... a voice I know. Or should know? Did know? Will know?

Ugh. It hurts. When I focus on the voice it pulls me toward the light and it's too hot, too uncomfortable. There's pain there with that voice. No, it's much nicer here in the dark on the sea, thank you very much. I'll stay here.

"Victoria, please," the voice says.

The voice has a quality, something about it that makes my heart ache, and suddenly I need to be closer to it. I know it's going to hurt but I can take it. The pain and need in that voice is more than what I'll feel when I go back. I can take it.

The voice pulls me but the blackness clings, holding me down, struggling to keep me. Some part of me really does want to stay here. It's comfortable. Too comfortable possibly. Maybe? Tajss. Tajss is pain, Tajss is hard. What is Tajss? A place? A state? It's something... where I belong?

Bright.

Ow, so bright!

The deep ache settles into me, pulsing into the core of me, unrelenting. I don't want this; it's too much. It's hard. Too hard.

Something cool in my mouth? Mouth, is that what that is? Right, yes. Water.

I drink a few sips, but then it hits my stomach which roils in response, rejecting the intrusion at first. Nausea sweeps through, pushing away the clinging unconsciousness where I'd been drifting along, ignoring my body and its travails.

A soothing touch trails across my forehead, cups my cheeks, so I blink rapidly trying to clear my eyes. Everything is bright and blurry and pain. It takes time. How long I have no clue, but I feel it moving along like I'm barely in touch with it. Honestly, I'm not sure I'm here at all.

"Victoria," the male voice says.

Male. I know the voice. I know it, but who—

"Victoria, wake up, please."

"Lo-t-h-or?" I ask, mouth too dry despite the water.

My mouth is as dry as sand, my throat raw and croaky. My head pounds, body aches, and all those pains are anchoring me here, pulling me into the overly bright moment. Dragging me, willing or no, to him. The one man who will take care of me. Back to him.

"Yes," he says, his voice barely a whisper.

"Did... you... get it?"

It. Right, it was... something. Something needed. Important. I know I should remember what it was, but all I can recall through the pain is that I needed it. It. Magical, mystical *it*. The thing that will make all this pain go away.

"No," he says, his voice catching on that single syllable.

"Oh," I say, blinking more until at long last I can see his face at least mostly clearly.

He's such a handsome man. For an alien, I mean. No, I don't mean that. He's handsome, period. That jaw! My God, so strong. His brow is high and prominent in a very good way that makes him look highly intelligent. The scales that cover his face reflect the sunlight and they're so beautifully colored. While he looks a deep sandy tan, each small scale is edged with soft colors that make me want to trace each one of them with soft kisses.

Except for the effort. Yeah, that's way too much work. Not now. Maybe later...

"I'm sorry," he says.

"It's fine," I say. Suddenly my hand is touching his jaw, tracing the line of it.

I don't recall telling it to, but I really like the sensation. It's oddly pleasing. My fingers tingle as I drag them along.

"I'm not done," he says, resolve in his eyes and voice. "I need you to live. Stay with me."

"It's fine," I say, unable to think of anything else to say.

It is fine, it will be fine, one way or the other. I'm tired is all. Need to sleep, rest, get away for a little bit. It's pulling, calling to me with the soft beauty of release.

"I'll get you the epis," he says. "A couple of days, that's all. It won't be long. I'll find it."

"I know you will," I say, trying to lean up into him, but it's so much effort.

He's so damn far away, ugh. He gets the message though because he comes to me and his lips touch mine. Then the blackness comes back and I'm drifting. Unhitched from time

MIRANDA MARTIN

but more from the pain that my body is going through. That's nice. The blackness is a relief. I'll take it.

"Damn it, Vickie!"

I'm jerked from a sound sleep, heart pounding and cold sweat covering my eight-year-old body. Something crashes, followed by the sounds of breaking glass.

"Jake, no," Mom yells. "No, don't, I'm sorry—"

"You'll be sorry," Daddy yells and the sounds don't stop.

They assault my ears as I pray for him to stop. Someone to stop him. Anyone. He's such an angry, bitter asshole. It's not right. This isn't right. None of it is.

When my door slams open I dive under my blankets to hide...

"Hey," Amara yells, storming past, hands balling into fists.

She walks right up to one of the other pilots and the instant he turns around, she belts him across the jaw with her fist. His head spins around from the force of the blow, and the other pilots with him gasp, then laugh.

"Whoa!" one of them cries out.

"Don't you ever do that again!" Amara yells.

"I didn't do anything!" the pilot yells.

I watch, breathless, from my position on the floor cleaning up the broken pieces of the beer pitcher.

"Right," Amara says. "You didn't just grab her ass? You didn't make her drop that beer?"

"I did—"

"You did and we all saw it. You treat a woman with

respect, you hear me? You don't and next time I'll kick your ass in front of all your friends for real."

Amara is a legend. She's so strong, fiery, unafraid of anything. I can't believe she's standing up for me. She glares at the other pilot a moment longer, then turns and kneels in front of me.

"You okay?" she asks.

"Yeah," I say, voice quavering.

"Good," she says, picking up pieces of glass and putting them on the tray for me. "Don't let these assholes treat you bad. If they do, you tell me, okay?"

I nod mutely, unable to speak. I wish I could be like her… but that's not me. I'm not brave, nor strong, nor anything but me. Looking over her shoulder, the look that pilot gives her makes my muscles quiver as cold fear spreads across my limbs.

If only…

23

LOTHOR

*T*he suns set but still I run. I know one place that should have epis growing and it's not far. I have to get there soon. Victoria murmurs in my arms. Occasionally she twitches and twice she has cried out in pain or surprise, I do not know.

All I can do is hold her close against my chest and run. Run through the pain. When my breath comes in ragged gasps, I keep running. When my legs burn, I keep running. Any time my will flags I look down. I do this for her. It doesn't matter how far it is, how hard it is, I do this for her.

Shifting her to one arm I use my free hand to dig out a piece of smoked guster meat, pop it in my mouth, then shift her back to both arms. Chewing while I run brings a fresh burst of energy that I use for all it's worth.

Finally the suns rise again and I know I'm close. A massive dune rises ahead and I adjust my path to circle it. On the far side there will be a cliff with a large crack in it. That crack will lead me to the tunnels where there will be epis.

There has to be. It was there before but that has been

years and years. Epis can grow long after the passage of a zemlja if it's not eaten by other animals.

Something is wrong.

I stop my run for the first time in hours, looking around. Something... What is it? The sand shifts on the dune. Subtle... a tiny rivulet of it drifting down toward me. Every nerve tingles while I look from side to side, searching for what feels off.

Nothing. The sand rivulet stops with no further sign of trouble, but that feeling doesn't subside. The edges of my scales itch and I can't figure out why.

I take another step forward, trying to resolve myself to keep moving. I don't have time to drag this out. Victoria moans, a soft pitiful sound, and shifts in my arms.

The ground rumbles.

No.

Sand pours down the dune in wide sheets as the ground tremors.

No, no, no!

Cursing silently, I run. The ground jumps once and I leap as cracks form under my feet. The tremors grow more violent, and then the rumbling sound comes.

This is bad. Really bad.

Looking around, I need to figure out where it's coming from as fast as I can. I know what's going to happen sooner or later, and my only hope right now is to get out of its way. Glancing back, the cracks are widening and the ground is buckling.

Okay, it's behind me.

Bad. Right.

Leaping into the air, I spread my wings and glide as far as I can while trying to keep one eye behind me, an almost impossible task, but I'm at least aware of its approach.

How big is it? That's going to decide our fate. If it's a big one...

No, I'll figure it out. I have to.

Damn those other Zmaj for not helping....

I land hard, sinking into the sand. Then the ground bucks and I'm thrown into the air in an uncontrolled toss. I can either gain control of my unintended flight or I can protect Victoria. There is no choice to be made at all.

I curl my body around her as we tumble over and over. Tucking my tail up and under, I form a ball around her, bracing myself for the impending impact.

We hit hard. Pain explodes in my left shoulder, stars cloud my vision, and we roll over and over. The ground continues to rumble beneath me. I gasp air through the pain. When I check on her, she's still out and doesn't appear to be harmed.

Good.

Quickly getting my bearings, the unintended flight has pushed me toward my goal. We're almost to the far side of the massive dune. A few dozen steps away is rock—solid, craggy rock. It's our best hope; it's the only place I can stash her so I can try to deal with the monster hunting us.

Granules of sand bounce in front of my face as the rumbling increases. It's now or never. I burst into motion, running for the rock. The ground beneath my feet bucks up and down, making it hard to keep my footing.

Cracks form, racing along with me. I leap, wings wide, gliding as far as I can. The wind pushes against me. I'm not going to make it. The cracks below me are widening. Swinging my tail left, I adjust my flight and barely land on a solid piece of ground. Large cracks drop away into darkness on either side of me.

Crouching, I leap, and as I do the remaining ground crumbles away and the monster emerges. It screeches as it bursts into the open air. Dirt, sand, gravel, and rock pelt against my back, and I feel a dozen cuts through my protective scales. The crack in the rock ahead is close, so close. I can stash Victoria here and then pull the monster away.

A few moments. It's all I need. Enough time to get her safe. Time to free my arms to fight. A burning itch on the back of my neck is the only warning I'm not going to make it.

Instinctively I leap to the left, twisting as I do, rolling so Victoria is on top and I can see the monster. It's massive, writhing body flailing at the air. Its gaping maw opens as it screeches, revealing thousands of razor-sharp teeth capable of boring through solid rock, making the tearing of flesh nothing.

The zemlja slams its length down, mouth snapping open and closed, trying to capture its prey. Capture us.

It hits the ground with so much force that a ripple effect explodes out from the point of impact. As I crash down on my back I'm thrown back into the air by it. Pulling my legs up, I form the most protective shell I can around Victoria.

I bounce several times, hitting and going back up before skidding to a stop at last. There's no time, so I leap to my feet as the creature rises back into the air, wriggling around and listening.

Zemlja are blind, hunting by sound. The moment I move it will know where I am. Holding stock-still, I don't dare to breathe. Maybe it will give up and search for easier prey.

It slides down, slipping back below the earth. A small flame of hope flickers in my core. This is better than I could expect...

Victoria cries out in her fever dreams.

The creature screeches, all but flying back up into the air, taller than a building leaning toward the sound.

I run. There's no choice as its jaws snap closed where a second before we were standing.

I run, pushing myself for more speed. Faster, must be faster.

I run, zigging then zagging, trying to stay one step ahead of the monster.

There, a few more steps and we'll be on the solid ground. The crack in the bluff calls, offering its semblance of safety. Have to make it. Must get there.

My scales tingle and I duck and roll without further thought.

Its jaw slams shut over my rolling body. The smell of its breath rushes over me, a nauseating odor of rotten flesh and filth.

I keep rolling, angling to one side to avoid it slamming down. A zemlja isn't against eating its meal crushed to a pulp.

It crashes down and we're airborne once again, but this time we're flying toward my target. Twisting my body around her just before impact, my back cracks against the rock bluff and we slide down.

Everything hurts. It's hard to breathe. Every breath is a stabbing pain. I'm certain something broke inside, but there's no time for pain. No time for anything but the fight.

Forcing myself to my feet, I look at Victoria and time stops.

Her pale face, sunken eyes, and matted hair are the most beautiful sights I've ever seen. The bijass rages, laying claim as my dragon awakens. This creature would threaten her. It would take my treasure from me.

This monster wants a fight? Then a fight it will have. I alone am the most apex predator on this planet. No matter its size or its difficulty, no one and nothing will threaten my treasure.

Time rushes by as the moment passes. I slide her gently

inside the crack in the bluff, take a painful breath, and turn to face my opponent.

It's raised up in the air, four times my own height, bending toward me with all those rows of teeth bared. It screams, but this time I match its roar with my own.

I reach behind ne and my hand grasps empty air. My lochaber is gone, lost somewhere in the run for the bluff.

Protect her. Save the treasure.

I run straight at the beast empty-handed, nothing but my will and the strength of my body to fight it.

It thrashes and snaps but I dodge its massive mouth, which is big enough to swallow me whole. I run under its writhing body then move to the side and past it.

Have to lead it away. Away from her. Buy myself space to fight.

Moving past, it twists around with me. Its jaws snap so close the monster's outer lips brush my wings, but I lean forward in time to avoid being pulled in.

It screeches, anger and frustration as if the monster can feel such things, or perhaps I'm projecting my own feelings onto it. A moment later the suns are blocked out as its shadow falls over me completely. Tucking my head, I shoulder roll to the right.

The ground rocks with the impact of its massive girth. I roll to a stop, coming up on one knee. It's rising back up but opportunity is open before me right now.

I take out my skinning knife, the only weapon I have to hand. I run at the creature while it raises its body into the air.

I reach where its lower half is still below the ground and run up the length of it. Its body is made of concentric, over-lapping scales. Each scale is the length of my body before being laid over by the next. The scales protect it. My small knife won't penetrate them... not directly.

It climbs into the air, raising upright, and I slide backward. I've gone as far as I can. Leaning forward, trying to find a handhold with my free hand as I slide down it, I reach the overlay of two scales and drive my knife between them.

The knife slips in easily and I twist up, desperately hoping this works.

Its body writhes beneath me and the knife slips free. I'm free-falling along its side, grasping hands finding no purchase on its slick scales.

Hitting the ground so hard the wind is knocked out of me, new pains explode. My lungs refuse to inhale. I'm surrounded by air I can't take in a single breath of, but I climb to my feet. Eyes blurring, body screaming in agony, one thought pounds with every beat of my hearts.

Save Victoria.

Air rushes into my lungs, my vision clears, and the primal purpose burns bright.

"You will not win," I growl. "She is mine."

As if it understands my words it retreats, pulling below the earth, its body sliding down before me. Its mouth will soon be in reach though, so I run back, giving it wide berth.

As I run I look for an edge, any advantage to turn this fight and at last I spot one. My lochaber.

It lies on the sand a dozen paces away. Angling toward it I run, willing myself to be faster. I'm two strides away when suddenly I'm airborne.

Dirt and sand fill the air. I'm tumbling head over heels. The zemlja rises up below me, mouth an open maw impossibly wide. Time slows to a crawl. Each grain of sand is detailed in base relief. Every clod of dirt, every pebble. Each tooth climbing toward me in slow-motion is outlined and illuminated clearly.

My mind races, looking for a solution. A way out before it all ends here and now.

No.

I will not fail.

"Victoria!" I scream her name, making it my battle cry.

Chills run across my scales and I make a desperate bid for success.

Spreading my wings, swinging my tail, I turn myself in the air so that my feet are pointing down into the monster's mouth. As we close with each other I kick out.

And catch myself, forcing its mouth to remain open by planting my feet on either side of it. It screeches, disgusting odors assaulting my senses, making my eyes water.

Muscles strain as it fights to close on its meal. My legs quiver, threatening to give, but Victoria drifts through my thoughts, giving me strength.

I cannot fail. Cannot lose her.

The monster shakes, throwing itself from side to side, trying to force me down and into its gullet. My feet slip and come to a rest on the first row of razor-sharp teeth, but I hold.

The strain is unbelievable. I don't know how long I can hold like this. I need to turn the tide. I need my lochaber. Something. Anything before my muscles give out and I fall into the creature's stomach.

Impossibly it opens its mouth wider and I start to slip. but it takes the pressure off. I throw myself to the left and out of its mouth.

Sliding down the side of the monster I'm pounded by the ground. New bruises, more broken parts, but none of it matters.

My lochaber glitters just beyond the tips of my fingers. Reaching out, my fingers brush against it, almost there. Digging deep I roll toward it, grabbing it as I pass over, and keep on rolling.

Away. Space. I need space, room to think, room to fight.

Coming to a stop again I spin around, staying low before

rising to a knee. The zemlja rockets up, stretching impossibly far into the sky. It screeches so loud now my ears pop. Resolve forms as I tighten my grip on the shaft of my lochaber.

"Mine," I growl, leaping forward.

I run at the monster even as it leans over and tracks the sound. It pulls back and then thrusts its body forward, intending to smash me beneath its weight.

As its shadow covers me, I dive forward and roll out of the way. It hits the ground and I'm thrown up into the air by the force, but this is all part of my half-formed plan.

Spreading my wings, I turn my fall into a glide and luckily catch a breeze. Tilting to one side, I bank around until I'm over the zemlja's body. Closing my wings I drop, landing lightly on top of the creature and running toward its head.

It twists underneath me, so I throw my arms out for balance. It screeches then raises up again. I run up a steep incline until my feet start to slide.

My plan has to work; it's now or never.

Leaning over as far as I can I move back, adjusting the grip on my lochaber until I slide past the overlap of another set of scales. I drive the lochaber blade up and under the overlapping scale. The much longer blade penetrates deeper than my hunting knife and it screams in pain.

The zemlja bucks hard, writhing its body in impossible contortions. I'm thrown off its back, sliding down the side. I grab the shaft my lochaber and my feet dangle over empty air.

"Die!" I scream, all my rage pouring out in a single, focused word.

It has to die. I have to kill it to save her.

The shaft of my lochaber bends, never meant to take my not-inconsiderable weight. It bends until there's a cracking sound. The zemlja twists, pulling me up and flinging me across its back. I slam against it on the opposite side, barely keeping my grip.

The wooden shaft cracks again. It can't last much longer. This has to end... now.

I scrabble, trying to find purchase against the beast, heaving myself up with the shaft of my lochaber. Somehow I manage to get onto its backside again and I twist the lochaber as I do. The creature screeches, but this time I'm rewarded by blood spurting out from between its scales.

I shift my weight, trying to drive the blade in deeper, but my foot slips and I fall. My face slams against the beast and stars explode in my vision. Gritting my teeth, I hold on by the shaft of my lochaber, dangling off the side of the monster as it swings itself around.

I'm slammed against it repeatedly. The creature's blood splatters in my eyes, blinding me. I can't orient myself. Can't tell if I should let go or continue to hang on.

The decision is made for me an instant later. The lochaber shaft gives a final crack and then I'm falling.

As if stuck in some kind of repeating loop, I slam against the ground again. Sand explodes around me as it cushions my fall some, but then something in my right wing snaps causing excruciating pain.

Wiping my eyes clear I climb to my feet, holding the remains of the broken shaft of my lochaber in my hand. The zemlja screeches, twisting toward me, its maw opening as it strikes.

I'm too hurt and tired to run anymore. This has gone on long enough. It ends now. My treasure needs me.

Looking down into the red-black emptiness of its looming throat, the light reflects off the razor's edge of so many teeth that I could never count them all.

Calmness spreads across me. Certainty.

It opens wider and I leap into its mouth wielding the broken staff's sharp edges. I drive the stick up toward its brain, coming in through the soft, unprotected roof of its mouth.

"Lothor!" Victoria screams from the distance.

I roar as I enter the creature's mouth and then I'm being covered in gore and slime as the shaft pierces deep. It shudders, thrashes, then drops to the ground. I climb out of its mouth, victorious, albeit covered in grotesqueness.

Exhausted, I drop to my knees, breathing heavily. Then I look up and see Victoria stumbling across the sand a dozen paces away when she drops.

VICTORIA

Something pulls me out of the fever dreams. The ground shakes and I'm bounced up and down. That must be what it was.

A screech so loud it makes my ears pop cuts through the air. My head explodes with pain as I struggle to rise and find its source. The pain is so much my vision blurs. My arms shake, weak and unwilling to hold me, so I fall flat.

Rock. Cool, soothing rock scrapes my face and I don't have the energy to care about the scrapes, only enough to enjoy the coolness. The ground rumbles, making my head bounce up and down, which does nothing to ease the pain.

Damn it, give me a break, will you?

Sighing, I gather my will and force myself to rise again... though this time I'm more successful. My eyes are blurry still so I blink rapidly trying to clear them. Shapes move not far away. Big shapes, huge shapes, too big for Lothor even.

The screech happens again and somehow its even louder.

"Ah!" I cry, eyes watering, head splitting. I grab it, trying to keep it from dividing in two.

When it passes I wipe away the tears and now, at last, I can see. But I don't believe what I'm seeing. Lothor is fighting a zemlja. Alone.

He's dangling off the side of the massive creature, hanging on by what looks like the shaft of his lochaber. He's struggling, or not, I don't know.

My heart is in my throat, and when he the shaft breaks and he falls towards the ground I avert my eyes. I can't see this. I can't lose him. I don't want to see.

Lothor grunts, somehow still alive. Of course he is, he has to be...

Barely daring to breathe I look over and see him standing before the creature. The thing is ten or twenty times the size of him. It's huge, one of the biggest I've ever seen. He stands before it holding a sharp stick, the broken shaft of his weapon.

The zemlja rises into the air, gaping maw of a mouth opening wide. It strikes like a snake, slamming down so fast it blurs. Something that big shouldn't be able to move that fast. It's not fair. It takes me an instant to register what is happening.

"LOTHOR!" I scream the instant it hits me.

He disappears into its open mouth, gone...

The zemlja shudders, shakes, then falls over to its side, causing another quaking of the earth. Struggling to my feet I stumble forward, unable to stand straight, the stupid soft sand grabbing my legs, pulling me down making it even harder.

The zemlja shifts and my blood turns cold. It can't still be alive. It twitches and then Lothor climbs out of its jaws covered in grotesqueness. He drops to his knees, breathing heavily. I run forward, but I trip over my own feet. I cry out as I fall flat on my face into the sand and get a mouthful of it.

An instant later I'm swept up into his arms. I don't care he's gross. I don't care about the smell. I only care that he's alive and I'm in his arms. I throw my arms around his neck and gasp dry, tearless sobs against his shoulder. I can't stop them. It's relief and absurdity all rolled into a mishmash that I can't process.

It's all too much to handle, but the one thing that matters is he's alive.

"You're fine," he whispers. "I've got you."

My sobs intersperse with laughter. He's comforting me. All that he went through and he's the one giving comfort.

"Don't ever do that again," I laugh-cry.

"I'll try not to," he says, laughing too.

He carries me forward until we're in the shadow of a cliff. The adrenaline of seeing him fight drops away, leaving exhaustion and pain in its wake. My head is pounding, my throat is parched, and every fiber of my body aches. Even my bones hurt.

I shift, thinking I can stand but my muscles quiver then spasm before I even try to get out of his arms. It's all I can do not to bite my tongue as my muscles betray me.

He smooths my hair away from my eyes and holds me tight as my body is racked by it. At last it passes and my teeth quit chattering.

"I'm better," I lie softly. "Mostly."

"The epis should be inside here," he says. "It will help."

Biting my chapped lips, I nod. It's time and I can only hope there are no more dangers for us to face. Who am I kidding? For *him* to face. I'm nothing but a hindrance, especially in the shape I'm in. I can barely hold my thoughts together.

"Okay," I say, voice cracking. "I can stand."

Lothor smiles and shakes his head. "No."

I try to mount an argument and force myself out of his arms, but despite my willingness my body doesn't bother responding. This isn't a fight I'm going to win. Already sleep is clutching at my awareness, pulling me down and away from all of this.

"Fine," I agree. Willing or not he's right.

Nodding, he carries me further into the shade then gently lays me down next to a tight opening in the bluff wall. It's a crack so narrow I don't think he can fit. His broad shoulders, tail, and wings aren't going to let him pass easily. He pulls out a blanket of fur, spreading it in the shadow, then lifts me up and places me on it. He gives me a skin of water then digs through the pack.

"Food?" he asks, arching an eyebrow.

"Oh no," I say, shaking my head and clamping down on the rising nausea at the very idea.

Frowning, he nods his understanding and then closes the pack. He turns and scans the area, one hand resting on his hunting knife and the other shielding his eyes.

"It should be okay," he says, to himself or me I don't know. "I won't be long."

"It will be fine," I agree, denying the fear whispering in my head.

I'm going to be alone out here with no protection and too sick to defend myself if I had any. What could possibly go wrong? I have to shut down the hundreds of terrible things that flash through my thoughts in answer. His eyes linger on me, his jaw tightening, then he nods.

"Be right back," he says, then turns sideways and slides into the crack.

I can hear his scales scraping as he forces his way into the opening. It sounds painful, but he doesn't make a sound. A few moments later only his hand is visible, then even that is gone and I'm alone.

Sleep and unconsciousness call to me but I fight against them. If I'm going to be eaten by some random monster I prefer to be awake to at least try to fight.

But it's a losing battle. My eyes lose focus and I struggle to make them see as I'm pulled down into the blackness.

25

LOTHOR

*I*t's a tight fit and I barely scrape through, taking on new wounds as I do. That's good though, because if I can barely fit, it limits the number of things that might be calling this cavern home. I pull the knife from my belt and wait for my eyes to adjust to the darkness.

I'll need to go deeper to find the epis. It won't grow so close to the light of the suns. One of the many strange things about epis is it only grows in utter darkness. I also know that there will be a flight of sismis nesting around it, if there is epis here. The plant grows from their dung. I'll need to be quiet.

Eyes adjusted, I see I'm still in a tight crevasse. The walls aren't even an arm's width apart. I make my way deeper and the light behind me fades. The walls widen out into a full cavern, big and dark enough I can't see the far wall.

Sliding one foot in front of another I make my way across, trying to avoid finding any surprise crevasses or holes. Straining my ears for any sound, nothing catches my attention. It doesn't mean that nothing is in here with me. Some of Tajss' greatest threats are silent stalkers.

Reaching the back wall, I slide my hands along it, barely able to see dim outlines as I look for a way farther under the ground. I'm close to giving up hope when my hands find an opening. This one is shoulder-width and I move into it easily. A dozen sliding steps in I see it. The soft blue glow, a telltale sign of epis.

A sense of relief rises as I move down this tunnel. The moment I emerge there's a rustling from above. Freezing, I look up and see a flight of sismis nesting. Between the creatures hang strands of blue-glowing epis, reaching for the ground and the nutrients of their refuse.

Carefully and slowly so as not to make any noise, I make my way to the closest strand. It doesn't last long once harvested, so I'll only take some for now. Taking hold of the long strand, I wrap it in my hand and move my knife close, slicing it off. The glow dims but doesn't diminish completely.

I turn toward the way I came in, still moving slowly. My eyes strain to see where I'm about to step before I move. The light of the epis is dim but provides some illumination. Almost there. I'm almost to the opening.

My foot hits a rock and it zings off, clattering its way along the floor and cracking against the far wall. Time stops for an instant. In slow motion I turn and look back over my shoulder. The sismis awaken, their wings opening. As they start to drop from their perch on the ceiling time races forward.

I run.

The sismis screech, aware of my invasion of their home. They drop into the air and dive toward me.

There is no fighting a flight of them. They're too small a target, and even if I were to kill a dozen of them, a dozen more would be tearing at my flesh. My only option is to run, fast.

The air is filled with the sound of their leathery wings

beating. Their screeches split my ears as they dive at me. I duck and weave the best I can, but there's no avoiding all of them. Their teeth and claws tear at me, my scales giving me only so much protection against their onslaught.

One of them gets caught between my wings, thrashing wildly, its claws tearing and teeth gnashing behind my head as it struggles to free itself. Still running, I reach behind myself, grasping the creature and tearing it free.

It screams, in pain or anger I don't know, but I slam it against the wall as I pass into the tunnel. The air is filled with them. They're everywhere, attacking from all sides, and all I can do is run blindly forward. I don't think they can get out of the opening I came in, which means they'll have another exit.

That's fine. It's light outside and they're nocturnal. If I can get into the suns' light they'll give up the chase.

Blood trickles down my back and chest, flowing freely from dozens of cuts. I ignore it, ignore the pain, pushing through he cloud of wings and flesh blocking my path. I cannot be stopped. She needs me, needs this epis.

A few more steps and the first rays of the suns' light break through the assault of leathery wings and furry bodies. Hope ignites in my core and I leap forward, slamming against the wall. Turning sideways, I scrape myself hard as I fight my way through the tightness and emerge into the light.

Chattering teeth and high-pitched squeals emerge from the cavern as the sismis vent their frustration at my escape, but none of them emerge. I hold my knife ready, gripping the strand of epis in the other hand, waiting to see if any of them make their way out.

Out here I have the advantage; their numbers won't be against me. At last they give up their chase, and I take a deep breath before turning and going to Victoria.

She's passed out again, her head lolling as I lift her up

onto my lap. Trailing my fingers along her face, I try to rouse her, but she won't come around. I tear off a small piece of the epis and place it gently on her tongue, pushing her mouth closed. She doesn't react for a moment and I start to fear she'll choke on it, but then she chews.

The suns drift lower and lower as I feed her one small piece at a time. As they set heavy on the horizon she rouses, her eyes fluttering open and meeting mine. She smiles, a real, full smile. The first I've seen from her in so long, my heart explodes too big to fit in my chest.

"Lothor?" she asks, shaking her head. "I had the weirdest dream."

Smiling, I swallow hard, forcing the lump out of my throat so I can answer her without my voice cracking.

"Really?" I ask.

"Yeah," she says. "You fought a zemlja, alone."

"I see," I smile.

She pushes herself to a sitting position and looks around, then rolls her shoulders and neck. She stretches out her arms and looks at her hands, turning them front to back in front of her face.

"I feel… better…" she says, head tilting to one side. "Epis?"

"Yes," I say.

"Oh," she says, shaking her head. "How?"

"By doing what was necessary," I say. "Shall we go home?"

"It was real?" she asks. I shrug, not wanting to seem a braggart. "You're… incredible…"

Her eyes are wide and something comes across her. I don't know what to say in response, so I say nothing. The silence stretches but it's not uncomfortable. I touch her face and she doesn't flinch away. I didn't even think about it before I did it, but when she doesn't react it causes a warmth in my core that spreads through my limbs.

I pull a piece of treated leather out of the pack and carefully wrap the remaining epis in it. It will keep for a week or two before we need more. I'll cross that bridge when we get to it. Now that I know where it is I can come better prepared to harvest it in the future. Maybe I can figure out some way to drive the sismis out, but they're better than having a pack of guster take up residence in there. If I'm careful and harvest during the day they normally won't present any difficulty.

Victoria is still weak, but she helps pack up the few belongings we have with us. We're ready to travel home. It's dark, but I don't want to stay here any longer. It's dangerous out here and I need sleep. I reach out and offer her my arm and she looks at me, frowning.

"You're hurt," she says.

"I'm fine," I answer.

"Liar," she says, moving in closer and looking over my various wounds. "Your wing is hanging at a bad angle, you've got more cuts and scrapes than I can count, and your breath is hitching."

"It's nothing," I say.

"It's not, but I have nothing here to treat you with," she says, shaking her head. "I can walk. We'll be slower I know, but you're in no shape to carry me. Especially if we run into anything. You'll need your strength for that."

I open my mouth to argue, but the wisdom of her words can't be argued with. It's further proof why she's my treasure. She has a keen intellect.

"Yes," I agree.

We stare at each other and on some level I feel the changes between us. A closeness; some of the walls she's kept up between us are coming down. She smiles and her eyes light up as she nods. She holds out her hand, which I take gratefully, and we head for home.

Our future lays out before us as we walk across the

desert, hand in hand. A future neither of us knows is yet to bring us our biggest challenge.

26

VICTORIA

*H*ome. Never in my wildest dreams would it have ever occurred to me that I'd consider a small cave with a makeshift leather door home. Yet the moment I see it my heart leaps and my breath catches.

Home.

Grinning at Lothor, I lay my head on his shoulder as we walk. At an unspoken word we both move faster.

The epis is working, faster than I expected even. I chew a fresh piece of it even now. It makes my nerves tingle and light up. The hair on my arms stands on end and a sense of euphoria washes over me. No wonder everyone wanted to take this; it's like a crazy drug that doesn't cloud your thoughts. If anything it feels like I'm thinking clearer now than ever.

When we reach the base of the cliff and my foot touches that ramp, for the first time a fit of giggling overcomes me. I can't help it. I don't know how else to process all the emotions that are a raging storm inside.

Lothor wraps an arm and his tail both around me, turning me into him, and I rest my head against his chest.

He's always cool to the touch, which is amazing when the suns are trying to melt everything on the planet.

"Are you okay?" he asks once the fit of laughter eases.

"Yeah," I say, hugging him tighter. "Better than okay."

"Good," he says, then without warning he sweeps me off my feet.

"Oh!" I exclaim.

He laughs and carries me up the path. Before we reach the door a blinding blur races out of the cave and leaps through the air. Lothor turns, blocking the incoming attack with a shoulder, but Sree is ready for this and lands lightly. She mewls as she turns a circle on Lothor's shoulder, thrusting her head toward me.

"Sree!" I shout, scratching behind her furry ears. "I've missed you."

She makes that sound that's almost a purring and closes her eyes. She's no worse for wear, not that we've been gone that long, really. It only feels like forever. She leaps toward me and I catch her in my arms, laughing. She nestles against my chest and together we walk into a mess.

"Oh," Lothor says, shaking his head.

"Wow, Sree," I say. "Showing your displeasure much?"

The place is wrecked. Baskets turned over, items of the small shelves knocked to the floor, even the food stocks have been raided and are scattered around. Sree mewls in my arms as if to say it's not her fault.

Lothor drops his pack and puts his lochaber in its corner. I put Sree down as we both set about making our home right. It doesn't take long before we have it put back to rights. Sree doesn't help, of course, but she does have the decency to look shamed.

I'm gathering up a pile of clothes when a waft of something awful hits my nose. Then my hand touches something and I yelp, jumping back. Lothor is beside me in an instant, keeping me from falling backward by catching me with one arm. He shifts me behind him protectively, his hunting knife out in his free hand.

"Something?" he asks, not taking his eyes off the laundry, then his face wrinkles up and his brow furrows. "Oh."

"Yeah," I say. "Something gross."

He pokes at the pile of clothes with his knife, shifting them about, until he reveals a rotting carcass of some small animal. Sree makes a screechy sound that sounds proud. She trots over to the carcass and puts a padded foot on top of it. She stretches her head forward, ears perked, her tiny face grinning.

"She's proud," Lothor observes.

"Sree, that is so gross," I say, shaking my head and swallowing hard to try and keep the bile down. "Ugh."

"I'll take care of it," Lothor says, pulling me up with him as he rises. "Go outside so you don't have to smell this."

I'm not going to argue. I don't know how long that dead thing has been lying in there, but the odor is awful. Stepping outside and waiting beside the entrance, a few moments later Lothor races out carrying the thing wrapped in a piece of cloth. He doesn't pause even for an instant, racing down the ramp and going up the nearest dune before throwing it, cloth and all, as far as he can.

I wait by the door, watching him walk back. He cuts an imposing figure, outlined by the suns behind him turning him into a shadow. My heart beats faster, my breath turns ragged, and it feels like something shatters and a floodgate opens.

He's my protector.

I know it with a certainty that I can't explain. I've been around Zmaj long enough to know how they are as a race of people, or how the women who were falling for them felt about them anyway. I never saw them that way. I didn't believe them when they said all those wonderful things about the men they fell for. I always thought they were high on their own hormones. That sounds mean now that I think of it.

I was such a fool. Shaking my head, I try to hold back the tears, but the emotional storm raging in my head takes over and my cheeks are wet. Stupid. A life of fear. Every decision I ever made was because I was scared, scared of what might happen, scared of what had happened.

Where did it get me?

"Victoria," Lothor says, running up the last of the ramp and sweeping me into his arms.

I sob, laying my head on his chest. My throat is closed off, and I can't speak or tell him I'm okay. I throw my arms around him and he holds me tight. His concern is palpable; I feel it against my skin and know I should say something, but I can't.

The storm has broken free and is running its course. He's tense, worried, but silent. Strong. So strong. Stable, certain, and patient. My God, his patience with me is incredible. I sob until it empties out and there's nothing left but a sensation of having been cleansed. I'm refreshed, reset as if, maybe, the demons of the past have lost their power over me.

I take a first step into a new dawn. My first step toward freedom from the shadows of my past. They may not be gone completely, but their hold on me is less. Their grip is tenuous, no longer the steel that bound me so tight.

The tears run dry and I look up from his chest into his fabulous eyes, losing myself in them. Into his steadfastness, his strength, his welcoming heart. Pulling his head down our lips meet, soft, gentle, growing insistent as the emptiness is filled with passion.

His arms tighten around me, squeezing me closer as if he wants to press our bodies into one, and I want nothing more than that too. My skin tingles, every nerve alive, aware of the warm suns assaulting every surface, the hot soft breeze—every centimeter where our bodies touch.

More. I want more.

Need more.

I drive my tongue into his mouth, seeking his, needing his.

I've never in my life needed anything more than I need him. Joining with him, becoming, even for this fleeting instant, one with him.

His tongue meets mine and it's an electrical storm lighting up the darkness. Everything is firing at once, over-whelming as our tongues wrestle, our bodies meld together, my breasts crush against his chest, my arms squeezing, and he carries me into our home.

Home.

Our home. The place we've made together.

Our safety. Our retreat from the world.

A space, like any other space, but this is ours. Created by us.

He shifts me in his arms and then kneels, lowering us toward the furs that serve as our bed. Ours.

Everything here is us.

As my back touches the soft fur I ease my grip around his neck, letting my fingers trail through his hair up to his small horns, tracing them up to their points and back down.

His soft sigh exhales into my mouth and I consume his breath, welcoming him in. Accepting him.

His hands run over my face, tracing the lines of my jaw, down my neck, and across my arms. His massive body hovers over mine, not putting his full weight onto me, but his dominating presence presses in and I want still more.

It's not enough. How can it be enough? He's mine. I need him.

Tracing the lines of him with my fingertips, our tongues never stop, our kiss never breaks. The bulging of his muscles create beautiful peaks and valleys that entice my excitement as my fingers pass over them, exploring him.

He uses his tail, tracing it up my legs, a teasing extra touch as his mouth remains on mine and his hands find my breasts. He holds himself up with his knees on either side of my thighs. That teasing tail makes its way toward my pussy but doesn't touch, only enticing, building anticipation.

I thrust my hips up into him, urging him toward more, pushing for it. The aching desire burns. I need more and I need it now.

Sensing my desires—instinctively or consciously—his hands roam between our bodies, driving down across my stomach. When he presses against my mound the pressure on my clit is delicious, causing me to gasp and break our kiss.

He rubs circles on my mound while his hands work my breasts and his tail trails up and down inside my thighs. I tangle my fingers in his hair as my back arches, responding to the pleasure.

Pleasure builds until I'm almost there, but it's too soon and not enough. I break our lips apart and push him back, grabbing the hem of my shirt and pulling it over my head. He loosens his pants and slides them down, freeing his massive, throbbing, hard cock so it bounces between us, slapping my stomach as it drops.

He grabs my pants, not waiting for me, and pulls them roughly down, moving along with them. An instant later he buries his face between my thighs.

His tongue is magic and I cry out my pleasure. It's too good to be believed. His skill is unlike anything I've ever experienced. He finds every fold, touches every nerve, fucking me with his tongue until I'm dancing on the edge again.

"Ohhhh!" I moan as he works, driving in and out, licking up my soft folds and circling my clit softly with his tongue.

Somehow he senses the exact right pressure, never making it too much; it's always right and keeps building me up to that inevitable cliff.

My hands roam over his body, feeling his muscles shift, swell, and relax as he works my body like an instrument. It builds and builds until I'm overwhelmed and swept along by my own orgasm.

My back arches, toes curl, and hands twist in his hair, holding him tight against me as it washes over me in wave after seemingly unending wave of pleasure. I'm left shuddering and weak on the floor as the final shockwaves pass through, and I'm able to ease my grip at last.

"Lothor." I whisper his name and he's there, kissing me with soft, gentle kisses.

His massive body covers mine, protective and warm. I wrap my legs around his waist, pulling him down. His cock is at my entrance and I need it, need him, need to be filled in the aftermath of that earth-shattering orgasm.

His large cock slides in easily. I'm well prepared for him, and as my body shifts to accommodate him a sense of not only fullness comes over me but of completeness.

At last we're as close to one as we can be and it's still barely enough. I want him inside me and I want to be inside of him.

We mingle with each other on some level beyond the physical. The barriers are low, my fears are distant, and for this brief moment in time at least we're becoming what our potential really is. Something more than the two of us apart.

Has all my life been nothing more than a journey to this? Is this my fate? If so, then I welcome it. I forgive the harshness of my path because without it I might have never ended up here, in his arms, with his cock thrusting in and out of me.

He lifts me up and we roll to our sides, but he never stops pushing in and out, an edge of desperate need to his grunts accenting each thrust.

"Victoria," he breathes my name and it's an incantation on his lips. "My treasure."

Warmth races through my body at the word. It's a claiming and I accept it as such. I'm his. In this moment I give myself to him not only physically but in every way I can manage.

The deep scars hold me back, but nothing like they have before. I welcome his claim where any other time I would have run from it.

I accept it and I give him all I can, meeting each of his thrusts with one of my own. Desire fans desire until we're both being consumed by the grasping need for each other.

We twist and turn as we meld. Another lift and twist and I'm on his lap with my legs sticking out behind him, and he's helping lift me up and down as I ride his hard shaft.

We go and go past any reasonable time. My body resets as we continue and a new orgasm builds. This one will be bigger still: it builds and builds and soon it will take me.

He climbs to his knees, keeping me impaled, and then we're against the wall as he continues pushing into me. Our needs are insatiable. I can't get enough of him. We kiss, we touch, we thrust, and it's so much more than sensation.

It's need, it's desire, it's joining, it's a becoming. It's not only sex but so much more.

His thrusts become urgent and his vocalizations deeper. Then he drives in hard and I'm thrown into the wash of a fresh orgasm as he lets himself go, dumping his primary seed into me.

We hold each other tight, softly groaning and moaning as

our pleasure climaxes until at last we're together. Kissing, touching, holding each other as his spent member softens and we're left staring into each other's eyes.

"I love you," he whispers.

I sense his trepidation at the words, but I also know he can't hold them back any longer. I bite my lip, staring into his eyes. Deep inside the fears scream, but I'm not going to be their victim any longer. Fear may have a hold in my soul, but I'm walking as far from it as I can. I'm going to bask in the suns of his love for me and I'm going to proclaim it.

"I love you!" It comes out as a yell, echoing off the rock walls.

His eyes widen, his head jerks back, and my cheeks burn. I didn't mean to scream it, but it came out with the force of my own release from the prison I've been trapped in for so long.

The corners of his mouth twitch and then twist up, and his smile is so big it goes from ear to ear. He laughs, pulls me into a tight embrace, then moves back and we kiss. A soft, gentle kiss confirming the words we've shared.

"I love you," he says between kisses.

"I love you," I say, keeping myself from yelling it but wanting to.

I want to go to the top of the highest mountain on the planet and scream it out for everyone to hear. I want them all to know that at last I've found the one with whom I belong. I've found the man I can trust, the one who will protect me forever.

If only it were as true as it feels in this moment.

27

VICTORIA

The next several months are wonderful. It's something I never thought I would say—especially not on Tajss—but it is and it's all because of Lothor. By some odd twist of fate, I ended up with someone so perfect for me I could never have imagined it. I can't even imagine being afraid of him anymore. His strength makes me feel safe. Protected. His arms feel like home.

No, I didn't get there overnight. It was definitely a process. A painful one at times, but so worth it in the end. It started with sex, with me chipping away at my own emotional walls, trying my best to soften the most obvious scars from my past.

Little did I know that the breaking of that physical barrier was only the beginning. It freed me in a way that allowed me to let Lothor in, allowed me to be vulnerable in a way I never had been to anyone. Not since my father, before I knew how to put up barriers. I didn't put them up consciously, but I kept up a shield to protect myself from everyone else in my life from then on.

How else do you deal with that pain? The betrayal of the

one who's supposed to protect you? I built walls to hide behind, to avoid the fear that was a constant of my childhood. The walls did their job, but also kept me from developing relationships that could have been deeper.

Until Lothor. If not for him I don't know if I'd ever have brought that timeworn shield down. Heck, without him, I'd still be with the Zzlo and wouldn't have gotten a chance to even try.

I can't stop the smile spreading across my face while I fix our pallet. We've fallen into a routine, but it's one I enjoy. It's the new normal and it's so much better than any normal I've known in my entire life.

Pallet made and straightened, I pick up the duster he helped me fashion out of bivo fur and go over the few flat surfaces. One thing about Tajss, there's not a lot of dust. Sand, everywhere and on everything, but not a lot of dust.

When I reach the small cabinet with its odd assortment I pause, looking at the items there. A broken mirror, a cracked brush handle. I avoid these items because they bother Lothor. He's never said why and we don't talk about them. I don't think he knows why he holds onto them. Gershom talked about how the Zmaj were all primal beasts and attributed it to the fact that they have no memory. A man, or in this case an alien, with no memory of the past is no more than an animal. Or so he argued.

It was one of his many and varied arguments to keep his followers from trusting the Zmaj. I'm so glad to be rid of him, though I can't help wondering what became of him. Of his followers. I had friends among them. Or as close as I ever came to having friends, which isn't close at all I suppose. Yay barriers.

Glancing around quickly to see if Lothor is close, I give them a quick dust and move one. I know he won't be far. He never goes farther than he can hear me shout without making sure I know it. I know I wouldn't be able to survive without him, but he never makes me feel like a less important part of our partnership. In fact, he consults me before doing everything important.

My life is full. Sure, it's simple. Hunting, gathering, cleaning—the bare bones of what a life is. On the outside, anyway, but the fact that I'm doing it all with Lothor... I can't put a price on that.

We've learned how to live together, how things work best. At this point, we're more than just the sum of our individual parts. We live, we laugh. We have a lot of really good sex. What else could a girl ask for?

Dusting and cleaning done, I set to work prepping the dried herbs for storage. It's easy work that my small fingers are much better suited for than Lothor's big sausage fingers. Snorting, I think of things and places his big fingers are much better for than this. As if on cue I hear his familiar footsteps, then he opens the makeshift door to our home and wraps his arms around my waist, nuzzling my neck.

"I was thinking, perhaps a hunt," he murmurs in my ear.

"Hmm?"

I layer my arms over his.

"But now I wonder if our time could not be better used..."

I half laugh, half gasp, as he lifts me from my stool and takes us down to the pallet without warning, twisting to cushion the impact. He immediately flips us once more, his mouth nibbling at mine, his thigh sliding between mine.

I hum in the back of my throat, returning his kiss, sliding my hands down his broad back. It's that same initial thrill I first felt racing through me from when we kissed for the first time, but it's even better now.

I don't feel that edge of fear, that tinge of uncertainty. I only feel good. Sighing, I skim my hands down to his butt, squeezing. He moans his encouragement.

That's something he's made very clear. Any and all touches from me are always welcome. It's easy to become addicted. His hand skims up to cup my breast, squeezing it firmly before sliding back down. Down to where his thigh holds mine apart.

His fingers press firmly, sliding up and down the seam of my pants. The pressure, the placement...

He knows exactly how to touch me. Exactly how to tease me. My moan is a softer counterpoint to his, my hips pushing back up against him. That's when he loses his patience. I'm giggling as he wrestles with my clothes.

"You do not need these in the cave," he complains as he finally gets them off.

"Yes, I do," I argue back, opening my arms and pulling him close again. "What if we have to run outside? What if some creature shows up? I'm not running out there naked!"

"I will keep you safe," he responds.

It's clear his attention isn't on the conversation anymore. He kisses the side of my neck, skims his lips over my sensitive collarbone, sucks hard on one nipple and then the other.

"Lothor," I complain, rubbing up against his now-naked erection.

It feels good to rub up against him like that. He knows I want more. Chuckling, he reaches between us, his fingers lightly sliding over my wetness. Deliberately too light for what I want.

Fine. Two can play that game.

Reaching down myself, I take his cock in a firm grip and he stills above me. I slide my hand up and down, twisting slightly at the top like I know he likes. His grip tightens on me. Almost there...

With a growl, he flips me over onto my front, shoving one of my thighs up and to the side to open me up for his thrust.

Bingo!

I cry out as his broad head slowly squeezes in, making room for himself. I don't think the fit will ever be easy, but I'm not complaining. I push back as he pushes forward until he's seated all the way, filling me right up to the brim.

Nuzzling his face against mine, he starts to *move*. I cry out, clenching my hands in the sheets, feeling overtaken. The pleasure rises fast and hard. Sometimes Lothor takes his time, spending what feels like hours teasing me, but other times he's like this. Impatient, ready to reach that mind-melting end as quickly as he can.

Needless to say, I fully enjoy them both.

My breath catches when he reaches underneath me, his fingers finding my clit, and I'm there. The pleasure suffuses me, sharp and gorgeous. Only then does Lothor allow his own release. He makes sure I'm never left unsatisfied.

Which also means I'm floating around the cave a lot because I find myself on the pallet at least once a day. Or against the table. Or the wall...

Lothor flips me over once more, his eyes focused on my face and he slides his secondary cock in.

I watch him as he watches me, the ride slow and sensitive this time. A wonderful counterpoint. This time, the climax is almost gentle. Lothor drops on top of me, kissing me lazily. With a sound of deep satisfaction, he allows his head to drop down on the pallet next to my own.

"Hunt," he murmurs. "We must hunt."

He sounds almost like he is complaining, drawing a smile out of me.

"Okay. In a minute."

"Yes," he agrees, squeezing my hip.

We lie there for a while, my hand absently playing with his hair. It would be nice to just lie there all day, but we can't, not if we want to eat. Lothor must go through the same thought process because he stirs not much later.

"Come. I saw signs of gretba nearby."

Oh good. Gretba are smaller, furry creatures that live in caves. A lot easier—and safer—to hunt than the larger creatures.

"Okay."

I clean up with a rag and some water—maybe we can make a trip to the oasis later—then dress quickly. Lothor does the same, grabbing his lochaber and knife. I grab mine as well. It can be used for self-defense, but I mainly use it for skinning and dressing the animals Lothor hunts.

"This way," Lothor murmurs, heading down the path that leads up to the cave.

There are a lot of smaller and larger caves around our own, with winding and confusing connections that often lead to unexpected places. When we first headed into one of the larger cave networks, I lost track of where we were and how to get back. I'm a lot better at it now.

Not that Lothor would ever let me go through the caves on my own. It still isn't safe, despite my larger knowledge bank. I'm not under the delusion that I could handle myself against all the potential threats Tajss can throw at us.

Lothor leads the way into one of the narrower caves, his eyes scanning the ground in front of us. I look too, my eyes now trained to pick up the signs that he looks for. Droppings in the corner. Some scuff marks in the dust and sand that's been tracked in. There's at least one smallish creature in here.

Lothor turns left, and then right, before holding up a silent hand to signal me to stop. I still, scanning the dim cavern in front of us. There's a crack above that lets in small stream of light, though it still isn't well lit. There are also a good amount of rocks and debris to hide behind.

However, from what I can see, this is a dead end. There aren't any obvious exits, though it's possible there are small cracks that other creatures could fit through.

A hiss comes from my right, jerking my attention to the dark shadows. Narrowing my eyes, I can just make out the pale gray fur and large glinting eyes. Lothor has silently made his way over to its hiding place. So silently that I didn't even realize it until I looked.

Sometimes, he's almost spooky like that. I wince at the whistling sound of his lochaber swinging hard and fast, and then the hissing abruptly stops.

When I first saw one of the fluffy creatures, I felt bad about killing it. That was before it hissed at me, showing gleaming teeth, and I remembered that most, if not all, of the creatures on Tajss aren't exactly potential cuddle buddies.

I still don't like killing them, despite knowing it would bite my face off. They're cute, but living out here in the desert, you quickly realize survival doesn't really allow for too many softer emotions. Besides, we don't take more than we need.

I walk over to Lothor as he pulls his blade out, cleaning it on the creature's fur. Pulling my knife I crouch down and set about field dressing it as Lothor has taught me.

Better we do that here rather than back in the cave. The blood makes a mess, but it could also draw predators, which is not a great idea. We don't want anything attracted to our home by the scents of fresh blood. Once I have it dressed, Lothor cuts into its middle and skins it. Between the two of us, we have the carcass ready to transport in no time.

After Lothor taught me how to properly skin, dress, and harvest meat, I got plenty of practice. This one creature is more than enough meat for the two of us, but not enough to store long-term. So, when we bring it back, we cut it up and cook all of it.

It'll keep fine for a day or so after we add all the seasoning and keep it in the coolest place in the cave, a natural hole in the floor. When the prey is large, we preserve it, smoking it using techniques Lothor taught me and using lots of salt. Or the Tajss equivalent of salt. I have accidentally put some of it too close to the fire and burned some batches, but Lothor didn't get mad though.

"How will you learn without making mistakes?" he asked. "I know exactly how many I have made. Especially at first."

Despite his patience, I felt terrible. I'd learned how dangerous it was to hunt, how much time and the effort it took. Wasting the product of his work made me feel awful. I'm a lot more careful about it now. Today, with this small kill, we're eating the fruit of our labor within an hour of killing it.

"It is good," Lothor remarks, taking another bite with relish.

Sree mewls from her own dish of lightly cooked meat, as if in agreement. I smile and take a bite. My experimenting with the different spices and herbs has paid off.

"Do you think we can go to the oasis?" I ask. "I'd like to wash if I can."

He nods, looking out of the open door. I know he's judging the time by the amount of light still out there.

"Yes," he agrees. "We can fill waterskins as well."

True. We're not too low yet, but it isn't a good idea to let it get there. Once, I accidentally spilled the last of our water when Sree leapt up from my lap, chasing a tiny animal only she could see. The trek to get more water without any to take with us was not one I ever want to repeat, thanks.

After we finish eating, Lothor grabs four empty skins, and I grab two. Water is heavy. I can't handle more than two of the skins, even with Lothor helping me across the sand. Honestly, almost carrying me across the sand.

I grab a basket too—no use leaving good fruit or herbs behind if we find them. Sree mewls a complaint when we get up to leave once more, but she doesn't follow. She knows what the skins mean and doesn't want to take the journey with us.

"Must be nice having water brought to you," I murmur, reaching down to pat her soft head.

She rubs her face against my hand, purring, then flops down onto the pallet. She extends her claws, picking at the bedclothes and bunching them up, then sets her head on her paws to wait for us. Lothor chuckles.

"She is turning lazy," he remarks, stepping outside. "Soon, she will not run but roll."

I laugh, glancing back at Sree. He isn't wrong. She's definitely more round than she was when I first saw her. Hmm. Maybe it's time to put her on a diet. It would probably spur her to hunt for herself more, but at least she'd get some exercise.

I'm on autopilot as Lothor wraps his arm around me when we get to the bottom of the path. He spreads his wings and leaps across the desert sand, his wings helping us almost fly, or close enough to it. We've traveled this same path many times now. I'm sure Lothor has traveled it more than he would have before he stumbled across me.

I smile to myself. Well, if we're going to have this much sex, we're just going to have to get to the oasis more often. It's thirsty work! Not that Lothor has complained. I chuckle and he glances down questioningly.

"Nothing," I say, cheeks flushing.

He makes an understanding noise that's a cross between a hiss and a growl. It's familiar now, but not that long ago it would have frightened me. How much has changed since then! Leaning my head into the crook of his neck between his head and his shoulder, I close my eyes and enjoy the sensations of the wind in my face and the sinking of my stomach with each leap he makes.

Maybe I'm used to traveling the desert now, but the trip definitely feels shorter than it did at the beginning. Still, the sight of the green oasis is no less beautiful. The view from home is sand with more sand. The rare lush green outpost is a welcome change of scenery. Also, I can already feel the crisp, clear water on my skin.

Once we're at the edge of it, Lothor sets me down and leads the way inside. He goes much faster with me now, secure in the knowledge that I know which plants are safe, which aren't. Which are edible and which ones think we're edible. Ironically, some of the carnivorous plants are actually safe to eat. If you're careful not to be eaten by them first.

I stop and pick some herbs and a few berries as we go, but the pickings are slim today. We'll have to come back later, when they're riper. When we reach the edge of the water, I immediately chuck my clothes, ready to jump in.

I push my pants down, having to wiggle a little to get them completely off. Hmm. I poke at the roundness at the base of my belly. Maybe Sree isn't the only one who needs to go on a diet. Lothor has fed us well, much better than the mystery meats and gunk the Zzlo would bring for me to cook.

I crouch and pick my clothes up, intending to take them in with me to wash, but an odd dizziness hits me, followed by a punch of stomach-rolling nausea. I gasp, listing to the side, barely catching myself with one hand before I fall on my face.

"Victoria!" Lothor's strong arm catches me, holding me in the crook of his elbow. "What is it?" he demands, turning me to face him, his eyes worried. "What is wrong?"

"I..." I shake my head, taking a few deep breaths. My

stomach settles, the wave of nausea passing as fast as it came. "Maybe the meat we ate was bad? My stomach turned over..."

I trail off as another possible explanation hits me. Nausea. An expanding waistline. I do a quick calculation and realize I haven't had my period in...

Going on two months.

"Lothor," I whisper, head spinning, making me light-headed again.

"What? What is it?" he questions, his grip tightening, his gaze frantic with concern.

I take his hand, laying it over the new curve of my belly.

"Lothor...I think we're...having a baby."

He blinks and then looks down at my stomach. He shakes his head, his expression as floored as I'm sure mine is in that moment.

"A...baby?" he repeats, his hand pressing against the swell of my belly. We haven't said that word before, but I can tell he gets it right away. "Baby," he repeats, concern giving way to awe.

Awe and a joy that matches my own growing happiness.

"A baby!" he repeats again, dropping to his knees to lay his head against my still mostly flat stomach.

I laugh, combing his hair back from his face.

Lying here naked in his arms, the suns reflecting off the water, a soft rustling breeze passing through the plants, knowing a new life is growing inside of me... I want to absorb every detail; I want to keep this moment for all of time, because I don't think it can get much better than this.

If only it would be like this forever. If only... but nothing ever is...

28

LOTHOR

*L*eaping behind another dune, I keep the guster in sight while staying downwind of it so it doesn't pick up on my presence. It is currently alone, following the trail of others in the sand. Its single-minded determination to follow that trail tells me it did not mean to separate itself and perhaps it is close to rejoining the herd. Which means I cannot waste time in my attack.

Even if that were not the case, I would still be inclined to be efficient with the hunt. I do not like leaving Victoria alone for too long. One of the few times it is necessary to do so is while I hunt, especially prey as dangerous as the guster.

We agreed that it would be too much of a risk to bring her along now that she is pregnant. In my head, I know she is much safer in the cave. However, being apart from her leaves me anxious and restless. What if something happens with the baby? What if danger reaches her even in the cave? What if she needs me and I am not there?

I increase my speed, less careful of stealth and distance, and needing to bring this hunt to an end. Propelling myself forward, I attempt to reach its head before it clears the dune.

When I look ahead, I realize we will soon be traveling through a narrow path through rocks. There will not be room to maneuver in that corridor.

I must stop the guster before it reaches the protection of the rocks. Dropping my attempt to find a strategic strike, I spread my wings and leap up, whirling my lochaber over my head into position to stab down toward the middle of its back. It won't be a killing blow, but it should catch the beast's attention.

The blade sinks into its back, my feet land on it and I push off again, leaping to the side. It screams, an odd hissing edge to the shriek. Pulling the blade out of its thick hide as I leap off its back it swings its large head, razor-sharp teeth snapping on empty air where I was a moment before.

It swings its hefty tail and I barely dodge the blow, feeling it barely skim my back. At least I have successfully stopped its forward momentum.

Unfortunately, now it knows it is being hunted and it does not take kindly to the knowledge.

Whirling around, it charges, its enormous webbed feet hitting the sand hard enough that the ground vibrates beneath me. Taking a deep breath, I brace my feet, bend my knees, and wait.

I stare into its angry eyes as it bears down on me, at those glistening teeth as it opens its mouth in preparation. Ready to bite down on my flesh.

Wait...

Now!

I spring into the air, its teeth barely missing me as it snaps its jaws shut, only closing on air. I slice down the back of its head and neck, my lochaber not penetrating deep enough to hit anything vital but the blood loss will be significant.

Flapping my wings to keep myself in the air, I lift my

lochaber and slice down its spine before touching down on its back and leaping off once more.

It hurls itself to the side, attempting to impale me. Its spikes scrape against my side as I quickly roll out of the way fast enough to avoid a potentially fatal wound, though I still incur some scratches.

I need to finish this or one of its attacks will eventually land. I cannot be hurt or killed. It is not only Victoria depending upon me now. Resolve hardening, I circle around the creature, bouncing from dune to dune as it tries to follow leaving a trail of its life blood behind.

There.

It slides, losing purchase as it tries to keep up with my nimble maneuvering. Shifting midair, I pull the lochaber back and swing it in a shining arc.

By the time the creature's attention is back upon me, the blade is sinking into the side of its neck. It jerks back and I let the weapon go in favor of leaping back, gaining enough distance to protect myself from its wild flailing.

Blood spurts out of its new wound, splattering across the sand as it panics, knowing it is fatally wounded. I stay well out of its reach as it decides to attack, its movements slowing. It had already lost a significant amount of blood even before this final blow.

It tires, snapping and hissing, then its steps begin to falter. With one last huff of breath, it lies down in the sand, its sides rising and falling slower. And slower. I watch, waiting until I am absolutely certain it is dead.

A dying creature is almost more dangerous than one that is healthy. Watching it warily, I step closer. When it does not move, I grip the handle of the lochaber and pull my weapon free with a huff of effort.

The body does not move, apart from a slight shift caused by me. Confirmation of its death. Time to harvest what I can carry. Taking out my knife, I get to work. It takes longer than I expect it to, though perhaps I've just become accustomed to having Victoria with me.

Smiling, I remember when she was first learning how to skin and dress my kills. She would furrow her brow, wrinkle up her nose, and make a retching sound while she worked. I am certain she was not aware of making those faces and noises, but her feelings never stopped her from doing what needed to be done. She is very good at it; her small hands are more dexterous than my own.

Cutting the last piece of meat, I wrap it and pack it for the trip before I clean off the knife and my lochaber using the sand. Then I am ready for the journey back, laden with enough food to fill even my ravenous female. Grinning, I set a hard pace.

Having someone to come back to is a luxury I will never take for granted. I look up at the positions of the suns in the sky. Perhaps I will have time to take Victoria to the oasis after all. If we—

A motion at the corner of my vision interrupts my train of thought. Stopping and turning to see what it is, I see a plume of red sand clearly thrown up to the sky by something. Odd...

Shifting course, I aim to intercept the plume.

Though I quickly realize it is traveling in the same direction I was. I frown, increasing my pace. It could simply be a coincidence, but I don't know what the plume originates from yet. My stomach clenches as I climb that last dune. Cresting it gives me a clear view of source of the plume.

I trace the moving burst of sand down to a small, glinting point racing across the sand. A transport. The shape of which is all too familiar. My stomach turns over and cold races across my scales as bile rises into my throat.

Zzlo. It is a Zzlo transport. And it is racing straight toward home.

I drop the meat without thought, leaping as far and hard as I can, using my wings to help me glide. I have never traveled this quickly before. I leap the last segment of that journey home. I do not think I have ever had an incentive so immediate, so all-consuming.

Victoria. Victoria and our unborn child. She is waiting for me to return, sitting unprotected in that cave. I cannot believe that the direction in which the transport is traveling is a coincidence. I do not know how they found her location, but I know they are trying to kidnap Victoria once again.

The air burns in my lungs, the sand scrapes against me, and my wings ache with hard use. I do not care. I need to force as much speed as I can from my body. Gritting my teeth, I push even harder. Faster! I'm not fast enough.

The Zzlo transport is disappearing into the distance. Growling, I tilt my head down and *move*. All the while knowing I will not be fast enough. But I cannot give up. I have to push.

By the time I reach the path leading up to the cave, the transport is nowhere in sight, but I see odd scuff marks along the normally neatly hidden walkway. The bijass surges in my thoughts. I'll rip apart all of them, limb from limb.

I don't slow. Clenching my jaw, I bound up that last bit of distance, panic fluttering in my chest. The door is open, tilted oddly. Half broken. The blood rushes in my ears, my pulse a harsh thud.

Stepping into the cave, I feel as though I am in a dream. Or a nightmare.

The table is turned over, a chair thrown completely across the room. The food stores have clearly been rummaged through; some of the waterskins are gone.

Taking in the clear signs of a struggle, my knees give way and I hit the hard rock with a painful force that I barely feel.

Victoria. They took Victoria.

I feel hot, then cold. My mind is blank, unable to absorb the empty cave—the clear sign that the Zzlo have taken my Victoria. An odd glint on the floor catches my eye, but still no thoughts permeate my muffled mind.

Reaching out without thinking, I realize it is the mirror. The mirror I keep on the shelf...

A burst of old pain clashes with the new. Old loss, the scars of which will never be fully gone, fully healed. A flash of a pretty smile, shining green gold eyes... followed by a sudden...emptiness.

The pain... is too much.

Too much.

Snarling, I hurl the mirror across the cave. Rising to my feet, a surge of incandescent anger powers the shell of my body.

No!

Picking up the chair next to me, I hurl it against the wall, the sound of shattering wood barely registering. Gripping the shelf on the wall I tear it out, tossing it away, my hands reaching for something, anything else on which to vent my anger.

What are these things? What do they matter? Grabbing the door, I tear it fully off its hinges and throw it aside as well. It doesn't help. It's useless!

Useless!

I leave a trail of destruction behind me more severe than the Zzlo, rage clouding my thoughts completely. I barely register a small, furry animal streaking past, its gait somewhat odd. As though it is limping from an injury.

In that moment, nothing can penetrate the wall of anger. I feel... empty.

As though my hearts have been ripped out and torn to shreds. What does anything matter? Everyone I love only meets a terrible end...

I reach for something else to throw and find nothing. I have already destroyed everything. I drop back down to the floor, making a fist and punching it. Pain travels up my arm.

It's something. So I keep punching until my knuckles are slick with my own blood. I stare at the wetness on the floor, my chest rising and falling harshly.

Somehow, the sight of it reaches my thinking mind. What have I accomplished? I look around at the destruction, the clear evidence of my breakdown.

What did any of that achieve? I look at my torn-up hands, making a fist and releasing it, the rage, the despair, the utter emptiness still eating at me.

But there is something else now.

Purpose.

Resolve.

My eyes fall on the basket Victoria keeps near the pallet. Where she stores her clothing. I pick it up gently, the resilient weave of it having survived my frenzied attack. This... this will not be the end.

I may have failed my first love, but I refuse to fail my Victoria.

29

VICTORIA

I shift carefully, cognizant of the clinking of the chains. The less attention I draw to myself, the better.

I'm tossed to one side as the Zzlo driving takes an unnecessarily sharp turn. Gritting my teeth, I grip the chain tighter, the only anchor I have to keep me in place. The Zzlo chortle among themselves at the move, clearly in high spirits. They have managed to recapture their slave, after all. And this time they're being extra careful.

As soon as they brought me down to the transport, they secured me with the thick chain attached to my ankle. After the way I fought them in the cave, I can't pretend to be meek and nonthreatening. Not convincingly.

Even if I didn't fight trying to delay the inevitable in a desperate hope that I could give Lothor enough time to reach the cave, I know they would have taken extra precautions. They know, now, I'm a flight risk.

I stare at the Zzlo, their once-familiar features now again alien to me. Yes, I recognize them, but the horror of the situation is a lot sharper after a year of freedom. Freedom and happiness.

When they kidnapped me the first time, I hadn't been in the best situation, having followed Gershom into exile, trying to survive in the desert without sufficient food or supplies. Everyone I knew was having heat strokes, some were dying from it, but Gershom kept promising a bright future. I never believed him, not really, but I was too scared to go back to the City. Scared of the Zmaj and their massive size. If I'd only known then what I do now. Understood their true nature. But all I could see was my fear.

When they captured me then, it was trading one hell for another. The adjustment was easier. The contrast this time is starker. The difference now is me. I'm not the same broken, scared thing I was before. I'm better. Stronger.

My initial struggle wasn't enough to delay them effectively, but I'm not going to be so stupid as to keep resisting. Open defiance is not an option, not now that I can't be sure Lothor even knows where I am. I have to play this smart.

No matter how tight my chest feels, now much my memories are trying to rise up and paralyze me with fear, I have to survive. If not for myself or Lothor, then for our baby who is now dependent on only me.

I cover my gently rounded stomach with my hand. I will protect our child. At any cost.

I duck my head as one of them walks back to check on me. He barks something in their harsh, guttural language then nudges me with his boot, not at all gentle. I refuse to look up, refuse to feed into whatever he's trying to do.

When he gets no reaction, he turns and walks back to his seat in the front. Sighing silently, I stretch my legs out on the floor in front of me. They stashed me in the cargo area in the back, empty but for me and the things they stole from our cave. My heart clenches as I stare at the familiar objects.

They shouldn't be here. Shouldn't be with the Zzlo. It just looks wrong. Blinking back tears, I resolutely look away. God, please let Lothor find me. Or give me an opportunity to escape.

I know I can do it on my own now. The one thing I never would have thought of before, but now certainty fills me: I know I can escape. All I need is half a chance. I have too much incentive not to take the risk.

My hands clench on the chain as the transport swerves hard again. Their sounds of glee tell me the driver is doing it on purpose. They're enjoying tossing me around and making things harder for me. Assholes.

Grinding my teeth, I clench the chain tighter, fighting the irrational urge to choke one of the bastards out. No, it doesn't matter. I won't let them get to me. I keep my head down and wait and watch. At some point, they'll screw up. A chance, it's all I need. One chance to escape and I know it will come because now I'm ready. I'm not the scared, broken girl I was before. Now I'm strong and have so much more to live for.

I fan the embers of my hope, keeping it close to me as we continue to travel toward... something. I don't know what, but I have no doubt I'm not going to like it. Years ago, back on the ship, I watched a documentary show that focused on people who were kidnapped. It was a survivor's story, showing how they made it through their ordeals.

The takeaway was never to allow yourself to be taken to a secondary location. Apparently, it drastically cut the chances of being able to escape. I'm certain the creators of the program didn't have the Zzlo in mind, but I'm inclined to believe the advice still applies.

So, if there's a chance, I have to take it. I can't rely only on Lothor finding me, though I have no doubts he's coming, I can't rely on him getting to me in time. Unlike the survivors in that show, if I let them take me too far, they'll take me off the planet. How would I get back to Lothor then?

Lothor. My chest aches as I imagine him finding the empty cave. He would have been devastated. Tears cover my eyes, blurring my vision, and I take in deep breaths trying to keep them at bay. I can't give into that, not now. If I do I won't be ready.

My resolve hardens. I will get back to him. No matter what.

But as time stretches into hours and we are still traveling, doubts nibble at the edges of that strength, of that resolve. How far away am I? How can I travel all of that distance alone? How long would it take me? How will I survive?

I keep circling back to the baseline truth—it doesn't matter. I have to try. If I want any chance, I have to try.

Suddenly the transport jerks to a stop and I look up, pulled from my ruminations. The transport has holes in the metal walls, probably some kind of bullet holes. Looking through I see it's dark outside. They must be stopping for the night.

My heart picks up its pace. This might be my chance.

One of them comes through the compartment not bothering to even glance at me. He lifts the door open, letting in the fresh desert air, and I tense, watching for any opportunity. The Zzlo exit, jostling for position, leaving me chained to the wall, forgotten.

When one of them veers over toward me I quickly look away. He stops close. Too close. I don't know what he says, the words unclear, but the tone and the body language easily convey his intended threat.

When I don't react he takes another step closer. With nowhere to go, I curl up into a ball, preparing for a blow. I have to keep the baby safe. My breath is shaky as I wait for the pain. A second passes. And then another.

Seconds tick by in angsty anticipation as I wait for the blow I know is going to come, fear sending cold chills across my limbs. I must wait in that position for thirty seconds, but nothing happens. Finally, I hear a rustling sound and then the sound of footsteps moving away from me.

I wait another minute, my breathing the only sound. Loud and ragged. When I open my eyes, only the dark interior of the transport greets me. They even turned off the lights. Blood roars in my ears and for an instant I imagine what Lothor will do to them when he finds me, taking a perverse joy at my thoughts of them cowering in fear before my enraged lover.

The moment passes, the heavy cold restraints of the chains on my wrists cutting through the heated passionate imagining. Looking out the open door, they've started a large fire. Idiots. Why not send up a flashing signal of *here we are*!

It works in my favor though. I know he's coming, even if I have no intention of waiting for him to find me. Taking a deep, shaky breath, the scent of the meat sizzling over the fire drifts into the compartment and my stomach growls in response. My meat, food they stole from Lothor and me.

Lately, I can't seem to stay full for very long. I shift, moving as close to the open door as the chains will allow. One of them looks over at the sound, grunting, a large chunk of meat in its greasy hands, juices dripping down its chin.

It motions at me with the meat, cold beady yellow eyes locked on mine, it takes a bite and slowly chews it, grinning. That makes it clear they have no intention of feeding me.

Fine.

One night won't hurt me and I won't give them the satisfaction of letting them see it bothers me. Moving back to put my back against the wall, I close my eyes and wait.

30

LOTHOR

The sand flies under my feet as I follow the transport's deep tracks. It is heavy, which is in my favor, but it is also fast. Too fast.

Sliding down another dune while keeping my eyes on the distinctive furrows in the ground, despair threatens to overtake me, but I cannot allow it. Cannot give in, no matter what. I will not fail Victoria.

I will find her. I will bring her back safely. I will destroy those who dared to take her from me. There is no other outcome I will entertain.

Images of Victoria captured by the Zzlo, hurt, chained and afraid flash through my thoughts. My chest constricts and pain stabs into my left heart. It's almost enough to stop me, but I won't let anything stop me. She needs me. I grab the fear and make it fuel. Push myself to run faster, leap farther. I will be in time.

Anything less is too heavy a burden. I cannot allow fear of failure—or the terror of finding her hurt or worse—to overtake me. I know it is so great that it can. As it did when I discovered our empty cave.

Guster tracks catch my attention. They cross the transport's trail just ahead of me. Not slowing, I scan the area around me as I continue to follow the transport. I will have to keep a sharp eye out for the threat, but I cannot afford the time needed to scout the area.

My path is set in the wake of the transport. I will not veer from it; nothing can distract me from reaching her. If they reach their destination, they'll take her off-world, beyond my reach...

No!

Digging deeper, I push myself to run faster. My muscles burn, my breath becomes ragged, but I won't stop, I can't. The desert blurs around me, my single-minded focus keeping only the path I need to take clear.

Nothing else matters. Even when the suns set and I travel through the night, I do not rest or change my path. Traveling in the dark is not safe. There are too many predators who use the cover to hunt, but I cannot camp for the night. My greatest hope is that they will stop themselves and I need every moment I can take to decrease the distance between myself and the transport.

I can only hope my luck is with me, that the Zzlo have stopped for the night, that they are unfamiliar with the dangers they could encounter during their journey.

Because it is dark, I do not realize at first where I am until I pass a familiar rock formation. It is distinctive, even without the bright sunlight. I check the transport's path in front of me to confirm. There is no doubt; I'm nearing the Order's territory.

Pausing, I take a moment to catch my breath and get my bearings. I've had a run-in with the Order before, not one I want to repeat. A group of Zmaj, the only group I've seen since the Devastation happened, who work together. Years ago I came too close to their territory when hunting and ran across a patrol of them.

They made it clear I wasn't welcome there, in no uncertain terms. More than that, they had technology. Technology that allowed them to communicate with others. Technology and weapons. Since then they and I have agreed to avoid each other, which has worked out fine.

The Order could stop the Zzlo transport, I suspect, if they decided to involve themselves, but that's not something I can count on. No, I must assume the Zzlo are free to move as quickly as their transport will allow them to.

Every muscle aches, screaming from the abuse I've piled on it. I take a sip of water, roll my shoulders and stretch my muscles, then resume my run. I will not rest until Victoria is safely back in my arms.

It isn't long before my mind and body stop feeling, numbness settling in as I run. The moon drops below the horizon leaving an even deeper dark, the deepest it gets on Tajss for almost an hour, then the first rays of the prime sun peek over the horizon.

I do not know how far behind them I am, but the early morning light is a sure signal that the Zzlo will be continuing on their journey once more if they did indeed stop for the night. Which I hope they did. They had to. If they didn't….

No, I won't consider it. Nor can I slow. Faster. Run faster. Victoria calls to me, needing me. My arms ache to hold her, my heart aches for what she is going through. Pain doesn't matter. Nothing matters but reaching her in time.

I skirt another dune, going around it to avoid making myself a target. It is good that I automatically take the precaution, because as my view opens up I see the transport still parked. A burst of energy flows through me. Scouring the area I look for a small, delicate figure, but Victoria is nowhere to be found.

I focus on the transport itself. They must have left her

inside for the night. My hands clench into involuntary fists. Animals. They kept her locked up overnight?

As I watch, they finish breaking up their camp and start loading items into the vehicle through the still-open door. It closes with a loud clang that echoes over the empty desert. They're too far and I'm too late to save her now, but the hunt sings in my veins.

This is prey I will never abandon.

31

VICTORIA

I hold onto the chain to keep myself upright while leaning against the swaying wall of the transport. I'm thirsty and hungry, but more than that, I'm frustrated. They've given me no opportunity at all to run.

They never let me out of the chains. I've even had to take care of my business in a nasty pot in the corner. Even if they did, the whole night, they were directly outside the only way out. They weren't even considerate enough to all sleep at the same time. At least one was always on watch.

There is no air moving except for the soft whistling breaths that push in through the small holes that dot the sides. Sweat covers every bit of my body, and even the hard metal wall is hot, almost burning me as I lean my head against it. I keep my knees unlocked, swaying along with the transport as it races up and down the dunes of Tajss.

How am I going to get out of this?

Something clanks, followed by grunting and growling that sounds like cursing from the front of the transport. I lift my head, but not with any kind of real interest. It's probably another fight breaking out among those idiots. It's like they can't help themselves. Staring into the dark opening that leads to the front, I don't see any tussle in progress. Frowning, I move as far forward as the chains allow when one of them barks an order.

What's going on?

The transport turns sharply and I'm thrown across the cargo space, slamming into the far wall before the chain pulls me up short. The transport leans far enough I'm sure it's going to flip over. I'm lying against the far wall, my arms stretched over my head held by the chains fastened to the opposite wall.

Cursing, I hold onto the chain, struggling to get my feet underneath myself. It tilts back, slamming onto all four wheels and dropping me to the metal floor. Air escapes me in a grunt as I slam down, but it doesn't fully stabilize.

The driver smashes down the accelerator and we lurch forward, a loud humming sound coming from the motor like its straining the limits of what it can do. I don't think it's supposed to go this fast, even though it clearly has the capability.

What the hell is happening?

There's a heavy thud on the roof above and my heart leaps into my throat, an adrenaline dump causing me to shake all over as I struggle onto my feet. Lothor. It has to be. Somehow, he caught up. It has to be him, right?

The thumping sound is followed directly by another one. That's not Lothor…

I immediately lie down flat, keeping as much distance as I can from whatever is up there. Is something dropping down onto us from the sky? Hail? I shake my head. Not in a desert.

A blade punctures through the ceiling and I scream involuntarily, the curved blade stopping a few feet above me. Wait. I stare at it, my heart rate picking up. I've seen the like of it before, become more than familiar with it at this point.

That's a lochaber blade! A Zmaj weapon!

Just as I think it, the transport rocks again, and a harsh bang reverberates through, echoing off the metal walls. My ears are ringing, and I'm disoriented. Craning my neck around to look toward the front where the sound originated, I'm barely able to see past the open door.

A Zmaj is crouched on the front of the transport and there is a large crack splitting the windshield. A Zmaj, but it's not Lothor. Like Lothor and the others I've seen, he's large and well-muscled. His eyes are narrowed against the wind, his sharp featured face closed down.

Raising a large hunting knife, he hits the glass once more with the hilt. Another hairline fracture appears. I jerk as the blade above me screeches and disappears, pulled back through the hole. The Zzlo scream and yell. One of them rushes back and straddles over my prone form, jabbing up through the hole with his own short blade, but the Zmaj isn't there anymore.

Is this it? Will these Zmaj defeat the Zzlo?

The transport lurches to a stop and I scrabble at the smooth metal floor sliding toward the open door. The chains reach their length, jerking me to a stop so hard it feels like my shoulder is dislocated. I see the Zmaj in front go flying.

I wince and yelp, both from my own pain and in hoping he survives. The driver slams on the accelerator and the transport leaps into motion, though perhaps not quite as fast as before.

Struggling to my knees, I see that the hood in front is dented, likely from when the Zmaj leapt onto it. I wrap my hand in the chain, using it to pull myself to my feet and try to prepare for whatever maneuver the Zzlo tries next.

It's a good thing I do. He doesn't just turn this time. He jerks the wheel hard and does something that sends the transport into an outright spin.

My feet scramble against the slick surface of the floor as the Zzlo who came back here goes flying past me, not at all braced. I'm slammed against one wall, then the other, but somehow manage to keep my feet under me.

Shit!

Overhead there is more thumping and scrabbling sound. Somehow the Zmaj is still on top of the transport.

As if on cue the lochaber blade pierces the transport once more. way too close to my head for comfort. I pull away from it, fighting against the momentum created by the spin. The blade slices through the metal with a harsh grating sound so sharp and loud it cuts past the intense ringing in my ears.

White-knuckling the chain, I watch the blade slide in further, cutting a longer line, screeching the entire way. I can't believe the metal of that blade is sharp enough to cut through the steel of the transport, no matter how rusty and abused it is, but I'm watching it happen.

Suddenly the blade pops back out. Gone. The Zmaj is gone.

Shit.

The transport stops its crazy spin with a suddenness that slams me against the wall. Twisting as I fly through the air, I'm barely able to turn so my ass hits first and not my belly. I have to protect the baby.

"Ow!" I yelp as my butt hits hard.

I'm going to have bruises on my bruises. The transport lurches forward as the driver stomps on the accelerator and it takes off straight again. The vehicle is definitely more than a little beat up from the attack, but I see no more signs of the Zmaj who did the attacking.

My heart falls. That's it. They didn't succeed. I'm still right where I started—

I stop mid-thought, my eyes focusing on what I'm actually looking at. The tear the lochaber cut into the side of the transport runs almost to the side. Right to the edge of the bolt that holds my chain. The Zzlo who was thrown around by the spin rises to his feet, groaning.

I scoot over to the side, hoping my head blocks the damage. Turns out, I don't need to be so careful. He moves to the front of the transport without even looking, joining in on the escalating loud bickering up there.

While they're distracted, I look at the bolt. There's a bit of metal still holding it in place, but maybe if I wiggle it… Gripping the thick head of it, I keep one eye on the Zzlo as I try to dislodge it. It moves slightly. My heart rate picks up, my palms sweating.

If I pull it just a little more, it'll come loose, but it'll also be obvious that the chain isn't attached anymore. So I leave it where it is. The transport slows. Are we stopping?

A clanging, banging sound echoes back from the front. Looking through the open door and out the front windscreen I see there is steam pouring out of the engine from beneath the misshapen hood. It clatters louder, sputtering, and as the vehicle jerks with one final despairing bang it cuts out and lurches to a stop.

I freeze, not making a sound and trying to look innocent. Not that they're paying me much attention. They ignore me as they open the door and pile out, arguing and pushing at each other. Outside the door I see a couple of them look back the way we came, clearly concerned that we broke down too close to the attack.

They disappear from my line of sight, moving around the vehicle. Turning, I see them gathered at the front of the vehicle. It's hard to see them through the dirt caked onto the windscreen, but there's a loud screech and the light is blocked off so I'm sure they've opened the hood. Coincidentally, shielding me from view.

This is it. I'm not going to get a better chance. I grip the bolt, pulling it out the rest of the way. The chain clanks loudly as it unavoidably drops to the floor and I hold my breath, standing stock-still. I glance to the front then out the open door, but no one seems to have noticed.

Exhaling softly, I carefully wrap the chain around my forearm. I can't get the lock off from around my ankle without the key, which means the chain will have to go with me, unless...

I look toward the front of the vehicle, weighing the chain. It's heavy. It'll slow me down. I have to make a quick decision. Do I look for the key that might be up there or run while I can, even impeded?

Shaking my head, I make my decision and creep to the front of the vehicle. I'm going to be handicapped enough out there without this chain dragging me down. Butterflies dance in my stomach as I pass through the door.

Hoping I'm not making a mistake, I search through the trash piled throughout the vehicle in the front, wrinkling my nose at the offensive smells assaulting my senses. I touch something slimy and jerk back instinctively, suppressing a yelp.

Pushing aside some scraps of paper and containers reveals a dead thing rotting under the trash. God, they are so disgusting! They're even worse than they were.

Gritting my teeth, I return to digging through the mess. Finally, I get lucky as my hand closes over something hard and cool. Bingo.

Pulling out a long, thick cylinder, I push it into the corresponding latch on my ankle and the red light next to it turns green and it clicks open.

Yes!

Careful not to make a sound, but hyperaware of every second passing, I slide my foot out of the cuff and set it down. Staying in a crouch I slide over to the door and listen.

They're still arguing in the front. Multiple voices. I can only hope that's all of them.

Taking a deep breath then holding it, I dart for the open door to the outside, stepping onto the hot sand. Remaining in my crouch, I do a quick sweep of the area, getting my bearings.

One of their arms flails into view around the side of the vehicle as he emphasizes what he's saying, but he can't see me from this position. Okay. I sidle along the side of the vehicle, stopping at the corner to peek around the back.

Nobody.

Okay. I won't be able to survive in the desert alone for long. I've got no water and no food, but maybe the Zmaj who attacked might be willing to help me. I don't know them, don't know if they'll be friendly, but I have to try.

Here's to hoping the enemy of my enemy is my friend.

Taking a deep breath, I run forward, following the trail the transport left behind. Without it, I don't think I'd have a clear idea of where to go, not after that spin.

I run in a crouch, circling the first dune I come to so as to get out of sight as fast as possible. At this point, I'm far enough away from the Zzlo that speed matters more than making noise, so I don't worry about any sound my feet make as I slog through the sand.

God, this is excruciatingly slow!

I feel like I'm in one of those dreams where I'm running forward and not actually moving at all. The next dune is big, too big to circle, so I climb it. The air burns in my lungs, the suns beating down on me, my leg muscles already quivering, but I don't care.

I don't slow. Reaching the top, I slip and slide down the opposite side of the dune. It isn't comfortable, and the sand is hot and gritty against my skin, but I know it'll be faster and that's all that matters right now.

I slog up another dune, scrambling, hunched over as I fight my way through the sand that I would swear is trying to grip me and stop all forward progress as if it were sentient and out to stop me.

When I reach the top, I stop to catch my breath. Wiping away the sweat and shielding my eyes, I scan the area ahead, but there's nothing. Sand and more sand—welcome to Tajss. Damn it. Exhausted, I plop down and slide down this one, but as soon as I do I hear a distant cry of alarm behind me.

My heart clenches. They've found out I'm missing.

Stumbling to my feet at the bottom, I start climbing another dune, thinking about the very clear trail I've left. There's no way to hide it though, so I let it go.

Damn it, where are those Zmaj that attacked? Finally fighting my way to the top of this dune I stop again and take a moment to look around. Desperation rising, the Zzlo know I'm gone and it's not going to take any special skill to follow the trail to recapture me.

My eyes stop on a straight, tall shape, an anomaly. It's the same color as the desert sand, blending in with the land-scape, but it's too straight. A tower. It's some kind of tower.

A burst of almost painful hope blooms inside me as I rush forward, stumbling and struggling to stay upright as I work my way down the dune. Everything hurts, my body is screaming at me, begging me to stop, but the cold in the pit of my stomach knows better.

Stopping and resting isn't an option. Come on...

Behind me there is a guttural cry of discovery. My heart seizes and I throw myself forward, fighting for each step as I sink into the sand again and again.

Too close. They're too close!

Digging deep, I increase my speed as much as I can,

Despair trying to take hold, I keep my gaze fixed on that tower. If I can just—

Large hands clamp down on my biceps and I scream, throwing myself forward.

"No!" I cry out, trying to yank myself free, fighting. "No!"

Struggling wildly, another Zzlo takes hold of my legs and lifts me up. I wiggle and squirm, bucking in their arms, but it doesn't do any good. One of them covers my mouth with a hand, muffling my screams as they carry me away from the promise of that tower.

I stop screaming, my breath catching on a sob as the tower moves farther and farther away.

LOTHOR

I shut down all thought, focusing only on the one thing that matters: forward momentum.

Run.

Leap.

Extend my wings and glide as far as possible. Stay focused. My path are the tracks, the tracks are my path. Move, move, *move*.

I run through the entire day, the double suns beating down on me, then through another night. My mind hardly feels attached to my body any longer, though it still moves. Almost of its own volition.

I am my purpose; my one goal is to move. An image of Victoria floats in my thoughts, pulling me forward, helping me push past the bounds of exhaustion.

Up another dune. And then another. And another.

The suns beat down upon me, not impressed by my plight. Another dune. Another. I will never stop, not until she is safe in my arms again.

I crest another dune, ready to slide down and continue, but something breaks through the blind my single-minded goal has created. A reflection of light off of something metallic. I blink, focusing once more on my present surroundings and I slow, staring at the scene ahead.

At this point, I am unsure if I am dreaming or if I have actually reached the Zzlo transport. Have I found Victoria? A sudden realization comes over me, a burning wave of it, and the rage explodes out of the tight containment I forced it into in order to function.

I sprint the last bit of distance between me and my target with renewed energy, not a second wind but a tenth or twelfth. The transport has broken down, but it there are odd signs of damage. Two Zzlo are working at the front, trying to repair it.

Another two have opened a compartment underneath the main cabin and are pulling out smaller transports with big, fat wheels arranged in a line, clearly designed for one or a maximum of two riders. Those four aren't my goal. The last two ignite my rage.

They're walking up the ramp into the transport carrying Victoria between them as she struggles to break free. I don't bother trying to hide; this is not time for subtlety. Gritting my teeth I race forward, bounding down the side of the dune with wings spread wide, leaping forward in bounds.

One of the Zzlo by the engine notices and shouts in alarm, jerking up and banging his head on the bent hood. The two who were taking out the smaller vehicles abandon their job and charge me, reaching for weapons at their sides.

I roar a challenge, not slowing.

I reach one as he draws a club and slam him with the blunt end of my lochaber. He stumbles back, swiping at me with his club, but hitting only air. Sweeping the lochaber low, I swipe his legs out from under him.

He hits the ground with a grunt, exhaling air, and I slice

his throat. He clutches at it with both hands, but there is no doubt it's fatal as I whirl to face his counterpart.

A zinging sound followed by a burning smell comes from behind me and I shift as quick as I can to one side, but not fast enough. Something burns along my ribs, skimming past me. I snarl. Projectile weapons.

Turning to face the shooter, I hiss and leap at him as he fires again, his weapon emitting blue flashes. The bolts sizzle and burn through the air. I twist mid-flight and the first passes by harmlessly, but another hits my left wing.

Numbness spreads through it fast, reaching my back. I can't hold it open and lose control of it. I crash to the ground and roll to one side, keeping myself from becoming a still target. Stopping in a crouch, I spot the one with the gun. I must reach him quickly.

Jumping to my feet I run, zigging and zagging side to side. He's barely missing his shots. Even as I watch him, I'm too aware of the others rushing toward their backup vehicles with Victoria bound in between them.

Gritting my teeth, I leap, trying to cover the distance between us to save time. The Zzlo tracks my flight with the gun, preparing to fire, but it is too late.

Landing in front of him, sand throwing up into the air, I bring my arm up under his, shoving the gun up and causing the shot to go wild.

Grabbing my hunting knife with my free hand, I stab him in the forearm. Shrieking, he bares his sharp teeth; at the same time he loses muscle control and drops the gun directly into my waiting hand.

He swings with his other arm, landing a hard blow to my hip with a club. Ignoring it, I flip up the gun, pressing it up against the underside of his chin and press the trigger.

His head explodes, the mess splattering everywhere as I turn to the others.

"Lothor!" Victoria screams, struggling between her captors.

"Victoria!"

They've already tied her to the back of one of the vehicles, which roars to life and lurches forward.

Her frightened eyes meet mine as she turns to look at me. The dark circles under her eyes and the tightness around her mouth hurt me, and I use that pain to fuel my rage. Every muscle quivers, ready for action. I rush forward, closing the distance so I can leap onto the moving vehicle.

If I hurry, I may just be able to—

My leg buckles underneath me, a burning pain slicing across the front of my right thigh. Landing hard, I roll behind the broken-down transport rather than simply falling to the ground. Curse it all, the last two Zzlo.

Victoria's cry took my attention and I forgot about them. Stupid. I do not have time for this! Lying down in the sand, I look underneath the vehicle.

There and there. I crawl underneath it, gritting my teeth at the pain in my leg, my side, my hip, but I will not be feeling any pain at all if I do not take care of them. Then who will save Victoria?

Taking a deep breath, I let it out slowly. I need to make this count. Zeroing in on the legs closest to me, I pull the trigger twice.

One, two.

The Zzlo cries out, clutching his knees as he drops to the ground in a fetal position. Revealing his head. One more shot and he is gone.

I shift to the other Zzlo, who has realized my position, and I pull the trigger. Nothing. It is out of charge.

I'm an easy target in my current position, and it will take me too long to shift back into my previous position. Leaving me with one real choice.

Not wasting time, I roll out from beneath the vehicle and grab for the fallen Zzlo's gun. The air sizzles with crackling bolts of energy as the remaining one fires at random, apparently not bothering to aim, or else I'm very lucky.

I keep rolling, grabbing the gun as I pass over the downed enemy, tucking it against my chest and continuing to roll. Coming to a stop I aim fast and shoot, aiming for his midsection, but he leaps to the side, rolling behind the transport for cover.

Tossing the gun aside, I leap onto the top of the vehicle. Guns are useless things—a coward's weapon. A warrior isn't afraid of close battle.

There's a flash of blue from the left as he tries to hit me, but he shoots wildly, without thought. By my count, he should be near empty on his ammunition. Running across the top of the transport I leap into the air, wings wide, swinging my lochaber with every intention of removing his head.

It swings through empty air as he ducks, stumbling backward. He fires again but it goes wide. He stops moving, taking aim as I land. My one hand is on the ground, the other gripping my weapon tight, and I lower the blade toward him.

Time stretches as I stare down the monster and his gun. I watch as his finger tightens on the trigger. There's nowhere for me to go, no way to dodge it. The muscles in my legs tense, my feet dig into the sand, and I press down, intending to leap. My only hope is that the shot doesn't hit my head or anything vital.

The gun clicks and nothing happens as I launch into the air.

Good, he's out of charge.

I land in front of him, lochaber stabbing at his torso. The Zzlo yells, using the useless gun to block my blade. Metal on metal rings loudly, echoing across the sands. It screeches as I lean in, trying to bear him down with brute strength, but Zzlo are strong too.

I pull back, whirling my lochaber in front of myself, circling my enemy. He feints in but pulls back before I can block or connect. Without the gun he is no match for me. It is only a matter of time and he knows it.

Time I don't have. Victoria screams, the sound distant and barely to be heard over the roar of the engines carrying her away.

The bijass surges forward, a red fog taking over my mind. This creature will not keep me. Roaring, I throw my warms wide, welcoming his attack.

He swings, using the gun as a club, aiming for my head. I duck under the blow, knocking it to one side with my lochaber while bringing my fist up under his jaw.

A sick crack resounds, vibrating through my arm to my shoulders. Blood spews from his mouth as well as teeth. His eyes go wide, then blank, and he falls to the ground. Dead or unconscious I don't have time to figure out. He's not a threat for the moment, and they have Victoria.

Spinning on one foot I run. The plumes of sand are distant, too far, carrying her away.

I run, arms and legs pumping as I chase the machines. Pouring out everything I have, I push my already-exhausted body beyond any limits I've ever tried before.

I run. Hearts pounding. Breath ragged. Vision blurring. I run until my legs give out.

I drop to the sand, body aching, breathing harsh, unable to rise. Muscles quivering, soft like the kedi's fur.

Failed.

I failed.

Again.

The bijass rages, pushing me to fight, to keep going and I try. I push off the sand, rising to my knees, but when I stand my legs give out again and I fall face-first into the sand.

The bijass retaliates in an explosion of images, flooding me with memories, reminding me why I'm unworthy of Victoria. Showing me how I've failed before, just like now.

Emotions, images, the touch of soft hands, laughter...

Joy.

I clutch at my head, the burst of memories not without pain—as if dead, bruised parts of my brain are waking after a long sleep. Which is the case, is it not?

"Nermana," I gasp, trembling as she coalesces in my mind.

Our life together sharpens and her death reemerges. The pain, the despair... ancient memories, but the pain is as fresh. As is the blow of failure of being unable to protect her from the disease that ravaged her body.

The patina of age does not diminish any of it, and the emotions blend with their counterparts in the here and now. Despair, loss, failure. Unworthy. I was unworthy of Nermana's love. I'm unworthy of Victoria's.

I could not keep either of them safe, my duty as a mate. A failure. I am a failure. Muscles shaking, refusing to work, I sit up and the pain beats at me.

It is so much more agonizing than the physical wounds, but my thinking self slowly reasserts itself. Nermana is gone, but Victoria still lives.

Growling, I push myself to my feet. Digging in my pouch I pull out a faded piece of epis, pop it in my mouth, and chew. The energy of the plant flows through my limbs, giving me at least a little lift.

Am I going to admit defeat and allow her to be taken by those animals? Or will I fight?

Groaning, every muscle screaming in agony, I pick up the lochaber and force myself to my feet. I must save her, but I must also face reality.

They are too far for me to catch them. It is an impossible task for my beaten body. If they reach their ship before I get to them, they'll take her off-world again, and then how will I ever find her?

I need help and I know where I might find it.

I turn back in the direction I came from forcing myself forward. My feet stumble at first, but nothing will stop me. No pain, no doubts, no reservations. I will make them listen; they will help. They have to. I can't lose her.

VICTORIA

I'm thrown roughly onto the weird bike-looking thing despite my fighting them every step of the way. They're too strong and I'm too scared to risk the baby growing in my womb.

"LOTHOR!" I scream, until one of the Zzlo slaps my face, blurring my vision with tears.

"He's going to kill you," I growl defiantly.

It grunts, raising its hand to backhand me, but the other one grunts something in their guttural language, pointing. The one who slapped me looks over his shoulder, grunts, and then hooks the ties binding me to the machine before jumping on and starting the motor.

"VICTORIA!" Lothor bellows, his deep voice echoing across the empty desert.

My heart leaps at the sound of it. Seeing him sends my spirits soaring. He's so close… if only I can slow them down before they get me away from him. Thrashing myself back and forth, I try to destabilize the bike thing. I know it will hurt if it falls, but I don't care. I'll do anything to keep them from getting away with me.

The Zzlo laughs at my struggling and the machine lurches forward. Sand sprays up from under the tires as it digs in looking for traction. Good, maybe it will get stuck!

Suddenly it catches purchase and leaps forward. I'm jerked back so hard something snaps in my neck and my vision is clouded by stars. As it clears and I can see again we're racing across the desert, up a dune. Turning back, I can see Lothor fighting the remaining Zzlo.

"LOTHOR!" I scream, the sound tearing at my throat as it rips from my heart to his ears.

He disappears as we drop down the opposite side of a dune. My stomach is a tight knot, my adrenaline pumping hard. Lothor was clearly hurt, and there were still two of the Zzlo left for him to fight.

A new anxiety sinks its sharp teeth in. Is Lothor going to be okay? He's clearly the superior fighter, pushing the Zzlo with me to flee rather than fight, even though they outnumbered Lothor. Hell, they had guns to boot, but he's hurt. Tears fall down my face that I can do nothing about,. My arms are bound to my sides and my legs are hooked onto this infernal machine.

Guns. They had guns and it didn't stop him. I saw him take at least one hit but all it did was make him angry. Was he slowing? He didn't seem to be moving as easy and he still had at least two of the Zzlo to fight. He's in the middle of nowhere with nobody to take care of him.

At this point, I'm more worried about him than me. If anything happens to him... even if... seeing him and then being ripped apart... it makes it worse.

Hopes dashed. Once again.

I glare at the Zzlo in front of me, wishing my hands weren't bound and that I was physically stronger. It sucks to not only have a lower skill level, but also to be weaker in general. Here on Tajss, even the *plants* are sometimes stronger than me. I shake my head, trying to get it on straight once more.

Figuratively. Fine, I'm weaker. That's a fact, so I have to be smarter. That's the only path I have here. Okay.

Lothor wasn't able to extract me from my captors. I have to accept that loss. Maybe he'll catch up again, maybe he won't, but now that I know for a fact he's on our trail and we no longer have their main transport... maybe I'll have an opportunity to at least slow us down. Lothor needs time and I need to find any way I can to give him that.

Luckily for me, they didn't really have a chance to dwell on my escape after they caught me. Lothor attacked too soon after. Maybe that will change later. Maybe they'll catch me trying to slow us down and take their anger out on me, but I have to do it anyway. If it might help, I have to.

Forcing myself to keep my wits about me despite my worry and fear, I try to stay in place on the back of the bike as we ride. The up and down of the sand dunes punctuated by the occasional rocky section doesn't make for a smooth ride. Still, I don't particularly want to lean against the Zzlo in front of me, even if it might be more comfortable. I'll take the bruises, thanks.

My backside hits the seat hard as we fly over another bump in the sand. Ouch. Somehow, I'm in an even more uncomfortable situation now than I was before the attack on the transport. Great.

My stomach clenches tight and bile rises in my throat as cold chills race through my limbs. I push it aside, along with the hunger and thirst. Closing my eyes, I focus on breathing, in and out, doing my best to calm myself. I don't want my blood pressure soaring. I'm worried that it could affect the baby.

I must find a way out of this quickly. Though any possibility of that seems like the dimmest of hopes, I won't let that hope die. I'm not only fighting for my life anymore; I've got so much more depending on me now.

We travel the rest of the day, not stopping even once. It's obvious they were spooked by Lothor. Was it him that caught up to us before or some other Zmaj? The first attack on the transport seemed like it was more than one person. If it was others, then who? My thoughts drift back to that tower-looking structure I was trying to make my way to. Some other Zmaj warriors maybe?

One way or another maybe the Zzlo will think twice about Tajss being easy pickings from now on. I can only hope. Bastards.

Eventually the suns dip below the horizon and the day turns to night. The Zzlo call out to each other and slow down. Traveling through the night is dangerous. Predators are more difficult to see, as is the terrain itself, though if they were to drive right into one of the big holes left by the giant worm things it wouldn't hurt my feelings.

They must decide traveling at night will be more difficult than risking Lothor showing up again, because they come to a stop. I'm fine with this, the longer we take getting to the final destination, the better.

The Zzlo I'm riding behind gets off and grabs me, jerking me off. The ties holding me to the machine pull him up short, tightening on me, and I yelp as he tries to yank me free.

"Idiot!" I yell.

He growls and says something that sounds like a cross between a belch and hiss before setting me back on the machine and undoing the bindings. He then jerks me off of it again, setting me on my feet, but my knees are shaky after the poundings and I drop to the ground.

I don't react or move when he attaches a chain to the cord around my tied-up hands, linking the other end to the bike.

He takes out a bedroll from one of the side bags and wanders over to the other Zzlo to help make camp.

Glaring, I shift around on the sand, leaning against the bulk of what I can only classify as some kind of advanced motorcycle-like contraption. They lay out their bedrolls and start a fire, pulling out water and provisions. Neither of which they offer to me. I turn away, my stomach growling.

I swallow, my mouth and throat so dry that even that is difficult. Sighing, I lean my head against the still-warm vehicle. I'm getting weaker already.

At this point—hungry, thirsty, and pregnant—I know I won't make it far on my own even if I manage to run again. If only they hadn't had these backup transports when the larger one broke down! There would have been no way they would have outrun Lothor, not with his desert-specific adaptations...

Wait.

I lift my head, staring at the vehicle I'm literally chained to. Sure, it effectively halts all attempts at running, but they should have thought about the vehicle.

I glance back at the Zzlo.

They're awake, talking to each other. I can't do anything now. They're sitting too close. It's too risky. No, I have to be smart about this, so I wait. And watch.

Lucky for me, they slack off now that their leader isn't here to keep them in line. It was the one thing I could hope for and mostly count on. If my time as their captive taught me anything, it's that the Zzlo are nasty and lazy. If there's any way to get out of work, they're going to find it.

Time creeps by while they talk and argue. One of them cuffs the other one, hard enough I hear it crack over here. That one leaps onto the hitter and they roll around on the ground wrestling and grunting like animals.

I can't tell that either of them actually wins in any

discernible manner, but they stop after a bit and return to their seats by the fire. One of them looks at me and says something that leaves the other one guffawing. My cheeks warm as a soft burning fire ignites in my core, and I grit my teeth.

You're going to regret this when Lothor finds you.

Finally, after what seems like it must be hours, the fire dies down and they both get into their respective bedrolls, neither of them staying up to keep watch. Perfect.

I watch, not moving or making a noise, waiting to make sure they're both asleep. Moving too soon could wake them. I close my eyes, pretending to join them in sleep and listen to their breathing.

Eventually, the rhythm of their breathing evens out and the movement stops. I wait longer just to be sure. The moonlight brightens as I wait until everything is cast in an eerie silvery light that I stare at through slit eyes.

When I open my eyes, they're fast asleep. If I weren't chained to the bike and on my last leg, this would have been a good time to make an escape. Heck, if I were secured to the bike toward the top, I might have tried to just take the thing and ride away. Besides, I'm locked onto it too low to make that feasible.

Staring at the monstrosity, I chew on my lower lip, thinking through my limited options. I'm no mechanic, but it has to be easier to break something than to fix it, right? Right. Hmm...

Reaching in, I loosen a wire here, pull out a hose there. As I fumble around, I find a small latch and open it. The soft silvery light illuminates some kind of circuit board. Score.

I wiggle a couple of the pieces loose, careful not to turn off every switch. I'm hoping I can break the thing down without them realizing that I sabotaged it. I stare at my handiwork. I've done just about everything I can to this thing.

I turn to the other one since they were nice enough to park it within my reach, though I have to stretch. Damn, I have to be really careful. The other issue is that it's on the opposite side of the vehicle from the one I just worked on, which means it's a little different.

Okay, move slow. I slide on my butt, dragging the chain binding my wrists along with me. Almost there. Almost...

The chain clanks and I freeze, my heart stopping in my chest. I strain my ears for any signs of my captors stirring. The seconds seem to stretch until my lungs scream for air and my heart goes from stopped to a full gallop.

One of them stirs, shifting. Did he notice?

Cold tendrils stretch through my limbs. Thoughts racing, I do the only thing I can think of: dropping my head to the ground and pretending I'm asleep. Unfortunately, my back is to my captors when I do and I can't see what's happening.

Wait. Now? No, wait more. A warm breeze blows sand into my face and I sneeze before I can stop it. Damn it!

A grunt behind me, more stirring. I'm screwed. Okay, well one sabotaged is good; it will buy some time. Maybe enough, it has to be... please all the stars above let it be enough.

I wait and then wait some more, every muscle tense, expecting at any second a rough hand to grab me or to be hit. Nothing happens and at last I let out a heavy breath. Rolling over, doing my best to make it seem like I'm moving in my sleep, I get to where I can see my captors.

Asleep. Those idiots didn't wake up despite the sound. My luck is holding!

Sliding across the last of the space, I fiddle around with the parts, hoping I'm doing something. I pull at a piece and my heart stops when it makes a distinctive and loud cracking sound. My eyes dart over to the sleeping Zzlo as one of them stirs.

I drop to the ground, eyes closed. I'm just innocently sleeping, nothing to see here. It takes all my willpower not to react when I hear more rustling, but the sound stops.

I stay in place, waiting, counting down the seconds before I crack my eyes open and look again. Nope, they're still fast asleep. The one who stirred is snoring and the other one apparently won't wake up unless I run over there and kick him.

That would be sorely tempting if it were at all possible. Sighing, I close my eyes and take a shaky breath. I give my handiwork a close once-over assessing if it's easily noticeable. Satisfied I've done all I can, I scoot back to my original place and lay my head down on an arm.

I don't want to risk doing any more. Hopefully, what I've done is enough to disable the things. Now I'm exhausted, but sleep eludes me anyway. The ground isn't exactly comfortable and I'm so worried about everything my thoughts won't quit spinning.

At some point, my body does decide to just shut down. Thankfully.

Something shakes me, hard, and I'm jerked from one nightmare into the one I'd left. I'd been dreaming that Lothor and I were running to each other but neither of us could close the distance between us no matter what we tried. The very air had become too thick for us to move closer.

I frown, squinting at the Zzlo as he undoes the chain. He ignores my glare, staring at the sky instead. He grunts something to the other one. It's still mostly dark, the very first rays of the primary sun only now illuminating the horizon, its rays barely stretching past the distant dunes.

They grunt at each other, moving quickly to pack up their essentials and load them on the transport bikes. The one with me jerks me to my feet, barking orders that I can't understand but he gestures violently at the vehicle, making it clear what he wants.

I suppress a smile seeing that they're clearly worried about staying in one place for too long. They should be; they know as well as I do what's coming for them and he's not going to be nice when he finds them.

Groaning, I settle onto the back of the transport, trying to act normal. Though I guess normal is relative, especially in this situation.

The Zzlo climb onto their respective vehicles and I hold my breath. Will what I did be enough? Closing my eyes I wait, sending out a silent plea for help to whatever powers there might be out there who will listen.

The bikes sputter to life without so much as a hitch. The back of my throat hurts as I stare at the betraying machine next to me. Damn it. I really thought that all I did would at least delay us. I barely register when we start to move. Despair swamps me in a black cloud of negativity. Hope is barely a flicker; too much has happened.

Ducking my head, I try not to think. There's nothing else I can do right now. My thoughts turn dark, sinking into dangerous territory. What if I can't keep from being taken to this final destination? Do I allow myself to be taken back onto that ship with them?

It isn't a question of whether I can handle it or not anymore. I have someone else to think of and I'm under no illusion about what will happen to my baby if it's born on a slaver ship. It would be born into bondage and most likely taken away from me as soon as they think he or she could survive without me. Maybe two or three years if I'm lucky. They'll sell my baby to the highest bidder.

I take a ragged breath, a sharp pain piercing my chest. No. I can't let that happen. I don't know how, but I can't let them take me, not alive. If I—

The transport jerks and I'm thrown up, almost bucking me completely off. I struggle to get a grip, my hands still bound. I look around, expecting to see rocks or something in the terrain that caused the jump, but then it bucks again, making an odd squealing sound.

There's another loud bang from up ahead and the other Zzlo yells something that sounds harsh and panicked. When I look over, I see why. His bike is traveling fast—really fast—and it's streaming smoke behind it.

He tries to turn it away from an upcoming rock formation, but it doesn't respond to his desperate attempts. A few feet away from the rocks, he bails, jumping off the vehicle and hitting the ground in a spray of sand as the bike hits the rocks. Hard.

The crash is loud as the bike impacts with the rock formation at full speed. A moment later it explodes in a massive fireball that roils up into the air. The heat of it flushes my skin as the Zzlo driving the bike I'm on tries to stop.

Above the roaring of the flames is the screeching protest of the bike we're riding. It shakes and shimmies as the Zzlo works the steering mechanism with frantic motions. Apparently giving up, he barks harshly then leans left as he forces the wheel in the same direction.

The bike leans, hard, until the sand looks like it's inches from my face as it continues to speed past. My heart leaps into my throat. I can't raise my arms to protect my face or the baby. Fear pounds through my veins. This isn't what I had planned. Are we going to crash too? I don't want to die in a fiery explosion. No matter how dark my thoughts were, I don't want to die at all! I've got my baby to protect somehow.

The Zzlo loses control of the bike and we hit the sand. I'm chained to the side of it and dragged along with it. The Zzlo tumbles away, not having any such restraints. Sand tears at my skin, abrasively ripping through that protective outer layer.

Sand fills my mouth, gets into my eyes. All I can do is close my eyes and mouth tight and offer up silent prayers that I survive this. The sand drags and I slow down, then finally the bike comes to a stop. Intense heat passes over me in waves, and when I open my eyes and see I'm only a few feet from the burning wreckage of the other bike.

I stare at the destruction. Wow. I guess all that fiddling around did do something. I'm numb. It's hard to process what's happening.

Suddenly one of the Zzlo grabs me by my shoulders in a too-tight grip and I cry out in pain. I'm covered in abrasions that feel like at least head-to-toe. He drags me across the sand as tears stream down my face.

He throws me to the ground in front of the other Zzlo who is howling and shaking his fists in the air. They bicker back and forth, then apparently forgetting me for the moment, one of them shoves the other who responds by punching back. That devolves the situation into a free-for-all.

I roll out of the way and take a deep breath. The longer they fight, the longer we delay getting to our final destination. It's all I can do to buy more time for Lothor to catch up. That dying flicker of hope sputters back to life. I do have a chance.

They fall to the ground, wrestling and punching each other. At one point one of them, I can't tell them apart yet, is on top beating the other's head against the ground. I'm certain he's going to kill his opponent. Which isn't a bad outcome in my opinion.

Unfortunately he doesn't before the one on the ground punches him in the throat and he falls to the side, holding his hands up in surrender. The one who was underneath gets to his feet and offers an open hand. They exchange guttural complaints or compliments, which I have no idea. They turn back to look at their broken vehicles, one in flames one dead in the water.

They look at the horizon, grunting and pointing at the sun overhead. It's obvious they're aware of wasting too much time, but neither of them tries to fix the vehicle. I'm assuming because they have as much knowledge of their inner workings as I do. Meaning diddly squat. It's not surprising, really. I spent enough time with them to realize they're scavengers. I don't think they can make anything of their own. Everything they have they've stolen from someone else.

One of them stomps over and grabs the end of the chain that's still attached to my bound hands. Turning sharply around, he drags me along behind him, not bothering to let me get to my feet first. He drags me for a few feet before looking over his shoulder and jerking on the chain and grunting.

Slowly I work my way to my knees, panting, sweat pouring off of my face and dampening the sand. My throat is so parched I can barely swallow, and every part of my body hurts.

"Water," I say, looking at the one holding my chain.

He grunts and jerks the chain, pulling my hands out from under me. I slam facedown into the sand, getting a fresh mouthful. Asshole. Pushing myself back up I spit out the sand and glare at him. He laughs. The son of a bitch laughs!

Rage hits me out of nowhere and I leap at him with strength I didn't know I had. One moment I'm looking at his laughing ass and the next I'm slamming into him.

Except I bounce off of him and slam back to the sand. Fortunately it's a relatively soft landing, hurting mostly my pride. He laughs harder and the other one joins the mirth fest.

"Laugh it up," I mutter, rolling back over to my knees. "We'll see who's laughing when Lothor finds us."

He jerks the chain again because he understood me or because he's a dick, I don't know, but this time I'm ready for him. I slide forward with it fast enough I don't fall on my face again. Struggling, I get to my feet, waver as dizziness passes over me, then finally I'm up and not about to fall down.

Ignoring me again, they turn and start walking, the chain dragging in the sand between us. Guess we're continuing on foot. Perfect. Nice and slow.

They set a fast pace, too fast for me, and I'm stumbling before we go more than a few feet. He doesn't slow; he's a dick like that. I try to keep my feet as I'm dragged along, but I don't move cleanly on purpose. The more I drag my feet, the more I thrash around, the bigger a trail I leave for Lothor to follow.

The sand is hot against my feet. The suns' light is even harsher without the wind from the forward momentum to offset it. I slog forward, focusing on staying upright. This is really the worst way to travel on Tajss.

We walk for what feels like hours. I don't know how long it actually is, but it feels like an eternity of hell. Thirst, hunger, exhaustion, anxiety, fear—none of it makes for a clear head. I'm not so out of it that I don't notice when they pick up the pace. Or when excitement enters their tone. I look up.

My heart drops at the all-too-recognizable hunk of metal in the distance. The ship I already wasted too much of my life in. Adrenaline pumps through my veins, fast and hard. Once we're there, once the ship takes off...

That's it. They'll never give me another opportunity to escape. Game over. I can't let them take me to it. I have to do something...

LOTHOR

*T*his is a bad idea. I can't trust them, but I have no choice. If they make it to their ship, she'll be gone and I'll have no way to save her. No matter how much I hate it, I don't have an option, so I push down the negative thoughts.

In part I realize that those thoughts aren't really me. They sound like me, seem like my own, but then at the same time, in some strange way they are different. They come from the bijass. The same thing that stole my memories of my former wife. The same instincts that told me I'd die alone.

No, it's not to be trusted. It's not analytical but primal. I'm not an animal, I'm a warrior. And a warrior knows when he needs help. It isn't weakness to fight with allies, it's intelligence.

Still, the Order is dangerous. I've run into them before and it wasn't pleasant. We have agreed to keep our distance once they made it clear I'm not welcome in their territory, and I did not welcome them into mine.

I'm desperate. I have to save Victoria, and they're my best shot. I can't do it alone, and I know they have some working technology. Hopefully they have enough to help. Or if they'll help at all. I can't make predictions with them; they don't act like normal Zmaj.

There is no demarcation indicating I've crossed into their territory, but I know I'm getting close if not there already. Pushing myself as hard as I can, my body is exhausted, but I won't stop until she's in my arms. Suddenly four Order warriors appear, seemingly out of thin air, though I know that is an illusion. It's no different than my own ability to bury myself in the sand and hide, though they take that skill to a new level.

Their flowing robes are the sandy-red color of the sand, and thus of most of Tajss. A deliberate choice to help them blend. They point their lochaber blades at me, staying far enough back I won't be able to hit them all at once.

"Why do you trespass?" one of them asks, the others standing silently still.

The only movement is the ruffling of their robes as a slight breeze blows around us. It takes me a moment to adjust to his voice, to the words. Victoria and I have fallen into a mix of our languages and I have not spoken to anyone except her in years beyond number. Hearing pure Zmaj spoken doesn't make sense for a moment, but it becomes clear fast enough. I keep my response simple.

"I need help," I say, admitting my weakness, holding my hands up, palms out toward him.

That seems to catch them by surprise. They glance at each other in silent communication.

"Help with what?" the biggest of them asks, harsh eyes glinting with suspicion. He must be their leader.

"Saving my female from the Zzlo who have stolen her," I hiss the last word, fighting internal urges.

Fight them—destroy them—they'll take what's mine—

Instinct thrums, pushing thoughts forward. It's urges

more than words, pushing me to react, to protect Victoria from these new males. My muscles hum with unspent energy as I struggle to control myself. The Zmaj surrounding me watch closely; it's obvious they're waiting to see if I act or talk. After a long moment the leader nods at the others and two of them move to either side of me.

"Come with us," the leader says.

It is not a question. They lead the way across the empty dunes. Uncharacteristic heat flashes through my body as we move away from the trail of the Zzlo.

"No!" I say, irrational though it may be. I can't go farther away from her. There is not time. I have to get to them before they get to their ship. "They are traveling and there is no doubt they are heading for their ship. There is not much time left to save her."

None of them respond. I turn my back on them to continue my pursuit alone. I don't have time for this.

"If you are too cowardly to fight, I will do it on my own," I spit my challenge.

The two next to me grip my arms and I jerk myself free. The one I assume is the leader moves in front of me. None of them draw weapons, but they've boxed me in. There will be no way out without a fight. The dragon inside hums the song of battle, certain I can take them all if that's what it takes to save Victoria.

The leader locks eyes with me. His are purple with gold flecks. He's bigger than me, broader in the chest and shoulders, massive biceps crossing over his chest. Fire rages, pushing me to take him, dominate him. The bijass—that fog of time—surges, eating rational thought. He places a hand on my shoulder and I growl.

"Name?" he asks.

Every muscle tenses, ready for action. Kill him. Destroy the one standing in my way. Inside the maelstrom I struggle for control, fighting my most primal nature. I came here for help. A warrior accepts help, a warrior works with other warriors. This isn't the way it's supposed to be.

Inhaling a deep breath, hissing it out through my nostrils, I push through and gain a semblance of control.

"Lothor," I growl.

He nods, tightening his grip on my shoulder. Coolness flows from that point of contact, spreading through my body and quenching the fire of my primal instincts. Muscles relax, my breathing becomes easier, and the bijass retreats before it.

"Betkar," he says, removing his hand from my shoulder. I look at my shoulder, then at him. I've never seen or experienced anything like this. "Come with us."

I glare, gritting my teeth.

"There is no time," I say.

"I understand," he says, and I believe him. Odd.

"You will help?" I ask.

"It's not up to me," he says.

"Then I don't have time for this," I move to step past him, but he blocks my path. Meeting his eyes, I growl, hands balling into fists.

"It's come too far," he says, the other warriors closing around me. "I have to bring you in first."

I don't bother with words. He's almost a head taller than me, which I take advantage of. I slam my head into his lower jaw. White-hot pain and stars explode, blurring my vision, but I don't wait for it to clear. I run, spreading my wings and leaping.

The warriors cry out in surprise and rage, giving chase as I bound across the endless sands of Tajss. I don't take time to look back, but I hear their pursuit. I've already wasted too much time. I should have known better than to trust others. Victoria is all that matters.

"Stop!" a voice yells, but I ignore it, knowing it's close.

Leaping into the air I twist my body, angling my wings to change my direction. Four of them are after me, but I can't stop. I have to save her.

Landing hard, sand spraying up, I coil my legs to leap again but I'm hit from behind, knocking me off my feet. My attacker and I roll across the sand, wrestling for control. Have to end up on top. Can't let him win.

Momentum slowing, I'm underneath. I slam my tail up and into the side of his head. He's knocked off of me, dazed. Arching my back, I throw my legs out attempting to get back on my feet, but two more land on top of me before I can complete the maneuver.

The fight resumes. I'm outnumbered, already exhausted and wounded. I fight, but it doesn't last long. In seconds I've lost. They force me to my feet, one keeping my arms twisted painfully up behind my back. Another approaches with ropes and binds my wings and arms.

"That was stupid," Betkar says, inches from my face.

His nose looks broken. Blood drips from it, and it's cocked to one side. His words are slurred as well. Good. I'll do worse the moment I'm free. I don't deign to answer, glaring at my captors. Betkir shakes his head and motions with his hands. Silently those holding me force me into motion.

They more or less drag me across several dunes until a rock formation comes into view. If I tilt my head to one side, I can make out a spire of it that's too straight to be natural. It takes me a while to catch it, though something about the scene keeps pulling at my attention until I do.

Obviously, this is our destination. Hidden in plain sight a tower was crafted to blend into the rocks around it, and I have no doubt that its heights offer a commanding view of the surrounding area. I knew these Zmaj were not to be trusted.

When we step inside the relatively cool building, they lead me down a hall and to another, heavy door. This place is clearly designed not only to keep watch, but to withstand an attack. The guard on one side of the door opens it when he sees our group approach.

Two stay on either side of me when we step into the office, and in front of me is Betkir. This office is strange. It's too nice, calling to old memories that have long been lost to the bijass. It tries to pull them from that fog of the past.

A large desk dominates the space. The desk is ornate, gaudy even, crafted of wood. The rarest of resources on Tajss, it's stained a dark color, almost black in its shading. The front of it is covered in intricate carvings. The walls are floor-to-ceiling cases with shelves on them that have various oddities on display, including books.

How long has it been since I've held a book? I can't recall the memory of them. Even the name comes back to me from some unimaginable distance across time and space.

There are stools in front of the desk and behind it is another Zmaj. This one is older, stern-looking, with a dull color to his scales that implies a great age. His eyes are a storm-gray color, but there is no doubt he's still a fit warrior. His presence dominates the room as he rises from his seat, leaning onto the desk.

He stares, looking me up and down carefully before he nods to the guard behind us to shut the door. He then turns his attention to Betkar.

"Who is this?" he asks.

I've no doubt he's made note of my injuries and weak points. There is no hiding them.

"I'm Lothor," I answer, shaking myself free of the two guards' grip and stepping forward.

"We found him coming toward the outpost," Betkar explains. "He asked for our help, but when we tried to bring him here, he decided to be… aggressive."

The one behind the desk grunts, his eyes moving back to me.

"Help with what?" he asks.

"My female was taken by the Zzlo," I say, struggling to keep my frustration at the delays under control.

"There are no females on Tajss," he says, eyes narrowing. "Why are you lying to us?"

The bijass rages forward with the accusation. Red clouds my vision, and I strain my muscles against the restraints binding me.

"I have one," I growl. "Either help or let me go."

"Where did this 'female' come from?" he asks, leaning in closer.

Come a little closer, I'll show you who's in control here. Wisely he stays right outside the range of where I can make contact.

"Her kind wrecked here," I say through gritted teeth, flexing muscles to test the bindings.

"Her kind?" he asks, tilting his head to one side. "Do you mean human? She's a human female?"

That stops me. How do they know the word she uses for her own kind? Are there others like her? Where are they? Other survivors? Victoria talked about the one she followed into the desert, but I assumed they were all dead. If these Zmaj know about them then perhaps they're not.

"Yes," I hiss.

He nods, straightening upright and appraising me again.

"The Zzlo have her?" he asks.

"Yes. We have to move and beat them to their ship before they take her off-world."

"You're too late," he says.

Cold chills race down my limbs. Searching his eyes, the icy grip of fear holds onto my heart, holding me tight. No…

"You can't know that," I say, my throat tight and mouth dry.

"Don't I?" he counters, tilting his head to one side.

"You lie." I force the words out to his ears, but even more I force them into my heart.

It's a lie. It has to be. She can't be gone. If she is, then somehow, I'll find her.

"What is she to you?" he asks.

"She is mine," I growl, the dragon burning hot as I lay my claim.

My blood boils, tensing my muscles. The restraints creak as I strain against them, loosening the slightest bit.

"We don't have time for this," he sighs, resuming his seat.

"Then let me go," I argue. "I have to save her. She is my mate!"

"How did she come to be with you? The humans are far from here. How is it you end up with one so far from the rest of their kind?" he asks.

"She was a Zzlo slave almost a year ago," I say. "When they landed on Tajss, I went to investigate and saw her." I remember it clearly, a memory so sharp and visceral I know I will never forget. "I could not allow her to remain enslaved, so I took her away."

"Took her away," the leader repeats. "I see." He considers me. "And she has been living with you?"

Clearly that is the case, but I try not let my irritation dictate my words.

"She is my mate," I say simply. "They took her while I was gone hunting."

He watches me, silent. I do not know what he is thinking, his face deliberately impassive. When he does speak an icy pit forms in my stomach.

"Why should we risk ourselves to help this human or you?"

Behind the block of ice in my core bubbles rage. I struggle to keep it under control but it's almost impossible. Flexing my muscles, I test the restraints again. They keep getting looser.

"The Zzlo should not be here. Slavers should not be here."

"Some would say humans should not be here," he counters.

A low growl escapes before I can stop it. The bijass beats at me, coloring my thoughts, my anger and despair swirling to the surface despite my attempts to stem the flow.

"You would stand aside and allow an innocent female to be enslaved?" I growl. "As I thought. Cowards. This was a mistake. Let me go and I'll handle it myself, as a warrior should!"

He snorts, shaking his head.

"The Order cannot involve itself in every matter," he answers.

"What purpose do you have, then?" I yell, struggling to control my temper while subtly working the restraints.

"That's not your concern," he says.

"Cowards, hiding behind your thick walls, letting the world out there go to hell," I yell, straining with all I've got against the ropes binding me. "All this time and I finally find hope, a reason to live. I'll not let you or anyone take that hope from me!"

Adrenaline pumps through my body, tightening every muscle. The restraints break and I'm free, roaring.

"Restrain him! Put him in a cell!" their leader yells.

The guards move forward, reaching. I grab the first one by his wrist, jerking him closer and turning into him as I do, throwing him over my hip. He flies through the air and crashes into the desk, forcing it back and tying up the Zmaj behind it.

The other guard ducks under my wild blow, coming up inside my reach, his fist connecting with my chin. My vision explodes then blurs, so I grab him with both arms and squeeze, trying to crush him.

Others join the fray, grabbing and pulling. I fight them all, hitting but being hit more. My vision clearing, there are six Zmaj in the room struggling to restrain me.

"Don't waste my time!" I roar. "They are taking her away!"

No one responds, ignoring my words as they continue to pile onto me until I collapse under the weight of them all. In moments I'm bound with steel instead of rope and then forced to my feet. They take me down a hall and through another door into a hallway lined with narrow ones, each solid panel with a small window cut to look in. Cells.

"Let me go!"

I thrash as they open the door, snarling as they throw me into the dim, cramped cell. I throw myself against the door, but it's already locked. There is nothing else I can do.

I pace the small confines, rage buffeting me, burning me up from the inside out. Victoria. I must get to Victoria.

Mine. They took what is *mine*.

Picking up the pallet in the corner, I throw it to the other side and it smashes to pieces. Reaching for something else, I find nothing. Clenching my fists, I scream my rage.

Circling the cage, I throw myself against the door, testing its mettle again and again, but it doesn't give in the slightest. I beat on it until my rage is exhausted. Adrenaline dropping, I'm left empty and lost. Sliding to the ground with my back against the door, black despair washes over me.

I've failed

Victoria.

Her name echoes in my mind. Images of her swirl in my

thoughts. Our unborn child, the swell of her belly backlit by the gleam of the double suns. The look on her face when she first stoically learned to dress a kill.

Victoria. "Victoria," I whisper.

Every muscle in my head throbs with pain. A hundred cuts covered in dried blood cover my body, but I'd take a thousand more to save her. It can't end like this. I can't fail her too.

Fail, fail, fail, fail, fail.

The singular thought echoes through my head, coloring my memories. Victoria grows distant as she is taken farther from me. She is counting on me and I'm trapped here. I shouldn't have come here. I should have kept running, I could have caught up to them. Somehow.

Don't be stupid. A warrior cannot win alone. Warriors work in teams, units. Yes, that's the word I'd lost. Units. It's how we fought before....

The memory is so dim it feels like it belongs to someone else, not me, but I know with an odd certainty that it's right. We fought in units... like those who captured me. Units, trained and skilled together, working as one. Stronger.

"Bah!" I scream, slamming my fists into the fair.

She needs me. It's hard to come back into myself, return to the present, but I slowly push everything back into the box it was once in. I do not have time for it. I need to *think*.

How can I get out of this cage? If they are not going to help, I'll save her myself. Rising to my feet, I inspect the cage with an analytical eye. Touching every surface, testing the bars, the door, with more than my blind rage. I stop when I hear footsteps approaching.

"Are you calm?" a voice asks through the small barred window on the door.

"Does it matter?" I ask.

There's a click and clatter then the door opens, revealing the one who was behind the desk. He looks me over with a critical eye, assessing if I've fallen to the bijass. His bulky form fills the door and I push down the instinct urging me to charge him, take him by surprise.

"Good," he says, stepping away from the open door and turning around. "We're going to help." Looking over his shoulder, he jerks his head at me. "Follow me."

I step out of the cell cautiously, expecting some trick. But there is no one waiting, and it seems to be legitimate. I follow him, hoping it's not a farce.

I'm coming, Victoria.

35

VICTORIA

*S*tumbling to a stop, I drop to my knees, bending over as nausea roils my stomach and I retch. The ship is right there and more Zzlo spill out from it. Numbness creeps along my skin as blackness swells in my thoughts. I can't let them have my baby. I can't.

I'm too late. Lothor is too late. There are too many of them now. It's too late to escape. Even if Lothor reaches me before the ship takes off, there are too many Zzlo for him to fight. If he makes it before... no, better I end up in captivity again than that. At least knowing he's out there, alive, is better. I think.

Tears fall onto the hot sand, accenting the black swamping my thoughts. They tug at the chain binding my hands and grunt. I should move. If I don't, they're going to get rougher, but I can't. I know what I should do, telling my muscles to get up and follow along like a good girl, but they won't respond. My body sends back a big fat *nope*, not going to do it.

I can't begin to care. It's over. I've lost. What else matters? There's no way in hell I'm going to let my baby be born into captivity with these animals, so why bother? I might as well let it end here and now.

Dirty, worn boots step into my line of sight. A quiver races through my body, my only reaction to the blow I know is coming. He grunts and growls while pushing at me with the toe of his hard leather boot. I retch in response, my empty stomach not even giving up any bile in its revolt. I'm too dry for even that it seems. He grabs my hair, pulling hard.

"Ah!" I cry as he jerks me to my feet. Wobbling, knees weak, stomach roiling, I glare at him and rage flares to life. "Lothor will kill you slowly."

Anger, hate, and rage all combines into my words and in my heart. For that instant, I believe it will be true. Somehow Lothor will find me. If I don't give up. If I'm smart and keep watching for any opportunity to slow them down. I don't have to escape; I have to buy time.

Resolved, the nausea and dizziness pass. He grunts and raises the back of his hand, but now I don't flinch. I'll take the bruise. *Do it, you son of a bitch. Let's see what Lothor does to you when he sees it.* I glare, daring him.

He does something that's never happened before. He hesitates, then drops his hand. I thrust my chin out, defiant. The other one grunts and growls something to him but he shakes his head, turning and pulling on the lead, forcing me to stumble along behind him.

We head down the dune, sinking in at every step and I don't hurry. I drag it out, buying every second I can, wiggling my hips each time I step forward so that I sink further into the sand. Many times they have to stop and lift me out as I'm unable to continue forward.

It's driving them nuts. We're so close to their destination and it's taking a hundred times longer than it should. I suppress a smile, not wanting to reveal my game. Each time I make them stop to help me is a little victory that I relish for all its worth. I can't beat them physically, I can't see a way to escape, but this? This I can do.

When we reach the bottom of the dune the sand is packed harder and my game comes to an end. Damn it. Blackness tingles at the edges of my thoughts but I can't give in. There has to be something I can do...

"Ow!" I cry as an idea hits me and I drop to the ground, landing hard on my ass.

It hurts, making my cry more real. My two captors turn and glare so I throw myself back, lying prone on the burning sand. The double suns are high above, forcing me to close my eyes too. I lie still, throat burning, body aching and tense waiting for a blow I'm sure is going to come. I don't really have a plan beyond this: lie here and slow them down.

I sense them come closer and I brace myself for impacts, but none come. They grunt and their shadows fall over my face. Guessing from the sounds, one of them shoves the other and then they get into an argument. Someone steps on my chest and instinctively I roll onto my side and curl into a ball to protect the baby.

Slitting my eyes enough to peek, they're rolling on the ground fighting with each other. I suppress the smile as fast as I can. This is even better than I hoped! They roll around and over each other; whichever one is on top at any given moment rains down blows on the one below.

I close my eyes and let them drag the time out for me. I'm starting to feel the effects of epis withdrawal on top of being dehydrated and underfed. My muscles ache with a deepness that I've never experienced before, which makes me as miserable as I've ever felt.

Oddly enough I hadn't even thought about epis all this time, but I have been busy trying to escape and survive. Only its absence made me think of it. There is a marked thing, morbid as it may be. I don't think anyone can survive epis withdrawal, so if I'm not rescued…

That's too dark a thought to finish. No, I will be rescued. Lothor will catch up to me. Keep buying time. That's my job. Buy time. Slow them down in any way possible.

The sounds of their struggle stop, apparently one or the other having come out on top in whatever game of dominance it is these monsters play with each other. Hooray for the winner, asshole. Their shadows loom over me, blocking out the suns. I don't bother opening my eyes or moving. No point in speeding things up for them.

I'm grabbed roughly, tossed into the air, and land with a whoof over a shoulder. Gasping for air, I struggle but to no avail. I'm carried along like a sack of potatoes. Great. My mind races for any way I can slow them down now. The last moments of my captivity by Tweedledee and Tweedledum pass too quick.

Staring at the open sand behind us, I do my best not to notice how empty it is. No signs of rescue. But I can't let that deter me. *Focus, Victoria, you've got one job and can't screw it up.* It's the only hope, if not for me then for my unborn child.

Guttural shouts sound as the Zzlo with the main ship notice our approach. Outside my immediate fears and concerns I notice how amazing it is these morons survive. How close have we been this entire time and they only now seem to notice our approach?

They must win their battles with sheer numbers when they do fight. Which makes sense, I guess, in the fact that they're the scavengers of the universe. They never pick a fight when they don't know the odds are heavily stacked in their favor.

Randomly it makes me wonder why they attacked our generation ship so long ago now. It is really out of character for them.

That thought is pushed out as I'm tossed on the ground, cracking my head on something metal. Stars fill my vision as pain blossoms and tears run down my face.

"Ow, damn it," I curse.

None of them pay attention to me, but judging by the tone of their voices my captors are being resoundingly congratulated for my capture and return. Of course they are. Gods forbid they had to cook for themselves. Or clean, which I'm sure they didn't do while I was gone. The odor drifting down the loading ramp from the open cargo bay door is testament enough to that.

After a few moments of celebration two of them grab me up and carry me between them. They don't bother undoing my bindings or even loosening them. Apparently, they understand I'm a flight risk now.

They carry me onto the ship. The darkness is cool and almost a relief to my aching body. If it didn't come with the cold certainty that my time is almost up it'd be even better. They shove me into a cell, not bothering to undo my bound hands before they slam the door, leaving me on my own.

The cell is damp, dark, and hard. No blankets, no pot, nothing but an empty ten foot by ten foot metal box. It's supposed to be a storage closet I think, but now it's my trap. Scooting along on my side, I get to the wall and work my way up to a sitting position.

The deep-down bone ache has settled in so much it's feeling normal. That's not good, or maybe it is. I know from when we first crashed on Tajss and a lot of people around me started taking epis what it means. It took a bit for them to figure out how addictive it is.

Addictive but lifesaving if you want to keep living here. It won't be long before the withdrawals really kick in. Morbidly I can't help but think it's a good thing I'm addicted to it. I don't think I could do what will have to be done if they get me off this planet. I'm not that strong.

Leaning my head back against the cold steel, Lothor's face drifts through my thoughts and then I'm bawling. There's no holding it back or containing the flood of tears. I'm sobbing, gasping for breath that keeps hitching, and wishing everything hadn't turned out so bleak.

All this time, I finally had it all. I finally have what I never would have dared to dream of, a mate who loves me more than life itself, a baby on the way. I was always so scared I never ever thought it could come to pass.

That's what makes this so much harder. Finally, my tears run dry. I can't cry that much when I'm so dehydrated my mouth and throat feel like they're full of sand. My head is pounding on top of all the other aches in my body. Staring into the dim room, my eyes drift closed and time passes.

A scream jerks me awake, heart pounding, as I'm torn from sleep to instant awareness. I try to rise but stumble when my hands don't move with me. What the—

My hands are still bound, numb from the tight restraints. Right, captured. Another scream echoes through the cell, bouncing off the metal walls, assaulting my poor ears and making my headache worse. Shaking my head to clear the cobwebs of sleep from it I rise, this time more carefully, balancing myself against the wall until I'm on my feet and steady.

The room seems even darker. It might be night outside but who knows. I don't think we've lifted off yet. I can't imagine I'd sleep through that no matter how wiped out I was. God I hope not...

Gunfire. That's gunfire for sure. We can't be off the

ground; even the Zzlo aren't so stupid as to fire their weapons on a ship in space. Or at least I hope so, for fuck's sake. On second thought, they're really not bright, so maybe they are doing something that stupid.

No. No way, I've no doubt I would have woken up. *Okay, breathe, Victoria. Deep, easy breaths, and think this through.* My muscles throb with the need to be in action. All the adrenaline pumped into my body when I was pulled from sleep demands action that I can't give it. My hands are bound and I've got nowhere to go if they weren't. I'm locked in this small room.

Leaning my head against the door to try and think this through it moves. I jump in surprise.

"You've got to be kidding me," I whisper, pushing at the door with one foot. It screeches loudly as it swings open. "Holy shit."

Peeking my head around the corner, an empty hallway meets my gaze. My heart rabbits, pitter-pattering so fast it's making me lightheaded. This has to be a trap. Some cool trick. As soon as I go sneaking out here one of those bastards is going to jump out, grab me, and grunt his alien version of "surprise."

It has to be, so I wait. My heart rate slows. The distant sounds echoing down the hall sound like a battle. Steel clanging on steel, guns firing, shouts and screams. These jerks aren't that smart. Even if they were, they would be too lazy to put that much effort into a surprise.

Still, I slide one foot out the door, cold fingers clenching my chest. Looking back and forth as fast as I can turn my head, I take another step, then another and no one jumps out. The sounds of battle grow louder until, at last, I make a break for it.

Memories color my thoughts as I run down the hall. I've

traversed this so many times before but never before did I run it. Never did I have a hope or a prayer of being free.

The sounds are louder as I come toward the end of the hall and the brighter light draws me forward like a moth to the flame. It's not super-bright, daylight-bright, so it's definitely nighttime, but the shouts and clanging of steel accented by the firing of guns gives me pause. I stop before turning the last corner, breathing hard but trying to control it so I can listen.

I'm close to being free now and don't want to risk it all. Is it Lothor out there? It sounds like a lot more attacking than him alone. Closing my eyes, I offer up a prayer to all the powers that might exist in the universe then peek around the corner.

The sight that greets me makes me pause. The Zzlo are fighting against several Zmaj dressed in flowing robes.

I stare, watching the robed Zmaj move *fast*. Faster than I thought was possible. Even the Zzlo's guns aren't a match for their battle skills.

Leaping and dodging, their lochabers strikes are never wasted. Fast and deadly. I don't know who these strangers are or if they're friendly or anything. Biting my lip, eyes darting around, I'm trying to take it all in at once when another Zmaj catches my eye.

A familiar profile. A way of moving that I would know anywhere. Joy punches through me at the sight of Lothor, quickly followed by a stab of fear.

His face is cut in so many places if I didn't know him so well I wouldn't recognize him. His bare chest is covered in blood and I can only pray that it's not all his. The soft moonlight highlights him, and it's clear he's a lot worse for the wear.

Still he moves and fights with the same ferocity he always does. No matter how badly beaten he is, he doesn't let it slow him down. As I watch, he kills a Zzlo and immediately pivots to another.

"VICTORIA!" he screams my name and my heart leaps into my throat.

It's raw and filled with so much emotion that goose-bumps race over up and down my arms and, unthinking, I step out onto the ramp.

"LOTHOR!" I yell, unable to stop a fresh round of tears at the sight of him.

That was dumb some analytical part of my brain throws out there, because as soon as I yell he turns his attention to me. Of course, idiot. God, am I really too stupid to live?

Two Zzlo don't miss their chance. One fires his gun and the other swings a wicked-looking club that has sharp spikes sticking out of it while Lothor is distracted.

Time slows to a crawl as I watch everything happen at once. As I take a step forward, that sensation of moving underwater, fighting for every inch gained comes over me. The blue lightning bolt leaves the gun, crackling through the air toward Lothor in slow-motion. The club arcs down toward his head, ready to deal a crushing blow.

His mouth opens, eyes widen, and he steps forward, muscles rippling. He holds his lochaber in one hand, raising it to block the incoming blow, but he doesn't see the shot coming at his back.

I try to raise my arm, try to point out the danger, try to cry out in alarm, but I can't move fast enough.

The moment stretches without speeding the actions. My eyes lock with his, my chest swells, his love flows across the distance, engulfing me. The passionate fire in his eyes warms my soul but the danger creeps closer and closer.

In less than a breath time leaps as if making up for the momentary slowdown. It happens so fast I can barely follow it. The club crashes against Lothor's lochaber, his muscles bulge stopping the blow, but a heartbeat later and the blue lightning bolt hits him in the back right between his wings.

He's thrown forward, arms going wide, eyes and mouth opening wide in shock and pain. The club resumes its arc down as his muscles give way beneath the strain, cracking into his head. He stumbles forward and to the side as if drunk.

My heart is a hard lump pounding in my throat, reaching toward him with still-bound hands, I'm stumbling toward him, but I've been noticed. Two Zzlo leap onto the metal ramp causing it to bow and rattle, throwing off my balance. I'm tossed forward into their waiting grips.

Too-tight hands grip my biceps with bruising force as I'm lifted off my feet and carried back toward the yawning maw of darkness behind me.

Lothor falls to his hands and knees, fresh blood pouring from the wound on his head. He looks up, our eyes lock, his mouth opens, and he roars.

The wordless sound echoes somehow across the open desert. It rings in my ears and my captors stop, looking over their shoulders, fear etched on their faces.

Lothor rises to his feet. Throwing his arms wide, he grabs the Zzlo with the club by the neck, lifting him off his feet. He doesn't look away from me as the muscles of his arms ripple and there's an audible snap, and then he drops the Zzlo to the ground dead.

Silent, he points at the Zzlo holding me, his eyes narrowing. His knees bend, crouching, wings spreading wide, then he leaps.

He soars through the air, dominating my vision and I'm sure that of those holding onto me as well.

The Zzlo are not brave. It's not something I would have thought in my years of captivity but now, having known true bravery in Lothor, I know them for the cowards they are.

They let go of my arms and almost as one they jump off the ramp to either side and hit the ground running.

Lothor lands in front of me and the steel ramp bends, screaming in protest at the force of his landing, but it holds. His strong arms wrap around me, the scent of him fills my nostrils, and my face presses against his cool scales that cover his chest. I'm safe.

Battle rages around us, forgotten. In this moment there is only the two of us as he holds me tight, claiming me even as I give myself over to him.

Tears fall free. My heart pounds while I listen to the double rhythm of his beating a fast staccato in his chest.

"Victoria...are you hurt?"

I shake my head, unable to force words past the lump in my throat. He pulls me tighter, hugging me close, the desperation in his hold mirroring my own.

He jerks forward, bending over me protectively and he grunts.

"Lothor?" I croak.

He growls in response, pushing me to arm's length and whirling around. His tail rises up and his wings spread, blocking my view of what's happening. His body jerks side to side at the same time I hear the now-familiar sizzling of the Zzlo guns burning through the air.

He roars, rage filling the air in sound.

His arms drop, his wings go limp, and he stumbles forward. Racing ahead, I grab him, but he's so much bigger and heavier than I am that I'm pulled down the ramp along with him.

When we reach the sand he's weaving back and forth, seemingly barely able to stand.

"Kill them," he hisses.

"Lothor, are you okay?" I ask, desperation making my voice crack.

"Numbing," he says, his voice thick. "Shots are numbing. Fight. Through. Kill. Them."

His chest heaves, his body shakes, and his tail shifts side to side between my legs, dragging across the sand.

"What do I do?" I ask, having no idea how to help.

"Hide," he growls. "Run, hide, away from ship."

I'm not going to argue with him. I'm not an idiot; even if my hands weren't still bound, I'm no warrior. It tears at my heart to leave him, but I know that the best thing I can do is remove myself from danger, leaving him free to focus on the enemy.

He straightens, though his left wing and arm are hanging loose as if he has no control of them. His right holds his lochaber, and I watch him tighten his grip on it.

"Ready," he says, but before I can answer he barks. "Now!"

No questions about it, I run. My first steps are blind, running with no clear goal, but as I move out from behind him I see a stack of supply crates not far and change my direction.

I don't look back, not even side to side. I run. I run for all I'm worth, pushing my battered body past any limits, running for that single target. Get to safety. Protect the baby.

I run past the crates and try to stop, sliding in the sand as I slip and land on my side. A blue bolt sizzles through the air over me. Damn, that was close. I can't get back up. I'll be a target for sure, so I roll to the side, coming to a stop behind the crates.

I want to look so badly, but that would be stupid. Even peeking around the corner would open me up to being shot at again, and this time I might not be so lucky. Pulling my knees up to my chest, I huddle down and listen. The battle rages behind me and I can only make guesses as to what's happening.

There is less gunfire than before, which I hope is a good

thing. The guttural cries of the Zzlo, the whistling of lochabers through the air, the thudding impact of blunt weapons... all are accented by screams of pain.

I don't know how long it continues. I tried counting heartbeats but it's pounding too fast and I lose the count.

It continues. And goes on. And on.

How many Zzlo are there? How many Zmaj did Lothor find to help? Who's winning? Is Lothor okay?

Breathe. Wait and breathe. It's all I can do. No, I can do one more thing. I can trust in Lothor. He found me. Impossible as it seemed, he found me. A lone man on foot while I was being carried away on machines that moved exponentially faster, yet he found me. He never stopped.

I knew he wouldn't. In my heart I knew, sure, but in my heart and in reality are two different things. Or they used to be. Not anymore. He's here. He came for me. Relentless, driven, powerful—my man.

My love for him still grows, acknowledging no boundaries, pushing to limits I never imagined possible. My mate. My love. I'm so damn lucky. I am truly blessed.

Resting my head on my knees, I listen and wait. The sounds slow, and then there's a round of grunts and commands issued by one of the Zzlo. I'd recognize their awful voices anywhere. At that point something behind the crates changes.

The sounds are different, not in any way that I can describe, but different for sure. A few moments later there's a loud metallic screech followed by the rumble of engines firing.

I'm swept off the ground, tossed into the air, and lightly caught.

"NO!" I yell, terror sweeping through me in a wave of nausea.

Opening my eyes wide, I'm in Lothor's arms. He doesn't

speak, face grim; he's running. Running as fast as he ever has. Leaping across the sand and *moving.*

He leans into the run, cradling me against his broad chest, and moves faster still. He's panting, face strained and covered in blood, a lot of which I know is his. None of that stops him or slows his pace.

The ground rumbles underneath us. Bucking and rolling.

Oh shit.

The whining sounds of engines grows louder behind us, but that's not going to cause this. There's only one thing that could do this to the ground.

"Lothor—"

We're thrown into the air and for a moment I'm weightless as I drift up and out of his arms. Lothor's hands grab for me, trying to regain control, his wings working the air. Sand and dirt explode behind him as the monstrous creature bursts out of the ground, stretching impossibly far into the sky, going up and up.

Tumbling through the air, I lose sight of the monster's emergence. In a strange, weird moment everything seems to stop. I'm acutely aware of everything, each detail standing out as if defined in some new form of sensory input. Each clod of dirt, every grain of sand, the exact coloration on the edge of every one of Lothor's scales. I'm hyperaware of everything.

Behind is the Zzlo ship, engines blooming out fire as they try to life off. The zemlja, obviously attracted by the rumbling caused by said engines, climbs into the air, its undulating body rising impossibly high. Lothor's hands reach toward me but aren't quite able to make contact.

In this singular moment of acute clarity, I run through a thousand scenarios desperately in my strangely calm way, trying to realize a way out of what I know is going to happen.

If only I could fly, if I had wings like Lothor. If only, if only, if only. Each idea is discarded as fast as it comes. None of them are viable. I am well and truly screwed, and as the final idea is tossed away I do the only thing I can.

I close my eyes and curl into a ball, covering my stomach in preparation for the impact that is about to happen. Everything speeds up to happen at once.

My stomach sinks as I fall through the air. Then, suddenly, strong arms wrap around me and I'm tumbling over and over but protected by Lothor's body.

We roll to a stop with him covering me protectively. It takes a moment to orient myself. My ears are ringing, then the night sky lights up bright as day as the Zzlo ship lifts into the air. The engines blast blue flames, and then there is a screeching sound so loud I cover my ears and it still cuts through my head.

The pain of that screech is indescribable. I can't think—can't process thoughts at all—as it goes on and on. Tears stream and bile rises in my throat the pain is so extreme. Finally it stops, leaving me gasping with a splitting headache.

Lothor touches my face, his fingers wiping away my tears, looking me up and down. When his eyes land on my restraints he growls and makes fast work of them with his hunting knife.

Hands free at last, I throw my arms around his neck and cling to him. I can't believe he's here. I don't ever want to let him go.

He cradles me against his chest, patient and silent, experiencing the moment with me. He kisses my forehead, my cheeks, his hands making small circles on my back while my own fingers trail across his strong shoulders and up to cup his beautiful, perfect face.

"I am sorry I could not reach you sooner," he murmurs, kissing the top of my head. "I needed help."

I shake my head, pulling back so I can see his face as I wipe away my tears.

"There is no need to apologize," I murmur. "You saved me. Saved us."

His eyes soften, dropping to my belly. He cups it briefly, but then pulls me in close again, his breath coming out in a harsh shudder.

"I don't know what I would do if..." He trails off, his grip tightening.

I hold him back just as hard, feeling safe again. A deep rumbling pulls us out of our reunion and Lothor picks me up abruptly and leaps forward. I hold tight while he takes us to safety.

"Lothor—"

He takes us down to the sand, covering me with his body. That's when the gust of wind hits us, sand pelting us harshly. Above us I see a sliver of sky over Lothor's shoulder, but it's enough to glimpse a large, dark shape rising up. The Zzlo ship. It picks up speed, but before it does, I see it's been severely damaged. It darts away with a resounding boom of sound. Gone. To keep dealing in slaves. I press my lips together at the thought, but there's nothing we can do about it now.

I take comfort that Lothor and the Zmaj he recruited did a good amount of damage before the remaining Zzlo were able to escape.

"Lothor," a new voice says.

Lothor pulls back, rising up with me secured against him. One of the robed warriors stands waiting for us, the others fanned out behind him. The ones behind us scan the area while also looking at us with a glimmer of curiosity.

The Zmaj who appears to be in charge looks me over before his attention returns to Lothor.

"We have done what we promised you we would," he says, his face almost cold. "You have your mate."

Lothor nods gravely.

"My thanks," he murmurs. "I will not forget."

The stranger's attention returns to me. My cheeks flush warm under the intensity of his gaze. He is openly appraising me in the most uncomfortable way possible. His eyes linger on the soft bulge of my stomach.

"She is pregnant," he says, a statement, not a question.

How the hell does he know anything about humans?

"Yes," Lothor says, as if not surprised at all.

The stranger purses his lips, frowning deeply. He's clearly debating something but taking his own damn sweet time to share it with us. At last he clears his throat.

"This will not be... easy," he says.

"What do you mean?" I ask, panic rising.

"Human–Zmaj pairings," he says, his eyes locked on Lothor though he's answering my question. "Are not easy on the female."

"Can you help?" Lothor asks.

"No," he says.

Tension rises between the three of us. I don't know if I want to scream, hit him, or cry.

"Why not?" Lothor asks, defiant.

"It is not in our skills," he says.

"Then who?" Lothor asks. "You know something. Say it."

His frown deepens further, a feat in and of itself.

"There are other humans," he says.

"The City," I say, filling in the blanks.

"Yes," he says. "Draconov."

"Draconov," Lothor repeats the word, not one I've heard before, but it seems to bring back memories for him.

The other Zmaj inclines his head, taking a step back.

"We will return to our outpost. If you cross our boundary, you will be dealt with as anyone else doing the same."

"I understand," Lothor returns, as stiffly as his stance would imply.

Without another word, the group of warriors turns and disappears swiftly. I know they don't actually disappear, but the coloring of those robes combined with how quickly they move means they're out of view faster than I would have predicted.

"Who were they?" I murmur, a little spooked.

"They call themselves the Order," Lothor mutters. Turning in a slightly different direction, he picks me up and flares out his wings. "Come. Let us return home."

I nod, resting my head against his chest.

That sounds perfect.

36

LOTHOR

I carry Victoria across the desert, but our travel is slower than I would like. My body isn't up to par. The abuse of the last several days has taken its toll. None of that matters, though. She is in my arms and that overrides everything else.

Instead of going straight to the cave, I go to the oasis. There aren't any food stores left after the Zzlo took her and ransacked our home. I'm sure she'll want to eat, and I'm hungry too. Stopping at the edge of the plant growth, I set her down but can't take my hands off of her, resting them on her hips. I tilt my head down and rest it against hers, basking in the moment.

"Lothor," she whispers my name, her fingers trailing white-hot fire along my cheeks, cupping my face between her hands.

I don't say anything. I can't form words, force them past the lump in my throat. I don't know how long we stand, touching, being with each other. Each passing moment of it is a treasure. She is mine, she is safe, we are together.

The moment is broken by the grumbling of my stomach,

demanding food. Victoria laughs and it's the most beautiful music to my ears.

"Let's get you fed," she says, smiling big.

"Yes," I agree.

"And a bath. I don't know what's yours and what's theirs, but you're a mess and I know I can't smell very good either."

My cock stirs as she suggests a bath.

"Of course, my love," I say.

I carefully forage through the oasis gathering edibles and collecting until we have sufficient amount for a meal. While we gathered we've both snacked on various berries and roots, taking the edge off our hunger and by unspoken agreement we strip upon reaching the water.

After undressing I pause, unable to do more than admire her. Her belly is swelling with the new life growing inside of it and it's beautiful. Her breasts are a little fuller. Though I know it's still early, already the changes are coming over her body.

She notices my stare and covers her belly protectively. A mother's instinct. My chest swells and my hearts beat faster even as my cock stiffens, which doesn't go unnoticed by her.

"Bath first," she laughs, eyeing my hard member.

"Must we?" I ask, laughing along with her.

"Absolutely. No way you're getting that thing in me while we're both so filthy!"

We walk into the water holding hands. The cool, azure liquid feels amazing against my scales but instantly dirties as the dirt and blood come off at its touch. She shudders as the water comes up to her breasts.

"Are you okay?" I ask.

"Yeah," she laughs. "It's cold."

"Let me help," I smile, moving closer and wrapping my arms around her.

She rests her head on my chest and I close my wings

around her, engulfing her. Slowly I move us toward the middle where the water is deeper. When it comes up to her shoulders I stand and let the natural flow of it work, washing away the layers of dirt and blood.

"This is nice," she murmurs.

I agree silently, not willing to break the moment. Eventually she looks up, smiling, and my heart melts. I was so close to losing her, but now she is here. Safe. Betkar's words echo through my thoughts about her pregnancy.

I hadn't thought of there being any difficulty. It's a subject we'll have to broach sooner or later, but for now I push it aside. It's too soon after having gotten her back to worry about future problems. I know, sort of, where the Draconov is or was, but I haven't traveled anywhere near it in a very long time. So long that I don't recall having been there at all. It's more like I have a vague memory of it and a certainty of direction.

Victoria steps back and I fold my wings, letting her move. She ducks under the water to vigorously scrub her hair, then explodes back up to send water spraying into my face.

"Oh!" she cries, "this is wonderful."

I laugh, unable to keep back my humor at her enjoyment of the water. Kneeling down, I duck my head under and then grab a handful of sand from the bottom and use it to scrub my scales free of dirt and the grime of battle.

"Let me help," she says, moving behind me. She splashes water up onto my shoulders, then scrubs at the hard-to-reach places. "Oh Lothor, you've been hurt so badly!"

"It is as nothing," I say. "Freeing you is all that mattered. My body will heal; my soul would never recover from the loss of you."

She pauses her scrubbing and wraps her arms around my chest from behind. I raise my tail between her legs and rest it on her shoulder, moving it side to side against her back.

"You say the sweetest things," she murmurs, kissing between my wings then resuming scrubbing me clean.

Idly I stroke her back with my tail while she works the grime out of my scales. When she finishes I turn around and pull her tight, my cock crushed between us. She gasps, her mouth parting and her eyes widening. She smiles, her eyes dropping to half-closed.

"I love you," I say, hooking under her legs and lifting her up.

"I love you," she says, throwing her arms around my neck.

My throbbing cock is at her opening, ready to lay its claim. She kisses me, pushing her tongue into my mouth while her fingers twine in my hair.

Our tongues dance with each other as I slide her down onto my primary cock. She feels so good I almost hit my release the moment I penetrate, and it's an effort of will to hold back. She sighs, burying her head into my shoulder, then biting me as I slide her down until she's fully seated.

We hold each other, neither of us moving, embracing the moment.

My cock throbs deep inside her tight sheath. Wrapping my tail around her back I hold her tight, freeing my hands to roam over her perfect body.

She gasps as I lift her up and lower her down while one hand works her breasts and the other I drive between us to find her pleasure point.

She throws her head back, panting, biting her lower lip as I play her body like the beautiful instrument that it is.

She's pulling herself up and down, thrusting onto me, grinding her hips against me as she bottoms out then rises off my cock again.

"Lothor," she gasps, moaning soundlessly. "So... good... fuck... me."

I obey. Her commands are my world. I fuck her, taking

back what is mine. Claiming her body while giving her my soul.

It doesn't take long. Her back arches and she cries out a wordless sound as her pleasure peaks. I can't hold it any longer either, exploding into my release until I'm left spent and exhausted.

Even my second cock doesn't want to rise to the occasion.

We kiss more, light touches, tongues dancing gently while my cock softens inside of her until at last I lift her off and lower her back into the water.

"That was amazing," she says, kissing my lips softly, fingers trailing along my cheek.

"You are amazing," I murmur, grabbing her hand and sucking her fingers before letting go.

She giggles, her cheeks warming to a soft pink color that I find delightful.

"Not with you," she says, her eyes turning serious.

My throat closes with inexpressible emotions as my love for her becomes an overwhelming force, so I don't bother trying to speak. Instead I pull her close and hold her.

"We should head home," I say after a long time has passed.

She agrees and we dry off, then dress. Shouldering the small amount of foodstuffs we've been able to collect, I lift her into my arms and set off for home.

The suns have dipped below the horizon before the familiar rocks of home come into view. Victoria is asleep in my arms, her soft breathing regular and even. Every time I glance down to check on her I'm struck by her natural beauty, which is now accented by the glow of pending motherhood.

Motherhood. I am to be a father.

My thoughts turn again to Betkar's words. The City.

Others. Dangerous at best not considering that Victoria herself was exiled by the rest of her kind. Will they hold that against her? Will they refuse their help? What do I do if they do?

Those future problems consume my thoughts as I cross the final distance to our home. When I'm at the base of the path to the cave I pause, cradling her in one arm and pushing her hair out of her face.

"Here we are," I murmur, waking Victoria.

She raises her head, smiling in relief.

"So soon?" she asks sleepily, unaware of the long hours since she fell asleep.

"Yes, love," I smile. She snuggles against me then moves and I set her down.

Hand in hand we walk up the small ramp to the cave. Unfortunately, when I set her down inside, the cave is just as I left it. A complete and utter mess. Victoria pauses in the door, her eyes wide.

"I... lost control when I realized they had taken you," I explain gruffly. "I apologize."

She shakes her head, turning into me and cupping the side of my face with her soft palm. I close my eyes, savoring the touch and the care in the gesture. I was so close to losing her. So close.

"Stop trying to apologize," she murmurs. I open my eyes to meet her own soft blue ones, the love in them so deep and clear that my chest aches with the sight. "I don't care about the mess. It's the last thing I'm worried about, okay?"

I nod, raising a hand to grip her delicate wrist and pull it away to kiss her palm.

"Well, I—" A small blur rushes into the cave, attacking Victoria head-on.

Victoria grunts, staggering back as Sree rubs her face against her, her small body vibrating with welcome.

"Sree!" Victoria laughs, cuddling her close. "Where have you been all this time?" she asks, smoothing the small creature's fur. "Seems like the unintended diet has helped you," she remarks.

It is true. Sree is significantly less round around her midsection. I would venture to say she looks fit.

"Come on," Victoria says, putting her furry bundle down on the floor. "Let's get to work on this mess, shall we?"

Sree mewls in response, following Victoria over to one of the baskets lying strewn across the floor. Taking a deep breath, I crouch down and start to help. It is my mess, after all. Focused as we are, we make quick work of much of the mess. Setting the pallet to rights, I turn to ask Victoria if she wants it arranged in the same place and realize she is frozen near the wall, kneeling on the floor.

"Victoria, what..." I trail off when I see where her attention is focused.

The mirror, the hair clip, the ribbon... my former love's possessions. Artifacts of the love I had for her. I kneel down next to her, staring at the objects. I held onto them all this time, even when the memories were hidden, weak shadows of the life we shared.

What do I say to her? How do I talk about this? Even now the memories of it are dim despite the breakthrough when I thought I'd lost Victoria. Looking at them something in me shifts. Some piece of my being clicks into something new, a part of me that I'd locked away. It opens me in some strange way I don't understand, but my love for Victoria is a palpable pounding, throbbing through my body with each beat of my hearts.

Her hand hovers over the broken mirror as if afraid to touch it. Slowly I touch the back of her hand and she looks at me. Swallowing hard, I speak.

"I had a love. Before." The words are hoarse, low. Victoria

looks at me with compassion written across her eyes and face.

"What was her name?" she asks, her own voice quiet.

Matched to my own.

"Nermana."

It feels odd to say her name out loud. Odder still to say it to Victoria, the past and the present colliding in some strange manner.

"What happened?" she asks, her tone gentle.

"I... I was not able to save her. We survived the Devastation, I remember that much, but it was hard." I shake my head, the memories too dim to see clearly. It's more of a knowing than any ability to see the past as it was. "She fell sick. Grew weaker with each passing day. I tried to save her."

I stop, closing my eyes as I remember that feeling of helplessness and my frustration and anger. The deep pit I fell into after she breathed her last breath, closed her eyes for the last time.

"Lothor." I open my eyes when Victoria places her hand on mine. "I know you," she says earnestly, the compassion in her eyes drawing me near. "I know you did everything you could have possibly done for her."

I take a deep breath, closing my eyes. The memories are distant and what I do recall feels as if it happened to someone else. A stranger's memories residing in my head, like a story I once heard but nothing that I experienced.

That's how I remember the destruction of our society. The loss of everything that mattered. The end of life as I knew it. Running, escaping into the open deserts because I knew it was going to happen? Maybe?

I don't know. It feels I had some idea ahead of it, some warning or something. There are still images that come to mind, but they don't make a whole picture. Bombs falling from the sky. Explosions. Roiling towers of flames reaching for the stars as big as the horizon.

Heated winds and death. Everywhere death. In the aftermath my body adjusted to the harsher conditions we found ourselves in, but hers only grew weaker, no matter how much I tried to help.

I hunted more, fed her all the meat I could find, found shelter for us so she could be out of the suns. It didn't help. Soon she could not keep the food down and then she entered a delirium where she did not always recognize me. A cruel twist of fate when I had so little time left with her.

Then, she was gone.

I do not remember what happened after that initial fall into the darkness. That memory remains a haze that I cannot see clearly.

"I... tried," I murmur, shaking my head. "But no amount of food or fresh water or herbs that I know are good. None of it helped. There was nobody to turn to for medical aid after the Devastation."

"Lothor...there is nothing you could have done."

I meet her eyes once more.

"How do you know for certain?" I ask. "Perhaps—"

"No, Lothor," she interrupts me fully. "I've met other Zmaj since we landed here on Tajss. I know there are no more Zmaj females left. There is nothing you could have done."

"None left..." I repeat, frowning.

How could that be? I think about my own wandering before I settled in this cave. Occasionally, I would pass another Zmaj or see one and stay clear, not wanting a possible altercation, but they were all male.

Could it be? Are all the females gone? If that is the case... I really could not have done anything more.

"I'm sorry, but I'm sure of it. There are none left," Victoria repeats. "Lothor." Soft hands cup my face, turning me toward her. "There is nothing you could have done."

I hear her, really hear her. Feel those words sink in, a balm to the still raw wound buried inside. And feel...the beginning of a true healing. I will never forget my first love, never forget the pain of her loss, but perhaps...perhaps I can heal. Heal and give Victoria the best of me. She deserves the best.

"Victoria," I murmur, dropping my head to rest my forehead against hers. "I... Thank you."

She smiles. I would do anything to keep seeing that love for me in her eyes.

"I only helped you see the truth, my love," she whispers. "Nothing more."

"It is...everything," I return. "I need..."

I close the small distance between our mouths, sinking into the softness, the *realness* of her. Mine. Reaching out for the strewn-about pallet, I pull it over haphazardly, just enough to cushion her back when I lay her down. She pulls at my clothing just as I divest her of hers, sinking into her warm welcome as soon as we are both free.

"Lothor!" she cries out, her eyes wide when I drive in all the way in one thrust.

I squeeze the roundness of her breast, sliding my hand down to the soft juncture of her thighs.

She gasps when my fingers start to work on her, my hips pistoning in and out. I watch her eyes flutter closed, her cheeks flush as I drive her to her first climax fast and hard.

When she reaches up to grip my arms, her short nails digging into my skin, I move even faster in her. Using my tail to toy with her hair, my hands work her breasts.

The sound of my hips meeting hers is loud and fast, mingling with our breaths. I shudder with my own climax, her tightness a test I cannot and do not want to pass. Picking her up, I brace her against the wall, my arm cushioning her spine and placing my tail as support under her ass as I push my second cock into her. Groaning, she wraps her legs around me, her hands sinking into my hair.

"Victoria," I moan, capturing her lips in another deep kiss, my body moving in and out at a more measured pace.

When I grow tired of that position, I arrange her on all fours, her knees cushioned by the pallet. Then I lay her back down on the pallet itself, raising her legs high and wide. When I hammer into her in that position, she bites her lip, arching up against me, squeezing down on my length in a velvet grip.

My orgasm tears through me, a rush of pleasure that has me dropping down on top of her, my erection jerking inside her. I feel as though I have been tackled by a heavy opponent.

Resting my head next to Victoria's, I try to catch my breath. She smooths her hand down my back, the caring gesture making me sigh. Rolling to my side, I pull her in close.

The pallet is uneven and I cannot fit fully on it because it needs to be straightened, but I do not care, not with Victoria in my arms.

I will forever feel this way. I kiss her soft hair, hugging her closer. She is... everything.

I do not know how I was so lucky as to have two loves. Whatever this twist of fate, my dragon has claimed her and I will appreciate my blessing each and every day.

37

VICTORIA

I roll over on the pallet, trying to find a comfortable position. News flash—there isn't one. Not with how huge my belly is. Sree mewls, resettling against my back with a huff.

"If you don't want to move, you're going to have to lie down somewhere else," I murmur, petting her silky head.

She just yawns and settles her head down on her paws. Sighing, I take a drink of the water that sits near the pallet. Being pregnant is no joke. Not that I would change it for the world. I rub my stomach, setting the waterskin down.

Sure, it sucks to be peeing every two seconds, sucks not being able to find a comfortable position to rest in, sucks feeling like a beached whale, but every time I think of the life growing inside me, I can't help but smile.

A tiny being, a mixture of Lothor and me. I can't wait to meet him or her. Can't wait to get to know the little person who's soon going to be the center of our world. I look up when I hear Lothor's familiar footsteps.

He smiles, walking over to me with a plate filled with fresh vegetables and meat. My stomach growls. I feel like I'm always hungry. Probably because I am. I roll to the side, trying to get to get up.

"Here, let me help," he says.

Lothor wraps one of his arms around me and easily pulls me up into a sitting position. I know it's stupid, but it makes me feel better that he can still move me around without breaking a sweat. Though I could probably triple in size and he still wouldn't break a metaphorical sweat. Maybe that's not the best gauge.

Sree moves again, curling up next to my hip. If possible, she dogs my steps even more these days. Like she knows I'm vulnerable and need the protection.

"Thank you," I murmur, kissing Lothor's cheek. "I'm—oh!"

I press my hand to my stomach, feeling a sharp pain as our baby protests against my movement with a hard kick.

"Is the baby moving?" Lothor asks, placing a gentle hand on my stomach.

"Ferociously," I say only half joking, shifting my hand to the side so he can feel the movement better.

His face is a mixture of delight and awe. I can't believe I was afraid of him. He's the world's biggest teddy bear. And I've become the sappiest person because of it, falling deeper in love with him every day.

Somehow he's managed to break through all of my barriers and reach a part of me I didn't even know could be reached by a man. With his help, I've finally come to terms with my past, with the fears that were instilled in me from my childhood, and now I can be fully present. I can love Lothor like he deserves to be loved.

"I am so excited to meet you, little one," Lothor croons, kissing my stomach. "We have so much love for you."

I smile, my heart aching in the best way. I feel so... full. Like I have everything right here. I'm so damn lucky.

I sigh and shift once more when there is a quick pain in my hip, there and gone. Lothor doesn't miss it, looking up at me with concern.

"Are you hurting?" he asks, sitting up to support me with his arm around my shoulders and curling his tail around my back.

"No, just a twinge," I reassure him, leaning against his strength. "Nothing to worry about."

He shakes his head, his expression turning troubled.

"There is much to worry about," he counters, seriously.

I sigh. He isn't wrong. I worry about the delivery more and more as my belly grows. I know he's thinking about the warning from that Zmaj who helped rescue me, but there are too many factors to consider.

"Yes, they have facilities in the City," I say. "But I was exiled from there because I followed Gershom. I doubt they'd welcome me back with open arms."

At this point, he knows the whole story, embarrassing as it is. He nods.

"Surely they would not turn you away?" he asks. "Perhaps we should journey there and ask for help," he murmurs, his hand protectively cupped over my stomach. "I do not have enough knowledge of the process to be confident in being your only support. What if something goes wrong? We need help."

I nod. It would be embarrassing to come back after I left the way I did and with a Zmaj mate of my own, no less. Then again, maybe that will show them that I really don't have any animosity toward the Zmaj.

"You're right," I agree, not looking forward to it. What's a little embarrassment if it helps our baby? Our child isn't even here yet and I know I would do anything for him or her. "When are you thinking we should go?"

"Soon. Not quite yet, but soon. I do not want to begin the journey too close to your birthing time."

Yeah. I don't particularly want to be in the middle of the desert when the baby decides to come.

"Okay."

Sounds good to me. A little more time with just the two of us before more people are around.

"Here—you need your strength."

"I don't think I'm weakening from a lack of food," I joke, taking the bite he offers me. "Mmm. It's really good."

He smiles, pleased with himself.

"Good. Here, have more."

He doesn't have to ask me twice. Between the two of us, we finish off the plate. Setting it aside, he shifts so he's sitting behind me, his legs bracketing my own. Leaning down, he kisses the side of my neck softly. I tilt my head to the side, giving him more room.

I close my eyes, leaning my head back against his shoulder when his hand slides down my shirt, gently squeezing my breast. It's a lot bigger now—along with everything else—but Lothor doesn't seem to mind.

Shifting, he lowers me onto my back, finally sending Sree stalking away with a complaining mewl. Lothor kisses my lips, his hands wandering my body, careful to keep his weight off me.

"You are so beautiful," he whispers, kissing me again.

"I'm fat," I retort.

"You are with child," he corrects, rising on his elbows. "And glowing with it."

I don't know about that. I feel like a sweaty mess. Maybe that's what he means with the glowing part, but when his hands start to move over my body, I stop thinking about all of that.

He makes me feel beautiful. Desired. Wanted. And very

specific parts of me are even more sensitive than they were before. A fact not lost on my mate.

As he covers me, sliding carefully into me, I hug him close, drenched in pleasure. And love. Happy. I'm so happy, I could almost burst with it. Everything has led me to this moment and it's perfect.

"Yeah," I smile, rubbing my swollen belly.

My stomach cramps and I grimace.

"Victoria, are you okay?" he asks.

Before I can answer the pain dials up to twelve, blinding me. I cry out, my voice shrill to my own ears and echoing off the stone walls.

"Victoria!" Lothor exclaims, cradling me against his body, but I'm dimly aware of him.

It passes as fast as it came, leaving me panting and scared. Sweat runs into my eyes mixing with the tears and I wipe it away.

"Sorry," I pant. "That was... painful."

"What was it?" he asks.

Shaking my head, I can't stop trembling. My stomach hurts, aches like cramps are waiting to happen. Lothor raises the waterskin to my lips and I drink it gratefully. Trepidation fills me as I wait to see if it's going to happen again.

"I don't know," I say finally. "It was... bad."

"We're going to the City," he says, a statement not a question.

"It's too far," I say. "They don't want me there."

"They will accept you," he says. "Or I will make them."

"Lothor," I say, shaking my head.

"No," he says. "Betkar knew something. He said this was difficult and I'm not stupid. We are two different races. That you're pregnant at all seems a miracle to me. I should have expected there could be complications."

"I'm fine—"

"No," he says, his tone the harshest he's ever taken with me, cutting me off. "No," he says softer, cupping my face. "I will not risk you. I will protect you, even if it is from yourself."

I open my mouth to argue, but what am I going to say? I'm not stupid either and I'm self-aware enough to know that it's fear, deep and probably irrational, that makes me not want to return to the City.

I left there under less than stellar terms, but do they really even know who I am? I wasn't somebody important. I was a scared little girl. Odds are they don't even know I was with Gershom. Maybe.

"Okay," I agree, but my skin turns cold and I can't stop myself from shivering.

Lothor pulls the furs up and around me, holding me tight.

"In the morning," he says.

"Do you know the way?" I ask.

He frowns, looking at the makeshift door of our home for a long moment before he answers.

"Not exactly," he says. "I'm sure I can find it."

"I'm sure you can," I agree.

Exhaustion settles in and it isn't long before I'm nodding off. Shifting around, I finally find a position that isn't too uncomfortable and I'm out.

When I wake up it's dark outside the door. Sree is curled up next to my stomach and snoring softly, which is ridiculously cute. I lie still, listening to Lothor's even breathing behind me. His tail lies across my middle, resting protectively over my stomach and his arm is over my breasts. I need to pee, but I don't want to wake them or break the magic of this moment.

I stretch it out as long as I can. In my condition it's a

super-human feat because I *really* have to pee. When the demands of my bladder can't be ignored any longer I attempt to slip out. Attempt being the key word.

When your belly is bigger than pretty much the entire rest of your body, nothing is subtle when it comes to moving. I get myself up on an arm, but by that time Sree and Lothor are both awake. Sree is upset, but Lothor helps me to my feet, makes sure I'm steady, then walks with me until he's sure I'm stable, only giving me privacy to handle my business.

When I'm done he puts his pants on and has his pack on his back.

"We should go," he says.

"It's early," I protest.

Nausea roils my stomach and there's an itch inside my head that I desperately want to scratch. Impossible but it's there, driving me nuts.

"I know, my love," he says. "I will carry you so you can sleep more."

"Carry me?" my voice cracks and stupid pregnancy hormones kick in causing tears to flow.

"I'm huge! I know your stupid strong but this is ridiculous!"

He stares blankly, shaking his head. "Victoria, what is wrong?"

"Wrong," I shake my head, unable to stop the tears, but then a cramp hits and I'm doubling over in pain.

He's there instantly, lifting me off my feet and cradling me against his chest until the cramp passes.

"Damn it," I growl, shaking my head.

Fear wars with my senses, but I have to do this. There's something not right and I have no idea what it is or how to fix it. I have to for our baby, no matter how scared I am, I have to face it.

"What is it?" Lothor asks, barely whispering.

"I'm scared," I admit.

"You have nothing to fear," he says with certainty. "I will destroy anyone that tries to harm you."

"It's not that…" I say, shaking my head. "It's… I'm scared to go back. To face my past."

"Oh," he says, silence falling.

There's a storm in his eyes, but more than that I feel it. I get it too, he's struggling with something that's never happened in our time together. Something upsetting me that he can't kill or beat the hell out of. We need these people.

And I'm stupid. I know it. I know I'm being a scaredy-cat and I've looked at every rational reaction and thought it all through, but none of that changes the fear that's riding on the edge of paralyzing.

Biting my lower lip, tears welling in my eyes, I struggle to admit defeat. To give in to what I know has to happen, to somehow face my fear.

Lothor's tail curls around, holding me tight and we stand in silence. I hold it all back as long as I can, then a single sob escapes and the dam breaks. Tears pour in an unstoppable torrent. I gasp for air, sobbing, and letting it all out.

All my bad decisions, every one of them was made in fear. I followed Gershom because I was scared. I stayed with the Zzlo out of fear. I watched them trade off my friends, silently afraid. Fear has ruled my life, and it's high time that came to an end.

Funny enough I thought I'd done that. Opening myself up to Lothor, accepting him, I thought had closed the door on fear, but here it is again. Like an old friend or more like an old enemy that keeps showing up even when you thought he was dead.

Eventually my tears slow then stop. The hitching comes out of my breathing and I'm left empty but clean. Lothor doesn't speak, only holds me and waits until at last I raise my head and look at him with bleary eyes.

"Okay," I say.

"Okay?" he asks.

I nod, biting my lip. "Yes, let's go."

He nods, silent, I assume not wanting to break the moment or maybe give me a chance to change my mind. I'm not going to; my decision is made. It's time to face the final piece of my past, for better or worse, this is it.

He sweeps me into his arms and as fast as that we're off. What happens next only time will tell. I pray that it works out for the best.

On the fourth day Lothor stops and sets me down when we reach the top of a dune. He hands me the waterskin then slips the pack off his back. He digs into our fast dwindling supplies and produces some leather-wrapped meat, holding it out to me for first pick. There are only four pieces left, not enough to last more than today if we don't find our goal.

"You should eat," I say, pushing it back toward him.

"I am fine," he says, shaking his head. "Please, eat, for our child."

He knows exactly which buttons to hit. I can't argue with it, so I take one piece and chew on the leathery meat. It's tough but flavorful thanks to his skill with spices. While I chew, I look around trying to spot anything that looks familiar. It's impossible, really. What do I orient myself by? Oh hey, I recognize that dune, it has this exact shape... except there's a constant breeze that shifts the sands all the damn time. Nothing stays the same on Tajss yet nothing changes.

What a weird contradiction this place is. Slowly I turn a circle until something catches my eye.

"What's that?" I ask pointing.

Lothor follows my finger and looks. I shield my eyes from the overhead suns, trying to make it out better. Something is glinting on the horizon.

"I'm not sure," he says.

"It could be..." I say, trailing off, afraid to say the words out loud.

"Could be?" he asks.

"There was a dome over the City," I say. "I remember looking back at it when we were exiled and it sparkled like that."

He nods slowly, thoughtfully.

"Then we shall investigate," he says.

I finish the meat and take a very small sip of the almost-empty water bottle before he takes me in his arms and we're off again. He's moving faster, a renewed vigor to his steps as he leaps and bounds us across the empty desert. Somehow he does this without managing to jar me excessively.

The suns are dipping to the horizon when he stops again. When I look this time it takes my breath away. The City. The glittering dome covering it calling me home. Fear wiggles through, weaving itself into my thoughts, but I'm not giving in to it. I've come too far to back out now.

"Can we make it by dark?" I ask.

"I think we can," he says, and we're off.

My heart pounds hard and a cold sweat accents my normal sweating. This is it, anxiety screams, and I know I should be afraid. I should be but I'm not going to be. What's the worst that can happen? They can exile me again. They're humans. Like me. They're not going to turn us away. Look at me, I'm huge! Who would turn the fat pregnant lady out into the desert? They're not monsters.

I hope.

And I keep reminding myself as I push through the anxiety that keeps trying to wrest control of my thoughts and mood.

It's not long at all until we're approaching the dome. Lothor pauses, looking at it, staring actually, and something is moving behind his eyes.

"What is it?" I ask.

"Memories," he says, his voice soft and distant.

"Good ones?" I prod.

He shrugs. "Memories, good or bad. It's all dim, like they belong to someone else. I was here, before, and seeing it with the dome reminds me of it, I think. There is nothing clear. It's all concepts and ideas that I should know this or a feeling I remember this, but nothing to back that up. No picture to go with the memory."

"I'm sorry," I say, trailing my fingers along his strong jaw.

"Bah," he scoffs. "I do not need memories of long ago. I have you, here and now. You are the only memory I need."

I laugh but mostly because I can't speak. When he says things like that, his words are filled with so much emotion, so much intention that it chokes me up. My heart swells, my chest explodes, and sensations dance across my skin like the light trail of a delicate touch.

When we stop again we're standing next to the dome. I guide him around to the airlock, distant memories of my own swamping my thoughts. Walking out this airlock with the rest of the exiles. Staring into the empty desert scared to go forward but too scared to turn around. The mighty, massive Zmaj warriors standing too close though they were nowhere near me.

Lothor sets me down and takes my hand. On the other side of the dome is a human. A man with a receding hairline, heavy wrinkles on his face, and a surprised look. He has a rifle close to hand but doesn't take it up at the sight of us. He turns his back and yells and in the distance. Someone seems to respond. He looks back at us and holds up a finger, indicating we should wait.

Wait. Of course, what else are we going to do?

"The City is a mess," Lothor observes.

"Huh," I say. "It looks a lot better than the last time I was here. Oh!" I grab my stomach as the baby kicks, hard. "Baby agrees."

Lothor snorts, curling his tail around my waist and resting the end of it protectively over my belly. It isn't long before a small entourage walks down the street on the other side of the dome. My heart races seeing the familiar white outfit.

Rosalind.

My inadvertent tormentor, the one who sent me into exile. Though in all honesty she didn't exile me. She exiled Gershom and I chose to follow him into the desert. As if he was some weirdly modern Moses leading us into some promised salvation. Except he wasn't. He was a small, scared man, as I was scared.

The airlock cycles open and Rosalind enters along with two Zmaj that I dimly recognize but I don't recall their names. We wait until the door on our side opens and they walk out.

"Hello," Rosalind says, walking boldly forward and extending a hand.

"Hello," I say, trying to keep my voice and hand from shaking as I take hers.

"Greetings," one of the Zmaj says, the one that stands closest to Rosalind.

That's right, she's mated to one of them too. She's grown older since I saw her last. Lines between her eyebrows, at the corners of her mouth, a touch of gray at her temples, but nothing diminishes the air of leadership she exudes. The sharp intelligence in her eyes.

"Greetings," Lothor says. "We come in search of aid."

Blunt and straightforward, that's my Lothor.

"The pregnancy?" Rosalind asks, eyeing my belly.

"Exactly," Lothor says.

"Of course," Rosalind says, her eyes meeting mine. "I remember you, but I don't recall your name?"

My heart is in my throat, making it impossible to speak. I stammer, trying to force the sounds coming out of my mouth to shape the simplicity of my name but I can't get it done.

"This is Victoria," Lothor says. "She was young and afraid, did not know that we Zmaj are safe and protective of females, so she inadvertently fell in with the one you called Gershom."

The two Zmaj males with Rosalind stiffen. No, Lothor is saying too much too fast!

"It's not... it wasn't... it's not like that," I stammer, the words coming faster than my thoughts can coalesce into a cohesion.

"I thought so," Rosalind says, pursing her lips.

This is it. She's about to send us away. I'm going to be on my own for this pregnancy. Damn it, it has to be okay. I can't let anything happen to my baby.

"I don't follow him anymore. I was stupid. Stupid and scared. I didn't know what a... I never hated the Zmaj. I was only scared. It's not my fault but I need help. I'm worried there's something wrong with my baby and oh dear God don't send us away! I need help, the baby needs help."

The words pour out in a jumble and I can only hope they're making sense. I'll beg, I'll do anything to help my baby.

Rosalind touches my cheek then places a hand on my belly. It stops the torrent of words like a dam and strangely I don't feel offended by her taking the liberty to touch me in such an intimate manner.

"Victoria," she says, her eyes arresting mine and forcing me to pay attention to her.

"Yes?" I ask.

"Calm down," she says. "We'll help you. Excitement is not good for the baby."

"You know about… you have experience?" I ask.

"Of course we do," she says. "Now come inside. We need to get you a place to stay and have the doctors look at you."

"You're not going to send us away?" I ask numbly.

"No," she says, not taking her fingers or eyes off of me.

"You don't hate me for what I did?" I ask.

"What did you do?" she asks, her voice soft.

"I followed him," I confess, the weight of it holding me down.

"Why?" she asks. In that moment it's like there's only the two of us in all the universe and her kindness and caring engulfs me.

"Because I was scared," I say.

"Scared of what?" she asks.

"Of them," I say, my eyes darting to the two Zmaj flanking her.

"Are you now?" she asks.

"No," I admit. "After the Zzlo—"

"The Zzlo?" The one closest to her interrupts the moment, cutting me off.

"Yeah, I was captured by them, trapped with them for… I don't know how long?"

"How did you escape?" he asks.

"I rescued her," Lothor answers.

"Well done," the other Zmaj says, speaking for the first time.

"They returned, recently, and I rescued her again," Lothor says, his chest puffing out and pride in his voice.

"Again?" Rosalind asks, her attention shifting to him.

"Yes," he agrees.

"We'll want to talk to you. We need all the information you have on them," she says. "But first let's get you inside and out of this heat.

As if on cue the cramps hit me again and I'm doubled over in pain. It's so strong stars fill my vision and behind them in blackness, deep and peaceful that I fall into, a welcome escape from the agony my body is in.

VICTORIA

"*Y*our baby is fine," Addison says, walking into the room with a clipboard in her hands.

Calista walks alongside of her, smiling.

"You're sure?" I ask, scooting up on the bed.

"Absolutely," Calista says.

"Oh, that's such good news!" I exclaim, tightening my grip on Lothor's hand.

"Well it's not all good," Addison says, looking over at Calista. "There's somethings you need to know."

"What is it? Is the baby going to be okay? What's going on?" I ask, panic rising.

"No, it's nothing like that," Addison says.

"First and foremost, stay calm. This isn't going to be easy to find out, but you need to know your baby is perfectly fine, a very healthy young one at that. So are you for that matter," Calista says.

"Okay…" I trail off, waiting for someone to explain the bad side to me.

Lothor hisses his disapproval of the entire situation but

remains silent, waiting. The sound of his tail swishing against the tile floor is the only sound for a long pause.

"I was the... first cross-mating," Calista says, exchanging a glance with Addison. "We've learned a lot since then, so this is nothing to worry about."

"Oh for the sake of all that's holy spit it out!" I raise my voice in frustration and fear.

"You probably think you're about to term," Addison says.

"Well, yeah, it's been about nine months, more or less. I know that's not exact and I don't know an exact start date, but still—"

I stop when Calista purses her lips and shakes her head.

"Zmaj gestation isn't the same as humans," Addison says.

"Gestation? What?" I ask.

"She means how long you have to carry the baby. The baby isn't going to be ready at the same time a strictly human baby would," Calista says. "It takes longer for a Zmaj baby to be ready."

"Longer? How much longer?" I ask.

"Three months," Addison says.

"Three months!" I exclaim. "I'm huge already! I can't go another three months!"

"Sometimes it's a bit less," Addison says.

"You're kidding me," I say, shaking my head. "This is some kind of joke. It has to be, right? How am I supposed to do this?"

"We have to get your diet under control first," Addison says, looking at her clipboard.

"My diet!" I yell.

"Victoria," Calista says, stepping forward. "It's fine, not that big of a deal. We've had many births here now and it's all worked out fine. We're here to help."

"Help? By what, telling me how damn fat I am? How I've

got to go another whole three months! I'm going to explode if I get any bigger!"

Panic is rising uncontrollably. Lothor leans over me, growling at Addison and Calista. Calista holds her hands up and backs away.

"Lothor, please," Calista says.

"She is not fat, she is with child," Lothor growls, his tail raising up and lying across my swollen stomach.

"We know," Addison says.

"Yes, we know," Calista says. "She's not fat, that's not what we're saying. Your diet has some deficiencies, that's all. We're going to get those corrected. That's why you've been cramping and having pains."

"Her diet?" Lothor asks, his eyes narrowing and tail twitching.

"She needs more vegetables, some fruits," Addison says. "She has some mineral deficiencies. Nothing threatening, but it will make the rest of her pregnancy easier."

"That is all?" Lothor asks.

"No," Addison says. "Of course not. She has to be on bed rest, strict bed rest. Humans aren't designed for the Zmaj gestation period. It's hard on us. Her body will need to be accommodated to for the rest of her term."

"I will care for all her needs," Lothor says, standing straighter and beaming with pride.

"Of course you will," Calista says. "We're here to help too."

"Three months?" I ask again, not wanting to believe it.

"It could only be two. It's difficult to tell what stage you're in," Addison adds, a note of hopefulness to her voice.

"Oh, that's so much better," I grouse.

"We'll make you comfortable," Calista says. "Trust me, there's an entire network of mothers here and we support each other through all of it."

"That's sweet," I say, but I'm not feeling it.

I'm still trying to process the entire two or three more months and strict bedrest on top of that.

"We'll leave you guys alone, for now," Calista says, ushering Addison out of the room.

Lothor hovers over me, silent, waiting for me to speak I'm sure. He adjusts the covers, then pours me some water and holds it up for me. Running out of things to do, he stands beside me and strokes my cheek and runs his fingers through my hair.

"That's a long time," I say at last.

"Yes," he agrees, leaning in and kissing my forehead while squeezing my hand.

"I can't do this," I whisper.

"You can," he says. Sighing, I pound the bed with my free hand. The baby kicks, hard, and I grunt in surprise.

"I saw that!"

"You did?" I ask.

"Yes!" he says, placing both hands on my stomach. "Our child is strong! It will be a great warrior. A leader for both our peoples."

His excitement and love is infectious and I can't stop the smile. It helps to cut through the despair that was trying to settle in. Our child. Placing my hands on my belly, I rub slow circles and I swear it feels like the baby presses a hand out against mine.

"Of course it will," I say. "She."

"Hmm?" Lothor asks.

"She," I repeat. "I don't want to call her an 'it' any longer. It's a she. We're having a girl."

"A girl," he says, staring at my stomach.

"Is that… okay?" I ask. I hadn't thought about him having any preference.

"Okay?" he asks, looking at me with open confusion. "It is

perfect! Our daughter. My only hope is she looks like you so that she will be the most beautiful female on the planet."

"You're silly," I say.

"No, I am lucky. Lucky to have found you, lucky you decided to be mine."

"I'm lucky too," I say. "Who knew after all this time that I'd find you."

"Fate did," he says. "Fate brought us together and fate will always bring us back to one another."

He moves closer and kisses me with every bit of passion of our first kiss. Hell, it might be more passionate as if he really does love me more now than he did then.

"I love you," I say, gasping for air when he breaks the kiss.

"I love you more today than yesterday," he says, as though he'd read my thoughts. "And less than I will tomorrow."

And it's true. I know it deep in my heart, I've found my mate.

THE END

ABOUT THE AUTHOR

USA Today Bestselling Author of fantasy and scifi romance, Miranda Martin's books feature larger than life heroes with out-of-this-world anatomy and smart heroines destined to save the world. As a little girl she would sneak off with her nose in a book, dreaming of magical realms. Today she brings those fantasies to life and adores every fan who chooses to live in them for a while.

She was born and raised in southern Virginia, but as a veteran she's traveled to places like Korea, Hawaii and good 'ole Texas. Now she's settled in Kansas, the heart of America, with her husband and daughters. Her favorite animals are dragons, unicorns and cats. If she's not writing, you can still find her tucked away somewhere with a warm blanket and her nose in a book.

Get in touch!
mirandamartinromance.com
miranda@mirandamartinromance.com

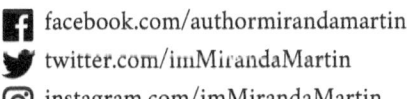

facebook.com/authormirandamartin
twitter.com/imMirandaMartin
instagram.com/imMirandaMartin

ALSO BY MIRANDA MARTIN

USA TODAY BESTSELLING AUTHOR

Red Planet Dragon's of Tajss Series
Red Planet Jungle Series
The Power of Twelve Series
The Alva Series
Dragon's & Phoenixes Series

www.ingramcontent.com/pod-product-compliance
Lightning Source LLC
Chambersburg PA
CBHW030937260626
47169CB00002B/517